From Square One

ALSO BY A. M. WOODY

They Hate Each Other

Exes & Foes

Most Valuable Player

From Square One

A. M. Woody

VIKING

VIKING
An imprint of Penguin Random House LLC
1745 Broadway, New York, NY 10019
penguinrandomhouse.com

Edited by Dana Leydig
Design by Lucia Baez | Text set in Dante MT Pro

Library of Congress Cataloging-in-Publication Data is available.

First published in the United States of America by Viking, 2026

Manufactured in the United States of America
LSCC

ISBN 9780593695449
1st Printing

The authorized representative in the EU for product safety and compliance is Penguin Random House Ireland, Morrison Chambers, 32 Nassau Street, Dublin D02 YH68, Ireland, https://eu-contact.penguin.ie.

This one is for the readers
who keep coming back
despite how many times
I've broken their hearts.
Sorry about that.
And thank you.

1

"I'm sorry."

The words come in a fragmented rasp that would make anyone with an adequate amount of red blood cells flush from their roots to their ankles. The world is a nauseating slosh of bright colors. I don't need the visual details to clock where I am, though. The pungent smell is a familiar nasal assault—cleaning chemicals, floral fragrances, my family's disappointment. That's the most potent one.

"Sorry," I whisper again. The words are featherlight on my tongue. "I took my supplements, I swear . . . I thought I was doing better . . ."

It's been a while since I was checked into the hospital. I'll probably always be as durable as frozen glass thanks to some prick named anemia, but I haven't had a fainting spell since I discovered the root cause of the issue last year—celiac disease. I *have* been doing better, especially now that I know which "gluten-free" brands don't taste like . . . well, not to be crass, but *dog shit* seems fitting.

So why am I here?

Discomfort burns through me. The moment I reorient myself, I'm leaving this sterile bed and heading home so I can inhale some iron-rich poultry and spinach. I shouldn't be here. I have an essay to write for English 11. An online quiz to take for US History. A house to vacuum. A brother to nag so he doesn't lose his graduation cap like he lost his full ride to college.

Though, I blame that blunder on his abysmal excuse for a best friend.

I blink through the murky veil above, squirming with irritation. I feel like each of my brain's commands are being relayed underwater. There's pain from . . . somewhere. I feel it radiating, pulsing like an exposed nerve. Maybe I tumbled down a staircase when I fainted. That misfortune would be relatively on-brand for me.

A face comes into focus, pale with astonishment. Unfamiliar brown scruff blankets his jawline. His tan face is flecked with healing nicks, like he had a brawl with a pocketknife, and his eyes are swollen as if he's been crying. But that can't be—I haven't seen my stoic eighteen-year-old brother shed tears since we were in our single digits.

"Riley?" he chokes out, sounding damp and faraway.

"Sorry. I didn't mean to faint." My voice is mortifyingly scratchy. I concentrate intently on his expression, confusion muddling my senses. "What happened to your face? Did Aaron drag you into a fight? I told you . . . stop hanging out with him . . ."

Logan smears his eyes on his ratty T-shirt. "You're awake," he murmurs, cupping my face gently. "I thought I killed . . ."

He bites the corner of his lip so hard that blood droplets bubble up against his canine tooth.

"You have a beard," I say. Because that's clearly the most important thing to discuss.

"Can you hear me?" he asks, and I can't tell if he's ignoring me in his disorientation or if my voice is too weak to register with him. "You've been out for two days."

I feel my ashen face paling further. No way. Anemic fainting only knocks me out for a few minutes—an hour at most. I blink at Logan, trying valiantly to slide the puzzle pieces together. "You have a beard," I repeat. I'm not sure why I'm fixated on his scruff. He's been trying to grow it out for years—how did it get to this length in a couple of days? And his arms . . . have they always been this bulky?

Logan rises to his feet, his chair scratching the tile floor. "I'll get the nurse."

The room is steadily taking shape. A vast window spans the wall, displaying an expansive view of the parking lot and distant cityscape. Golden light spills though the glass, creeping up the foot of my white cot, and several vases swarming with flowers sit on a side table to my left. Rectangular fluorescent lighting overhead pins me down like a spotlight. A muted TV displaying the US Open Golf Championship is mounted on—

Wait.

I squint at the screen. My head feels like it's been stuffed with snow—my sluggish thoughts aren't locking together with any coherency. They wouldn't host this in March. Not that I'm an expert in the world's most mind-numbingly boring sport, but Logan watches it every year in June.

Something isn't right. My skin is prickling, and my vision is haloed, like my body decided I don't have enough ailments and whacked me with astigmatism. When I examine the trees, fists hammer against my skull and confusion pokes holes into whatever visual stability I can scrounge together. It's not even spring.

But the leaves are full, and the sky is summer blue.

I reach for Logan as he retreats, tears of frustration scorching my eyes. "Wait," I plead. "Logan . . . was it really just a couple of days . . . ?"

Once again, he doesn't hear me, but that might be because someone is striding into the room. Someone who causes Logan's face to twist with vehemence. "I told you to stay away," he snarls.

The newcomer is lankier but taller, and he's clad in black—from his loosely curled hair to the shaded narcissus flower tattooed behind his studded ear to his jacket and slim-fitting pants. Two contrasting hues interfere with his aesthetic. Frost-gray eyes and a vase of red roses tucked to his chest.

Normally, the sight of this smirking nuisance would make me scowl, and I'd be preparing to fling myself protectively between him and my brother. But Aaron Beckham is different, too. He's always been annoyingly tall, but not to this extent. The tattoo is new, probably added to make him look more mysterious. His impulsivity drew my perfect, put-together brother into his orbit—the careless way he operates fascinates Logan.

Then the world is melting again, sounds tangling, sights bleeding together. Something hurts somewhere . . . and there's shouting. Logan's voice is elevated, and it's jarring even though I can't determine what he's saying. Logan doesn't yell. Especially not at Aaron Beckham.

That's my job.

Well, *yell* isn't the right word. But I give a mean glare and I scold Aaron to his face. Keeping this troublemaker out of my brother's life has always been an uphill battle, my warnings ignored, my threats laughed at. My words didn't sink in for Logan until he lost his golf scholarship after they were arrested for trespassing, and he finally admitted that Aaron was a negative influence and a corrupter.

The world crystallizes again, throwing colors into sharp relief. Aaron is leaning over me, his eyelashes long and dark, his arctic irises freezing me to the bed, his skin a smooth, snowy canvas. He's always looked as cold as his insufferable personality.

But his thumb is sliding along my jaw, and it's warm.

"Hey, sunshine," he says. He's probably here to poke and prod me while I can't complain. He mentioned once that "riling Riley" is his favorite hobby, despite how rarely we interact. Though he's never goaded me to the point of exploding. I don't have enough energy to detonate.

"Go away," I mumble.

He curses, and I realize Logan is wrenching his shoulder, cheeks flushed with anger. "Leave," Logan growls. "Or I'm sending you out the window."

Aaron's glare toward him is intense enough that ice crackles through my veins. He smacks Logan's palm away, and I make a choked noise of protest. "Touch me again and I'll break your fucking wrist," he whispers. "I have more of a right to see him than you do."

"He's *my* brother!"

"You're the reason he's here."

The red saturation melts away from Logan's face, paling his skin.

My frustration is insurmountable, made worse by my body's inability to follow my commands. "What happened?" I croak. "Why can't I move?"

Logan and Aaron whirl toward me, eyes widening. "Did he just speak?" Logan demands. "Wait, take the breathing mask off."

The *what*? How hard did I fall?

Aaron's horrifically long fingers lower a mask around my face that I hadn't noticed. "Riley," he says in a strange, unfamiliar voice.

Whenever Aaron speaks to me, it's in low, drawling tones, typically around the edges of a blood-boiling smirk. He's one year older, but he addresses me like a toddler because he knows it makes me prickly. This is softer. Kinder. "Try speaking again."

"Don't touch Logan," I snap. "I don't care how tall you are . . . I'll knee you right where you least want it . . . Stay away . . ."

My words sputter because Aaron's eyes are glassing with tears. "I can hear your voice," he says, his own wavering. "You're babbling and raspy, but I can hear you. Can you try talking again, Riley? The doctor is on her way over. Keep your eyes open, okay?"

All I can do is stare up at his pretty face in bemusement. Aaron despises me—he has for years, since I'm the only one who ever actively roadblocked him from being a bad influence on my brother. The way he's looking at me . . . Why does he seem so relieved?

I don't understand why he's here to visit me. He never has before. Though it's been a while since I landed myself here once I found the underlying reason for my fainting spells.

"Hey," he says, far too gently, his eyes brimming with an overwhelming emotion I can't comprehend. "You're okay, sunshine. I've got you. I'm here. I'm . . . Fuck, Riley . . . I'm so glad you're . . ."

He takes a shuddering gasp and bends down.

He kisses me.

The earth's rotation ceases. Everything is unbearably still. The smell of peppermint is the first thing I register aside from the throb of distant pain. Soft. His lips are soft, thin, insistent. *Peppermint.*

I blink, and suddenly, I'm lying on my bedroom carpet, and Aaron's tongue is nudging against my lower lip, and his fingers are notching my knee around his waist.

Peppermint.

I blink again. I'm back in the hospital. I focus all my willpower and sentience into my palm.

Then drive it up and slap Aaron Beckham across the face.

He staggers, expression etched with astonishment, like he didn't expect a counterattack. "I'm sorry!" I choke out, heat blistering through my cheeks. "But . . . but you really shouldn't have . . . I can't believe you would do something like that . . ."

Logan glances between us, equally bewildered.

"Riley." Aaron nestles himself onto my bed with a nervous smile that exposes the dimple in his left cheek. I've always wanted to poke it. If I ever do, it'll probably be with a knife, because I've finally snapped. Which—like, okay—I'm not *usually* violent, beyond the fact that I can't deal any real damage. I don't like confrontation, and I don't often get angry. But being around Aaron Beckham awakens primal, abhorrent instincts within me.

There's pressure on my wrist—Aaron's hand must be folded over mine, because my tingly fingers feel warmer. "It's just me," he says. "Don't you recognize your boyfriend?"

Boyfriend.

Aaron Beckham is a blight on my family. An ulcer I can't surgically remove. My parents verbally scolded Logan for hanging out with Aaron and risking his reputation as a golden child, but they've always taken the "passive parenting" approach in terms of enforcing consequences, so they didn't do much to stop it. I'm the only one who's ever looked out for my brother.

Even now—even when I'm limp in a hospital bed—Aaron is trying to get a rise out of me. Petting my hair, holding my hand, kissing me, calling himself my *boyfriend* . . . This fainting episode is one sick, amusing joke to him. He's mocking me.

Maybe I should congratulate him. In the five years I've known him, this is the closest he's gotten to making me explode.

"He obviously wants nothing to do with you, so get *out*!" Logan seizes the scruff of Aaron's jacket, heaving him off the bed.

"But . . ." Aaron looks like a wounded puppy, his eyes two giant gray moons. When he meets my gaze, his own flickers with something I've never seen before.

Panic.

This is a hallucination. A hellish nightmare. I need to sleep, and when I next awaken, things will start making sense. So that's what I do.

I go back to sleep.

2

My name is Riley Wilson. I'm seventeen. I'm a junior. I plan to attend the Ilitch Institute of Technology—a local college beyond the suburbs—where I'll earn my degree in computer science, because I hear it makes good money. After years' worth of medical bills alongside brutally expensive certified gluten-free food brands, financial stability is a reasonable goal. It's March. I'm single.

My name is Riley Wilson. I'm eighteen. I just graduated my senior year. I'm enrolled at some general education college thirty minutes north for the fall semester. It's June. I might be taken.

By Aaron Beckham.

I've been staring at my bedroom for ten minutes, nauseated by the change in scenery from what should be "three days ago," considering I was unconscious for two and monitored overnight in the hospital for one more. It's the same room—the chips in the wall, the furniture, the trampled carpeting. But it's painted sunset orange, my favorite color. Packing boxes are stuffed into the corner, filled with my clothes. Golden string lights drip down the far wall like a curtain, and the others have been fixed with artsy canvases that complement the room's warmth.

I massage my aching forehead. Who decorated? I'm not handy, and stopped trying to be when I broke my thumb while nailing up an honor society certificate. I've never understood which tools to use, or how to drill holes into things without hitting wooden beams, or how to properly balance decor. My dad has also been equally useless in this field, despite his best efforts to bumble his way to success. This paint job is far too neat to be either of ours. Professional.

I don't care enough to put money or time aside for sprucing up my living space. I only need a bed. That's what a bedroom is for, right? I don't need extraneous nonsense.

I don't hate it, though. I guess.

My eyes move to the calendar pinned on the wall. It's June, but the month on display is April. I don't just *forget* to switch a calendar over. In fact, I usually have to keep from flipping to a new month early so I can start planning my weeks out. Furthermore, half the month is empty—no notes, reminders, *anything*. It should be jam-packed with writing, but it's mysteriously vacant.

And what's with these moving boxes?

My head responds to my bewilderment with a particularly brutal throb, and I wince, shielding my eyes from the searing summer sun warming the windows. Trying to keep my frustration from swelling up into a burstable bubble. I've never had a meltdown, not even through the diagnosis process and accompanying life changes, so I don't need to start now. Yet my reality settles in my stomach as painfully as bread does. And pasta. And anything else worth eating. My body hurts beyond the usual joint pain—my bones feel weaker, like one good whack will shatter me.

Maybe it's because of all the bruises. The violet splotch spanning my thigh. The yellow tinge on my shoulder. The shrinking lump on my head. They all stem from the moment I was slammed up against Logan's passenger door after he drove through a stop sign, resulting in us getting T-boned. The other driver was fine, and Logan got away with scratches when his window shattered. It shouldn't have been a terrible accident.

But I wasn't wearing my seat belt.

Why wasn't I wearing my seat belt?

My head collided with the passenger window, and I woke up two days later, mostly fine aside from a major concussion. All my limbs came with me when I was pulled from the car, but I did leave something else behind.

The past fifteen months of my life.

I'm not sure why it's such a specific amount of time. I told the doctor that the last thing I remember is writing something on the calendar for March 15 of junior year. She admitted in all her years of handling trauma care patients, she's never experienced a case like mine. I woke from the coma slightly disoriented but behaviorally sound. Other than a blur that disappeared the longer I kept my eyes open, I experienced no vision problems or issues with balance or dizziness. I remembered what classes I was taking, who my teachers were, where I live, who I am. The MRI came back clear aside from a minor bit of swelling where I hit the window. By all accounts, everything is abnormally . . . normal.

So where are the past fifteen months?

I should be finishing junior year, but I've already graduated. My brother should be a senior, but he just finished freshman year at the community college down the road, where he's taking summer classes and works as a student assistant. Aaron Beckham also graduated despite his knack for setting fires. Breaking into restricted areas of the school, ditching class to buy smoothies, starting unnecessary fights with his condescending attitude.

I guess his grades being high enough to graduate isn't surprising. One thing that frustrates me beyond belief about Aaron is that he's smart. He could get a 4.0 GPA but doesn't care enough to put in the work because the end result isn't exciting enough. He must've done just enough to earn the cap and gown to make attending high school worth it. Along the way, he stirred up enough trouble to lose Logan his scholarship and put himself on my permanent *severely dislike* list.

So what changed eighteen-year-old Riley's mind?

I haven't seen Aaron since he kissed me. I've been too afraid to ask Logan for details because I'm not sure I want to know what fooled me into thinking that flirty, arrogant, self-absorbed jerk is worth my time. Which maybe sounds egotistical, but that's the thing about Aaron. He brings out my worst personality traits just by entering my thoughts.

After a few minutes of lying stock-still in my room, I fling myself back to my feet and start investigating. My dresser is completely empty. I move to my bedside table drawer and fumble through the clutter—gluten-free hand lotion, bookmarks, a cute wooden duck that looks like it was whittled, socks and gloves for when I get cold at night—

Wait. There's something stuffed in the socks. Candy wrappers? I shake the contents into the drawer, frowning, and the sight awaiting me causes every thought to evaporate.

I stare at them. They stare back. Menacingly.

Surely, I must be holding these for a friend. Though I don't have those, as far as I'm aware. I get along with people, but socializing has deteriorated since my diagnosis because I'm never sure where gluten is lying in wait to ambush me. Even though my digestive problems aren't as difficult to deal with compared to other celiacs', getting glutened makes me feel like I've been hit by a truck, the signs manifesting in symptoms like fatigue, brain fog, headaches, chills, and severe joint pain. The side effects of my anemia tend to flare up, too, worsening my tiredness and muscle weakness. Even sitting around others in restaurants carries risk if I touch the wrong thing, made worse by my finger-gnawing habit. I'm not close enough to anyone that I would be storing their . . . their . . .

I stare at the bottle peeking out of the twin sock. It stares back. Ominously.

I'm still in a coma. That's the only explanation.

I hear the dreadful sound of my bedroom door creaking open. Gagging from the mere mental image of someone finding me hunched over these items, I slam the drawer shut and smile awkwardly at the intruder.

It's Dad. His salt-and-pepper hair is rumpled and slightly saltier than I remember. Can fifteen months really make that much of a difference?

"How are you feeling, honey?" He's smiling, but his tea-green eyes aren't crinkled, so I can tell he's apprehensive. "You must be overwhelmed."

"I'm . . . fine." I divert my stare to my fingers. They seem fuller. I must have the iron supplements and my earnest desire to learn to cook to thank—every online forum I visited after my diagnosis recommended becoming best friends with my kitchen. I'm still not at the "average" percentile for weight or height, though I've grown a couple of inches vertically, thankfully. They measured me at five-foot-six at the hospital. "It's just a lot. Missing a year of my life."

"It's like the doctor said—give it some time, and you'll hopefully start to see results in the next few days or weeks." He scratches his fingers through my honey-blond hair, accidentally grazing the welt. I avoid flinching. "Keep faith, okay?"

I'm used to my parents trying to be optimistic around me. "How much is our insurance about to go up?" I whisper, scanning his face.

Dad's unruly brows furrow. "Don't worry about that, Riley. All you need to do is focus on healing."

"You always say that," I mumble.

"And I mean it." Maybe Dad sees the tearful frustration building in my eyes, because his own soften. He readjusts his rectangular glasses and props himself on my mattress, then rubs my knee. He's probably trying to soothe me, but another monstrous bruise spans my leg there, and his touch exacerbates the throbbing. "Ask whatever questions you want, and we'll do our best to answer them without overwhelming you, like the doctor suggested. Try to reestablish your routine so things feel normal. Mom and I will get the bills paid, and you can look after the house. Sound good?"

As if it hasn't always been this way. Over the past year in particular (or, I guess, two years), my obsession with cleaning everything to keep myself from getting sick evolved into me deep-cleaning the entire house on a regular basis. It's the least I can do to make up for the former hospital visits.

"Sounds good," I say.

I notice a shadow in the doorframe and look over to find Logan lingering in the hallway. He's bulked his upper body over the past year. The violet bruises under his eyes are intense from lack of sleep, and he keeps scratching at the maple-brown hair behind his neck.

Dad glances between us, then offers another nervous smile, and says, "Get some rest, honey. Let us know if you need anything." With that, he heads downstairs. Logan examines me in this thorough, cautious way, like I'm a land mine that might detonate if he treads on the wrong carpet strand. Like he's still not sure if he should believe my amnesia. I can't blame him, considering how perfectly functional I am.

Whatever Logan wants to ask me is trapped behind his tightly pressed lips. So I blurt a question I've been avoiding.

"Why did Aaron call himself my boyfriend?"

Logan's eyes glint with annoyance. He's quiet for a full fifteen seconds, like he's weighing his words. The silence scratches and claws at me, and every moment feels like another lost year of life.

Finally, he speaks. It's what I expect. It helps nothing.

"You and Aaron dated."

I wait for more explanation, my pulse fast enough to catch fire, queasiness stirring in my stomach. "And?" I accidentally snap. I throw my finger into my mouth and chew it, wincing. "Sorry."

"And what?" Logan peers at me with a level of intensity that's nearly accusatory.

I gnaw harder on my finger. "Are we currently dating?"

"Yes." Logan's voice is short and monotone. He clearly doesn't want to talk about this, but I can't abandon the topic when it's been eating at me since I woke up.

"For how long?"

His mouth twists downward with displeasure. "A year or something."

I nearly choke. I'm not sure how I could tolerate someone so awful for so long, especially after he ruined my brother's future. Logan was an honor student with perfect grades and attendance. He spent his free time studying in his room or toning himself at the driving range while my parents took me to doctor's appointments and tried to help me monitor my fluctuating health. Until Aaron infiltrated our lives and sent him careening down a path of delinquency.

"Um. So. Why did we start dating?" I ask weakly.

Logan reacts like the answer is on the tip of his tongue, but when he meets my eyes, his mouth freezes. His apple bobs in his throat. "You never told me," he says.

I'm chomping so angrily on my finger now that it's prickling with pain. After they were arrested, I determined I would never let Aaron Beckham into our house again. Despite being a full head shorter, I was resolved to shove him away with every ounce of strength my body would allow.

Or that was my plan. How could it have fallen apart so abysmally?

"Then what happened between you two?" I ask. "I know your relationship was rocky after the arrest, but I didn't think you *hated* him."

His fingers are curled so tight that his tan hands are bone-white. "I couldn't stand watching him hurt you," he mutters, turning away so I can't see his expression. "He filled your head with garbage and talked you into ruining your life. I know you, Riley. You're kind. Responsible. Selfless. But you were becoming somebody else, because Aaron corrupts anyone who gets close. I should fucking know. You tried to save me, and I didn't listen."

He's clawing into his jeans, like his nails tearing into his palms isn't enough to satisfy his anger. It's strange. Logan usually hugs his emotions close—it's like he's a different person.

"I don't know how he convinced me to date him," I whisper, more guilt raking my chest. "I'm sorry. For being a hypocrite. Telling you to stay away, then doing that . . ."

"He's a manipulator, Riley." Logan's voice softens—maybe he can hear mine getting choked up. "It's not your fault. But . . . this amnesia . . . maybe it's a good thing. A chance for you to start over before Aaron ruins your future, like he did mine." Logan peeks over his shoulder, strangely calm, considering he was just shaking with rage. "I can't tell you what to do, but here's some advice."

I wait, the taste of blood stinging my mouth.

"Stay away from Aaron," he says sharply. "I'm sure he'll try convincing you that you're better off with him. Don't be fooled just because you like his face."

Embarrassment surges through me. "Who said I like his face?" I squeak.

"You do, with your eyes, constantly. You could never stop staring at him." Logan gives me an irked look, and it makes me want to dive beneath my covers. If ever I stare at Aaron Beckham, it's because I'm imagining doing something horrible to him. Not because his eyes are winter gray and framed in inch-long lashes that could power wind turbines. Or because his skin is always smooth and silky for an eighteen—or, I guess, nineteen-year-old boy's. Or because his soft facial features stand in nice contrast to the sharp ridges of his jaw and collarbone. Or because he has a lopsided, mischievous smile that could skip the hearts of all straight men in his proximity.

"I stare at him for murderous intents and purposes only," I say, lowering my finger so I can massage away the pain. "But you're right. I won't let Aaron manipulate me. Things will go back to normal. I promise."

Logan's eyes lower from mine, and I swear I see the quickest glint of shame before he turns to the door. "That's all I've wanted for months, Riley," he mumbles.

Then he's gone, leaving me with my swirling thoughts and my pounding head.

3

I'm thirsty.

My dry eyes are latched on the empty water glass on my bedside table. I don't know why today is so difficult. I moved around a lot, I guess. Unpacking my clothes (my family has been vague about the moving boxes). Making two separate dinners (they tried going gluten-free with me, but I told them not to worry about it since the brands aren't usually as good). And just mentally reorienting myself to the present.

Now I'm thirsty. But I'm aching too much to move, and I can't tell if it's because I'm still sore from the car accident, if my anemia is flaring up, or if it's some irritating combination of the two. Maybe I should text Logan, but it's after midnight, and it sounds like he's been picking up my slack over the past year, so I shouldn't bother him. Without my calendar, I feel even more behind than usual—I need to investigate to make sure everyone has been keeping up with appointments and bills. My parents tell me not to bother myself with things like that, but they're both so flighty and busy with their jobs, I took it upon myself to keep the house standing.

I can fill my water glass. I can do that much.

I muscle upright and fumble through my drawer for ibuprofen. Not the liquid gels. I found out they have gluten the hard way. It was one of those brief, unexpected moments where reality backhanded me, and I nearly chewed through my thumb to avoid bursting into tears. Like, really? Why does over-the-counter pain relief need *wheat starch*?

I didn't realize how many things have gluten as a staple ingredient until I started meticulously studying labels. A couple of months—or, over a year ago—I had to throw away my hand sanitizers because they contained wheat amino acids. My finger-gnawing habit always ensures it'll get into my mouth somehow. I had to replace our sunscreens. My favorite shampoo. All as a precaution.

Now I get to deal with this nonsense on top of that nonsense.

Acknowledging it causes my eyes to burn.

Fifteen months. Gone. Just *gone*.

It doesn't make sense. I thought "amnesia" was a plotline showrunners used in cable television to freshen things up. Or Hallmark romcoms starring white city girls and whiter small-town boys. It's just a concussion, so the amnesia should be temporary, like the doctor told me.

I hope.

I shake two tablets onto the side table and rise to my feet, wobbling precariously. I've always felt brittle, though I started feeling better after my diagnosis and subsequent steps to correct my eating. Celiac disease wasn't their first opinion, mostly because my worst symptoms don't typically involve the stomach or check the common indicator boxes.

Some people might call me lucky because I don't have something worse. True, my treatment doesn't require much more than a particular diet and iron supplements. But just because it's easy to treat doesn't mean it's easy to live with. I have to be hyperaware of everywhere I go, everything I touch. I avoid places like bakeries because there could be flour remnants in the air. I need to have separate cooking supplies from my family—Tupperware, baking sheets, a toaster, wooden utensils, frying pans. I can't eat at most restaurants because cross-contamination is my number one enemy. Family events are a nightmare with people shoving homemade dishes in my face, telling me "a little won't hurt," and then being passive-aggressive when I refuse.

I need water.

I start toward the door when I hear a soft sliding noise coming from my window, like the frame is moving. I seize up, my heart lurching.

Someone is coming into my bedroom.

I should scream, but I'm so startled that I can only stare at my blackout curtain, slack-jawed. We don't have stairs leading to the second story. I don't have a balcony someone could vault onto. Am I hallucinating on top of everything else? Do I have more brain damage than they thought?

The curtain folds to the side, guided by a giant hand.

It's Aaron Beckham.

He's perched on a sturdy wooden branch belonging to the tree that stretches over my rooftop, dressed in a black T-shirt, jeans, and sneakers. He's got one foot through the window, and he's bracing the other against the branch to push himself into my bedroom.

He catches my eye.

"What?" I say.

"Hello," he says.

That's when realization slams into me, and I hurtle toward the panes in sudden panic, seizing his ankle. "Don't you dare!" I squawk, shoving him back toward the tree he's balanced on. "You're not allowed in my house!"

Aaron curses and wobbles, seizing the window frame to steady himself. "Surely this isn't attempted murder, sunshine," he says with a nervous laugh, like he's genuinely not sure if I'm about to commit voluntary manslaughter.

"What are you doing here?" I demand, clinging to his foot as he tries to wriggle it out of my grasp. Aaron buckles, intentionally drawing backward so I stagger into the frame. He snatches my wrist, his other palm still gripping the window, and smiles playfully as he pries my fingers off his ankle.

"A valiant effort to end my life," he commends. "But it won't work. Every time you push me away, I'll pull you in closer. It's a favor, really. Since your fingers are always cold."

He tugs my wrist until I'm nearly leaning out the window, the cool air of a mild summer's night unfurling across my face.

I'll smack him again, and this time, I'll do it so hard that he'll lose all his memories, too, and he can go back to seeing me as his best friend's irritable little brother who's always telling him to get lost. I mean it when I say I'm not violent, but he's basically breaking and entering, right? Who knows what kind of nefarious things he has planned?

Right as my hand is lurching out, he releases the window and grabs it. "I just told you," he says, his grin widening when my jaw clenches. "If you push, I'll pull. Is it just that you want your boyfriend to hold your hands?"

"You're not my boyfriend," I say fiercely, my heart pinballing between my chest and throat.

Aaron winces, like I've just backhanded him with my words. "That's news to me. Then, how are you going to get rid of me now that I have you in my evil clutches? I'd advise against headbutting, what with your . . . you know. All of that." He looks pointedly at the side of my head, where the lump is.

"What do you want?" I demand.

"To marry you and escape to the countryside eventually. But if you're referring to this exact moment, it's to talk to my beloved on solid ground." Aaron releases me and gestures to my bedroom. "May I?"

"I'm breaking up with you," I say instantly.

His slender black brows poke into his forehead. I hold his gaze, my own menacing. No hesitation. No room for manipulation. He can't sweet-talk me into making the same mistakes.

Amusement glitters in his eyes, though. "Okay," he says, nodding thoughtfully. I swear I hear a faint tremor in his voice, but when he swallows and continues talking, it disappears. "But as your partner of fourteen months, I should get to know why."

Fourteen months? That means we started dating shortly after he and Logan were arrested. That's an incomprehensible amount of time for high schoolers, let alone two people who don't like each other. "You're a bad influence," I say shortly.

I swear his ridiculous smile is getting bigger every time I open my mouth. "A bad influence you agreed to date," he points out, folding his egregiously long limbs atop his knees and nestling his chin into them.

"Have you considered that you like a bit of excitement in your perfectly sweet and innocent life?"

You'd think, with the anemia and all, that my face wouldn't be so hot with excess blood flow. But it is because he's right. I fell for it. I can see the truth in the way Logan spoke about us. "I don't," I say firmly. "I'm sorry, but whatever this is, it was a mistake."

The grin melts from Aaron's face, so slowly that it almost seems like he's fighting to maintain it. His head tilts sideways. He's studying me in that same careful, methodical manner that Logan was earlier, like he's seeking a hidden glint of recognition in my eyes. "Hate that word," he mumbles, voice muffled in his arms.

I crinkle my face with annoyance. "What?"

"Sorry."

I wait for an explanation. He doesn't offer one.

"Bye," I sputter out, and I slam the window shut, lock it, and throw the curtain over it before promptly heaving a shuddery gasp of relief. I did it. It's over. Aaron Beckham and I are no more. Now I just need to undo the damage I caused to this house during my period of . . . rebellion or whatever.

Tap. Tap. Tap.

The tension comes rushing back into my body.

Tap. Tap. Tap.

He's thrumming his fingers against my window.

I'll just ignore him. I have headphones around here somewhere. I pull out my drawers, a muscle twinging in my forehead. No luck, but whatever. I need water anyway. He'll be gone by the time I get back.

So I fill my water downstairs. I linger in the kitchen, tidying up scattered paperwork on the granite island, including some homework Logan left out for a summer class. The sight is relieving. It means that despite everything, he's still thinking about his future. Community college isn't "full ride to prominent university for a sport" levels of excitement, but at least he didn't give up after what happened a few weeks—or last year. Last year.

I wipe down the countertops with a sponge (just in case—it's clearly been a while since I cleaned). I return to my bedroom with a full water glass, fatigue blanketing my limbs.

Tap. Tap. Tap.

Voluntary manslaughter or first-degree murder? I wonder which I could get away with. I'm plotting his death, but the police don't have to know. I bet I'd have a good self-defense case, considering Aaron is committing a crime.

I storm to the window and rip the curtains back, glowering through the panes. Aaron is still crouched on that massive branch extending past the window, his handsome face propped in one open palm, his available fingers poking the glass. He waves at me with unbridled enthusiasm.

I unlock the window, yank it up, and snap, "I told you it's over. Respect that."

"I'd rather continue bothering you," he admits, his attention slinking away from my face to observe the rest of me. There's nothing important to notice—I'm in a tank top and sweatpants, so at least my knobby knees aren't on display. "I like the face you make when you're irritated. Your nose crinkles up and your eyes get squinty." He sighs wistfully. "It makes me want to bully you."

His words spark another level of anger. He's never gotten to me this easily before, but this week has been brutal, and I'm at my tolerance limit. "You want to beat me up?" I ask darkly. "Good to know I wasted a year of my life with you."

Aaron gives me such a skeptical look that it heats the hollows of my cheeks again. "You think that's what I meant by *bully you*?"

"What else?" I demand.

"I prefer to use my mouth."

"Ah." I roll my eyes, my scowl deepening. "Right. Insults sting deeper. Sure."

Aaron bursts into laughter with such force that I stagger back in surprise. Immediately, he vaults through my open window and onto my carpeted flooring. "I didn't mean that either," he says, his hands rising to combat my incoming shove. It's too late to stop myself, and the moment my palms touch his shoulders, he scoops them gently into his grasp. His skin is still warm, contrasting with his cool appearance. But then, everyone's skin is warmer than mine.

"Obviously, I only dated you because you threatened me or something," I snarl. "Your *bullying* won't work anymore."

"Since you're not getting the hint, I'll spell it out." Aaron pulls me until the tips of my toes are treading over his, and suddenly, his silky-smooth voice is combing the arch of my ear. "When I say I want to bully you, I mean I want to kiss every inch of you until you're begging for mercy. Make sense, sunshine?"

Goose bumps explode across my body in a disorienting rush of realization. We've probably kissed plenty, if we've been dating over a year. This bullying threat might be something he's actually followed through on. "Why are you still here?" I choke out, my thoughts so deep-fried with exhaustion that I can't offer any insults or warnings.

Aaron considers this. Then with his frost-gray eyes unblinking, he says, "Because I love you, Riley Wilson."

4

I stare up at Aaron Beckham.

Aaron Beckham stares back at me.

"Wrong," I say, because nothing else fits here. Nothing could make this make sense. How could Aaron, who only ever referred to me as a "little brat" when I was nearby, love me? We've spent the last couple of years glaring at each other over Logan's shoulder, him with a snide grin and me with annoyance.

Aaron is massaging my fingers, and the increased blood circulation warms my frigid hands. He's clearly doing it with little thought, like it's second nature. Like it's a habit nestled into his subconscious. "I'm not lying," he says, softer, without the cocky edge that's been grating on my ears. His eyes are so unwavering that I have to redirect my stare so my thoughts won't turn into mush. I fixate on the glittery black stud in his ear, then the narcissus flower tattooed behind it, then the curls.

Then the ground, because I don't want to notice anything else.

"Please let go," I mutter.

Aaron hesitates, the hopeful gleam dissipating in his gaze. His fingers loosen, and I slip my hands out of his. There's a long, tense moment of silence.

"Then it's true, huh?" Aaron smiles, but it's frail. Nothing like the usual impishness that shadows every grin he's ever offered me. "You don't remember. Not a single date. Single moment. Single word. It's gone. It's actually . . . everything we've been through . . . ah. Fuck." He forces his grin to widen despite how fake it is. "I don't really know what to do. Ha. This sucks."

My throat tightens. I'm not sure why. Anything we built together was clearly a mistake. But this smoldering, aching sensation is singeing the crevices of my chest, because Aaron's eyes . . .

He's hurting.

I hate how desperate I am to understand why.

"I . . . I'm sorry," I say, because apologies are all I'm good for. "But I can't see any way in which a relationship could be healthy for either of us."

"So ask." Aaron offers another smile as pained as his gaze. "I'll tell you. I'll *show* you."

He stands there, waiting. Logan's words come back in a deafening roar.

I'm sure he'll try convincing you that you're better off with him. Don't be fooled just because you like his face.

So I merely stand there, staring at the floor.

"Okay." Aaron draws a long, weighted breath, as if steeling himself. Sure enough, the soft, snowy texture in his eyes returns to being solid ice. It's not cruel, though, or unfriendly. It's more like he's resolved. "If this is how you need to cope, I understand. But . . ."

Suddenly, he's closing the space between us and frames my face in his warm palms.

"Are you okay?" he whispers.

I blink, so astonished that I forget to rip out of his grasp. "Am I okay?" I repeat, the words strangely foreign.

"You just woke up from a two-day-long coma after a car crash that wiped a year's worth of memories from you." Aaron's hands move along the sides of my head, gentle enough that it doesn't hurt when he grazes the swollen lump from where my skull connected with the window. "Break up with me if you want, but . . . but tell me what you need first."

I can barely process what he's saying. "I'm fine" is all I can scrounge together.

"Have you cried?"

I keep looking at him, because I'm behind, so far behind I can't even think—

"Where does it hurt?"

The world is swimming. I think I'm about to faint from the sheer sensation of being overwhelmed, but then I realize it's because a film of tears is clogging my vision. I can't get rid of it—whenever I blink it away, it lies in wait behind my eyes to surge forward when I'm least expecting.

I try to say, *Nowhere.*

What comes out is "Everywhere."

The acknowledgment heightens every ache in my body. My legs are sore—even standing is a bother. My ankles feel swollen, lifting my arms takes effort, and there's an undercurrent of constant, unending discomfort pulsing in my skull. It hasn't been this bad since before the diagnosis. I expect the car accident is to blame by setting me so far back.

I try to steady my breathing. I won't cry. I have no reason to cry.

"You can cry if you want," Aaron says, tucking me into his chest like I belong there, folding his arms around me like he's done it a million times. Instinctively, I slump against him, as if my body knows it's safe here in spite of my mind's insistence that it's not.

"Get out," I breathe, because he's Aaron Beckham, the boy who ruined my brother's future. Logan told me just hours ago that mine is next. Why is it that when my brother came to his senses, I lost mine? How could I allow myself to be swapped in as the new victim so easily?

"I will," he says, and I'm too drained to stop him from nestling me onto my mattress, then cradling my head and lowering it to the pillow. He's treating me so kindly all of a sudden—he must be trying to earn brownie points. I didn't take to his playful flirtation, so he's veering off course. It's a manipulation tactic.

"Did you finish unpacking?" Aaron ambles toward the boxes stacked in the corner of the room. "I tried organizing everything to make it easier—"

"What are you talking about?"

Aaron pauses. I stare at him from my pillow, my blood crystallizing into snowflakes. He doesn't answer right away, and everyone's hesitation around me—their silent contemplation that stretches for hours, like the wrong words might wound me—is driving me mad. Finally, he asks, "Nobody told you why your things are in boxes?"

A sense of dread expands in my abdomen. No way. I know what he's about to say, but it can't possibly be true.

"You moved in with me and my dads two months ago," he says, the confirmation a dagger between my ears. "After the accident, your dad asked me to bring your things here so you could heal at home. I figured you didn't need the added stress and did as I was asked." His pale eyes flicker with irritation. "They didn't tell you that you've been living with me?"

I can't hear myself breathing. My vision tunnels in as my eyes move to the dangling calendar, stuck on April, only half the weeks filled out. The reason I didn't flip it. The reason the boxes are here. The reason Logan has been so tense.

I left.

"No," I choke out. "I wouldn't abandon my family. I'm not that kind of person. That's so . . ." My chest is tightening, my breaths leaving in short, violent punches. I throw my hands over my eyes. It's too much. My inner child, who I've wrangled into silence over the years, is kicking and screaming. I want to damn the consequences and hit the wall until my knuckles break, or screech until my lungs give out. I threw away my responsibilities, my family, my life, and for *what*?

The bed creaks under his weight, his jeans grazing my sweatpants. "Breathe, okay?" he says, and he reaches out, like he wants to furl his hand over my back, before promptly wincing and seizing his own wrist to keep himself from touching me.

"The paint," I gasp out, a feeble attempt at distraction. "My room. It's painted. There are pictures on the walls. Your dads run a handyman business . . . Did they do this?"

"Their third partner did."

"Who?"

"Me."

I peek between my fingers, startled out of my near meltdown.

"They've apprenticed me since I was little," he explains. "I did summer coursework after graduation to cover some of the legal aspects, and they brought me into the business. Though, I can't handle larger cases until I have my contractor's license. I'm good at working with my hands."

Suddenly, the memory of opening my bedside drawer lurches to the front of my mind. I don't want to ask for clarity, but I'm so painfully lost, and Aaron seems like the only person willing to offer answers. Maybe they're all lies, or twisted truths, or exaggerations, but it's information I don't have.

I won't match his immaturity—I can handle this subject without acting like a blushing maiden. So I lower my palms, and confidently ask, "Did we really have sex?"

I blush immediately.

It's humiliating, but I can't help it. I've never dated anyone. I figured my chances of finding someone who could tolerate my severe eating restrictions and unpredictable roller coaster of physical discomfort would be next to none. If I ever saw someone interesting around school, I squashed whatever butterflies stirred in my stomach.

Aaron allows the silence to linger, and this time it's fully intentional, like he wants to tease me with the weight of anticipation. I can't look him in the eye—he's probably wearing the most gleeful, insufferable expression.

"Yes," he says, calmer and more matter-of-fact than I expect. "We've had sex."

My airway narrows. The thought of letting Aaron be intimate with me . . . I might panic again. "How many times?" I croak.

Aaron laughs, and I resist plunging my face back into my hands, because who am I kidding? I can't tackle this subject with grace and poise. "I didn't think to count," he admits, his teeth glittering under the golden lighting of the bedside lamp. "Should I guess? Or recount every memory in detail? To help you remember, of course. Or I can show you my poor, suffering back."

"Your back?" I squeak out, my eyes spinning.

Something strange happens. A sharp, lightning-like zap rips through my skull, so brief that I wonder if I imagined it. Then I feel . . . something. Skin. Under my nails. I'm raking my fingers down a stretch of flesh, but it's not my own, because I don't feel the sting.

I smack my forehead and the sensation evaporates.

"Hasn't your head been through enough?" Aaron asks with nervous laughter.

Vomiting isn't one of my typical medical issues, but I'm dangerously close to projectile expelling the contents in my stomach. I can't discern whether the nausea stems from self-geared anger or disgust at the thought of him touching me. I need this guy out of my room before he tells me anything else worth gagging over, so I fly to my feet, then seize Aaron's wrist and hoist him to his.

"I don't have any more questions," I say sternly. "You can leave now."

"You're kicking me out because we've had sex?" Aaron asks with a rage-inducing snicker. "Really, what did you expect? We've been dating over a year, we lived together for two months, and in case you didn't hear, I'm in love with you. Plus, you're a pretty blond thing who turns red when I tease you. Do you think I'm well behaved enough to keep my hands to myself?"

My mortification is so overwhelming that I want to rip my hair from my scalp. "I'm not some piece of meat!" I cry out, pushing him toward my bedroom door. Too late do I remember his promise to pull whenever I push, and sure enough, he gathers my wrists into one palm. Rather than tugging, though, he steps into my space, prompting me to backpedal into the door.

Aaron Beckham bends down, his frosty eyes sparkling with mischief. I can smell mint in his exhales and see the shininess in each black lock curling over his forehead. As if wanting to intensify my annoyance, he leans his lanky arm on the doorway over my head.

"What are you doing?" I sputter out.

"Listen—I want to respect you," Aaron says. He smiles again, but this one is flimsy and tired. He's not amused as much as he is exhausted. Or hurt. "I know you're in a lot of pain. I know you want me to disappear. And if it would help you, I would. But I won't let your family use your amnesia as an excuse to make things go back to how they used to be. I'm going to fight for you. So I can't always do as you ask."

Aaron draws my hands into his chest, his eye contact severe enough that I can only stand there and stare at him, transfixed.

"I'm sorry in advance for pushing your boundaries," he whispers. "I know you must be confused and overwhelmed. I can't even imagine what it's like to be in your position. I want to prove to you that I'm more than the person you remember me being. That I can help you through this. Not that you need it. Not that you'd ever ask for it."

His gaze flickers with a strange, fond exasperation. The sight settles like a haze over my agitated thoughts, dulling the sharp, angry edges.

"I can't give up on you just yet, Riley Wilson. I made you fall for me once. I can do it again. Even if I have to start from square one." He plants a kiss between my knuckles. "So please forgive me for being a brat. For catching you when you push, and forgetting when I'm staring at you, and asking you how you're feeling too many times, and showing up unannounced, and accidentally being too handsy, and whatever else I've gotten used to that may no longer be okay."

I don't know how to respond. I don't know what to think. Did he prepare this speech before he came here, or is he naturally this charming? Has he always been, and I just didn't know it?

"I know today has been a lot for you. I'll give you some space." With great reluctance, his hands slide away, and he heads to my bedroom window.

"J-just give up," I order, smearing my palm on my sweatpants so I won't feel the imprint of his lips against my skin. My head is still spinning with the words he just assailed me with. With the unexpectedly gentle tone of his voice. With the affectionate gleam in his eyes. "This is the last time we're going to talk, so scheming won't work."

Aaron is halfway out the window and pauses to peer over at me, his handsome face lighting with another roguish smirk I can't stand. "Good night, sunshine," he says.

Then he's gone, and all I taste is bitterness.

And the faintest hint of peppermint.

5

I come downstairs the next morning to find my mother pinballing around the kitchen, her dirty-blond hair in disarray, the buttons of her jacket mismatched.

"Late for a client?" I ask from the foot of the stairs.

She whirls around, her hazel eyes brightening. "Riley!" she cries out, sprinting toward me, her heels clacking noisily against the tile. She throws her arms around my shoulders and wrenches me into her chest, then squeezes tight enough that my bones cry in protest. "How was your first night? Did you sleep well? How are you feeling?"

Mom is always shifting from one thing to the next. Her frenetic personality would be fine if it weren't amplified by her flightiness. Thankfully, I only inherited the first trait, or my life would be in constant chaos. "I'm fine," I say—a blanket response that makes her click her tongue with dissatisfaction. But she clearly doesn't have time to try to pull a more accurate answer out of me, because she draws back.

"Make sure you get lots of rest," she says, bopping my nose. "Logan has class until some time and is working until two or something. Dad and I won't be home until late. I've overbooked myself."

She laughs with a dismissive wave.

"I thought you were doing better about making sure your appointments don't overlap," I say, my brow rising. "What happened to the calendar app I set up for you?"

"The . . . ? Oh, yes." She nods in recognition of my words. "I must've forgotten to upkeep it."

I swear she and Dad would leave their heads at home if they weren't permanently attached to their bodies. How Logan and I managed to develop a sense of responsibility under their care is an enigma. But then, I guess we both learned the hard way that we can only rely on ourselves, and sometimes each other. At least they made active attempts to be there for my doctor's appointments, but beyond that, they've always been a bit scatterbrained. "Sorry," I mumble. "I don't know why I left."

"Oh, honey. Why would you apologize for my incompetence? Besides, you're not to blame for teenage hormones." She pokes my nose again. That hasn't changed. Her constant need to fidget with me and tap my face and rumple my hair. "The point is that you're home and healing. I'm sure your memories will come back in no time."

Guilt is still bubbling in a pool at the bottom of my stomach.

"Rest up, honey. Oh, and there's a grocery list on the counter with my card. If you're up for it, maybe you can swing by the store. Only if you're comfortable getting behind a wheel, of course." She's backing toward the door, her cherry-red lips parted with a toothy smile. "Also, would you whip up dinner, if you're feeling well enough? It's been a while since we've indulged in your expert cooking."

"Expert?" I roll my eyes, smirking. The only reason I'm a half-decent cook is because I have to be or eating is a miserable experience. "Sure."

"Thanks." She's nearly sprinting to the door now.

"Wait," I call. She swivels, then blinks in confusion when I approach her. I undo the bottom buttons of her coat, then correctly match them. "Your lunch?"

"Oh!" She palms her forehead, then jogs to the fridge and seizes a lunch box from the bottom shelf. "My hero. See you tonight!"

Then she's gone.

I sigh, ambling to the medicine cabinet so I can pop some iron supplements before stopping by the kitchen island to examine the list.

I feel better today, so I can definitely do this. My legs are wobbly, my bones feel malleable, and I'm lightheaded, but it's not debilitating. Besides, everyone is out and about with responsibilities, and I'm sitting around with nothing to do but . . . what? Heal? Apparently, I've made myself useless this summer, since I'm not taking any classes or working a job.

I don't go immediately, because I'm still groggy. I hardly slept, tossing around, the memory of Aaron's fingers around my hands too heavy to ignore. The coolness of his breath in my ear—the reverberation of his voice through my bones.

Because I love you, Riley Wilson.

A full-body chill ravages me, forcing me to sit on the couch and bury my face in my hands. All he did was tease me yesterday.

And yet, he's the only person who bothered to answer my questions.

Maybe I shouldn't be too hard on my family. They're clearly being vague because they don't want me to feel embarrassed by my own actions, and the doctor literally told them to avoid overwhelming me with information. Their reluctance to engage with me about the past in too much detail obviously stems from the desire to protect me.

Still . . . I want to know anyway. The bad. The worst. Aaron's version will be skewed—a dim, blood-red light in this crushing darkness.

But it's still a light.

How did he convince me to move in with him? His dads just allowed that? Is he why I enrolled at some random college that wasn't in my top ten schools of choice? Why does he think he loves me?

What about me is worth loving, anyway?

There's a knock on the front door. I pry my face out of my hands, a crease surfacing between my brows. If it's Aaron, I'm slamming the door in his face. I storm toward it and swing it open, prepared to hurl the cruelest insult I can muster.

I don't expect to find a dozen people waiting for me.

"Welcome back, Riley!" they cry out.

I stare at them blankly.

"Woo-hoo!" one of them tacks on.

I have no idea what's happening. Looking closer, I recognize some of them from my graduating class. I might've had conversations with them in group projects, but otherwise, I don't have solid relationships with any of them. Yet they're all grinning expectantly, and two of them are holding WELCOME BACK signs that clearly took effort.

"Sorry, you're probably confused," a pretty girl in front says, laughing. I recognize her as the class treasurer, Amy Choi. She extends a hand, her onyx-black eyes crinkling with a smile. "Aaron told us about the amnesia. I'm head of the history club. You joined us for senior year. We still meet up over the summer when the museums get new exhibits, so we wanted to reintroduce ourselves."

She's trying to diffuse my confusion, but it only worsens the haze in my head. Since when was I in a club? I like history—it's my favorite subject, and I'm a glutton for a good museum—but I've always considered extracurriculars to be a waste of time. And what does Aaron have to do with this?

I only realize I haven't responded when they start fidgeting. "Ah, sorry," I say with a wobbly smile. "Nice to meet . . . or thank you for coming to see me. I'm sorry, I don't remember the history club. It sounds fun?"

"It is!" Amy says brightly, shaking my hand with enthusiasm. She reintroduces me to the line of people crowding my door. Everyone is staring at me, some of them with skepticism, like they don't believe I can't remember them. I notice movement in my peripherals, and my attention is drawn to the street curb. A scarlet pickup truck is parked beside my house, and leaning against the passenger door, gangly arms folded, a sucker stick jutting from his mouth . . .

I forcibly keep my face from gnarling with a scowl. I'm so distracted that when Amy says, "We'd love to take you for ice cream," I respond with, "Sure."

I can't swallow the word in time. I avoid ice cream shops religiously because they're as torturous to sit in as bakeries. Airborne gluten is less of a threat, but cross-contamination is nearly unavoidable with all the add-ins, the smell is intoxicating, and I haven't eaten today. I'll be starving and watching people lick ice cream I can't have.

"Actually, I have to go shopping," I blurt, lifting my grocery list. Suddenly, though, it's being snatched out of my hands. Aaron has appeared on the step beside me, his lightly curled hair poking over his forehead, accompanied by a black V-neck shirt and jeans. I've never seen him in any other color. He probably wants his exterior to match the all-consuming corruption of his soul.

Or he just knows he looks good in it.

"This can be done any time, can't it?" he asks, pocketing the grocery list. I'm still being stared at, so I swallow my biting words. "You should go enjoy yourself with your friends. Get reacquainted. I'll join up with you soon."

I want to growl that he shouldn't feel comfortable bossing me around. "Give it back," I order, but he's already sauntering to his truck.

"See you soon!"

My singular "out" of this situation has been stolen away, so I hitch a ride with Amy to the ice cream shop. Part of me wonders if getting into the passenger seat of a car will awaken anything in me—memories or primal fear or something. But it feels strangely normal, like it did when I was driven home from the hospital.

The shop has a worn-down parking lot and faded Christmas stickers on the windows. Several history club members try to buy me something, to which I can only apologize despite their insistence.

The history club doesn't seem offended that I can't remember them, and they're willing to catch me up. Apparently, we took trips to museums like the American Innovation Museum and the Wright Museum of African American History. Seeing so many people in school who have a shared love of learning is nice. Though it doesn't explain how I was convinced to join.

After enduring a few incessant questions about my amnesia, the club turns to a new subject—there's an updated Civil War exhibit at the history museum downtown. My skin tingles at the thought. Maybe

I'm basic, but it's one of my favorite periods to learn about. It sounds like they're willing to let me tag along despite my lack of memories.

"We'll have to leash you, though," one girl says, grinning at me. "Whenever we go on field trips, we lose you in the exhibitions. You get so into reading the placards that you forget to keep up."

The thought reddens my face. "Sorry," I say sheepishly, to which they all laugh.

"For what? It's funny." Amy tilts her head, her lush black hair spilling over her shoulder. "No offense, but it was clear you had never been in clubs before. It took a couple of months before you started opening up. Only because Aaron made you come to meetings, and he'd join us on field trips."

Her words are only spreading the heat from my cheeks into the rest of my face. Suddenly, something icy cold is pressing against my neck, and I squirm away, looking up.

"Hi, sunshine," Aaron Beckham says. He's standing on the checkered floor beside me, holding two pints of ice cream and wrapped plastic spoons. He puts one of each on the table, then drags a chair over and plops beside me.

"Why are you here?" I demand, narrowing my eyes.

"To harass my ex," he says with a syrupy smile that exposes his pointy canines.

Determined to ignore him, I turn to the pint he gave me, and avoid reacting when I realize it's a Ben & Jerry's certified gluten-free flavor. It's also my favorite—chocolate peanut butter split. Reluctantly curious, I peek at his own pint. Vanilla caramel fudge.

"You're not also gluten-intolerant, right?" I ask.

"Nope." Aaron wriggles his spoon through the plastic wrap, shooting me an amused glance. "One of the first times we kissed, you ended up feeling like you had the flu for a day. I went gluten-free after that. Been a little over a year now."

He says it with such nonchalance, like it's not a complete upheaval of one's lifestyle. I want to believe he's lying, but he even brought me a wrapped disposable utensil, so he clearly knows the drill.

I try to steel my heart because I can feel it fluttering. I can't let myself be ensnared by his manipulation tactics just because he chose to do something thoughtful. "Well, thank you for bothering, but we're not together anymore, so you should go back to eating whatever," I say, peeling the lid off the pint.

"What if I want to kiss you senseless?" His eyes glitter with feigned innocence.

"You won't, because I'll never give you permission."

"Wait, what?" Amy looks between us with thinly veiled dismay, and I nearly jump. I forgot she was sitting across from me. "You broke up? Weren't you just living together?"

I want to explain myself, but as I'm conjuring an excuse to stumble through, Aaron sighs with melancholy and leans his pale elbow against the table. "Unfortunately, Amy, my beloved can't remember a single moment of our precious time together. To him, I'm a lowly troublemaker who only exists to poison his soul." He reaches over to twirl one of my dark blond strands of hair, and I smack it away.

"Stay out of my life." I stab my spoon into my ice cream, and he nibbles his lower lip like he's holding back laughter.

"Like I said yesterday, I want to respect your wishes, but I can't make you fall in love with me again if I'm not following you around being sexy and mysterious."

I resist dumping my pint upside down on his head.

To my relief, the history club draws us into a conversation—the incoming seniors are asking for recommendations on who they should request for a school visit and seminar. I nearly jump in with a suggestion, but I'm not confident enough to add my two cents, so I stay quiet, nibbling my delicious ice cream, shooting Aaron exasperated glances. He's finished his own pint, and he's holding some kind of toy. A brassy-golden cube with cogs, wheels, and gears, which he fidgets with mindlessly. He notices me watching and smiles, then drags his index finger along the inner rim of a cog.

I wrench my eyes away, swallowing a scream of frustration.

As if I could ever fall in love with Aaron Beckham.

6

I don't mind socializing. Being out with people who I don't remember but are treating me kindly is nice. Not something I'm used to.

I'm starting to feel antsy, though, because I should be doing other things. Grocery shopping, for one. I should prepare dinner at some point, and the house needs a deep clean. Thankfully, everyone parts ways as I'm scrambling for an excuse to leave.

"We'll let you know when that exhibit is open," Amy tells me as we amble into the parking lot, Aaron's presence looming at my back. "I hope we made you feel comfortable."

"You did," I say, and I mean it. I must've enjoyed the club, considering how much they know about me. Like the fact that the Civil War and World War II are my favorite periods, even if they're cliché. Or that I had an obsession with Audie Murphy, and not just because he was, in all my improper honesty, a hot piece of ass.

I wish I could remember my experiences with them. A couple of times, I've gone to museums and wanted to ramble to someone about the knowledge I've collected over the years. To know that I finally found people as passionate as me . . .

I just wish I could remember.

"I'm going to work, but Aaron said he'd drive you home," Amy tells me, and my blood ices.

"I'll walk," I say instantly.

Aaron peers down at me, his offensively long lashes fluttering. "I'd sooner carry you home," he says, eyes flicking to my knees. I don't realize until then that they're trembling.

"I'm fine," I say, rejecting the mental image of being carried across town princess-style.

"Sure, sunshine." His frosty eyes soften, and he waits for Amy to walk out of earshot before continuing. "Maybe you should go home and rest now. I can go shopping for you."

I stare up at him, baffled. His expression is insistent, almost desperate. He's clutching my grocery list tight in his fist. "Don't infantilize me," I snap, making a swipe for it. He hikes it over his head, forcing me to dance on my tiptoes to try to seize it. "I'm not some helpless baby. Besides, I like shopping for my family. It's the least I can do to make up for everything. All the fainting episodes and hospital bills and leaving them to fend for themselves . . ."

The frustration unravels in Aaron's face, and the spark in his eyes dulls, like his life force is trickling away. "Okay," he says, lowering his hand. Immediately, I rip the grocery list from his grip. "But you're unsteady, so I'd like to come with you."

"Are you my mom?" I mutter, storming toward the sidewalk to begin my trek home. Judging by the wobble in my legs, it'll take about twenty minutes. Or so I think, until Aaron slides in front of me so abruptly that I nearly collide with his snug black shirt. I stagger back with a scowl, hugging the list.

"Don't be annoying," I order. "Or I'll—"

"You'll what?" Aaron asks, that familiar "delight at my expense" creeping into his voice. "You'll break up with me again? You'll call me *troublemaker* and *scallywag* until I cry?"

All the blood in my body is in my face, thick and boiling. "I hate you," I snap.

Aaron's mischievous smile fractures, and his pale eyes flood with sudden, unexpected grief that hitches the breath in my lungs. "I . . . I understand," he whispers. "That's okay. I have enough love to carry both of us."

His words shouldn't mean anything to me. Yet they strike a chord so deep within my rib cage that I feel the reverberation through my body. It leaves behind an awful ache rooted in my bones, so powerful that when I blink, my eyes are swimming with tears.

"Sorry," I hear myself breathe. "I didn't mean it."

Aaron grazes his face, which promptly twists with guilt, like he didn't mean to show me his pained thoughts. He steps forward and nudges my forehead back with his index finger, causing my neck to arch so I can look up at him. "Riley," he says in that soft voice, the one that stands in contrast to everything I know about him. "Don't apologize for things outside your control. Please."

"But . . ." Frantically, I massage the burn out of my eyes. "You looked really hurt, so . . ."

Aaron's hand slides down the back of my head, his touch featherlight to avoid aggravating the healing bump. "That's one of my favorite things about you," he says. "You just told me you hate me, and now you're about to cry because I'm upset."

"I won't cry," I say, trying unsuccessfully to sound sharp and irritated.

"It's okay if you want to." His touch skims along the curve of my neck, then drifts over my collarbone, his middle finger falling into the divot of the bone. "I think it's beautiful that you care so much about the way you make others feel. Even people you don't like."

His palm centers on my chest. I hope his fingers aren't pressing deeply enough to feel my heartbeat.

"As if I could let you go," he mumbles.

This must be how he did it. How he lured me in. By speaking sweet, honeyed words until every functional aspect of my brain was drenched in them, unable to form coherent thoughts. Paired with my deeply embedded fear that I'll never find someone willing to tolerate my lifestyle . . .

This is why I latched on to Aaron, isn't it?

I doubt he'll let me walk away, so I push his hand off my chest and fling open his passenger door. "Let's go," I say, blinking away residual wetness.

Aaron gives me an unusually sympathetic smile that only twists and gnarls my understanding of this situation. Whenever I think I'm encroaching on the truth, he looks at me a certain way or says something to unravel my progress.

He climbs into the driver's seat. I make sure to buckle my seat belt.

He takes me directly to the grocery store.

"Don't think this puts me in your debt," I warn him as I clamber out and beeline for the shopping carts. "I didn't ask you to be here."

Aaron beats me there, snagging one and rolling it into the store. "Have you considered that I just want to spend time with the person I love?" he asks with a pointed, entertained look.

I try seizing the cart from his grasp, but he merely muscles me away, smirking. "Quit using that word so casually," I order.

"Which one?"

I glare up at him as we start down the nearest aisle.

So then Aaron Beckham and I are shopping. Thankfully, he's quieter than I expect, but mostly because he's spending thirty hours reading labels on cans, bags, and packages we come across.

"A lot of this is for my family," I tell him, folding my arms. "They don't follow my food regimen, so I cook in twos."

"I'm aware."

He says it with enough annoyance that my defensiveness skyrockets. "It's not like they didn't try. I literally told them to stop."

"Because you hate feeling like you're inconveniencing people." Aaron's knuckles whiten around the shopping cart. "Your family should keep trying, especially if you're the one doing most of the cooking."

"It's not that easy—"

"I know, Riley. Trust me." He catches my wrist and shifts my fingers between his, beginning to massage away the cold shiver. "I'm just saying that if my dads can build a whole new cabinet just to store their future son-in-law's gluten-free cookware *and* avoid eating it when he's in the house, your own family should be twice as willing to make the effort."

I can feel my face deciding whether it should turn white or crimson. Not only did I take up space, but I forced his dads to readjust their lives to fit my needs? And what's with his casual use of the phrase *son-in-law*, as if he's already put a ring on my finger?

Maybe Aaron senses he's not getting through to me, because he draws a deep, exasperated breath, allowing me to pull out of his grip. His very warm, very steady, very large grip. "Let's keep moving," he says, pushing the cart onward.

Aaron gets a few certified gluten-free snacks for himself—dark chocolate popcorn, sweet potato chips, and gummy bears. I must've had an influence on him, because they're my go-to snacks in a pinch.

"I told you not to worry about what you eat anymore," I say as we approach the checkout aisle. "We're never going to kiss again."

Aaron smiles like I've said something endearing, then adds a pack of mints to the cart. I'm not sure why, but his lack of a snide comment worsens my blush. He uses his card to pay, because I didn't bring Mom's with me when I was blindsided by the history club. I note the total so I can pay him later, and then we're heading to his truck.

"Did you enjoy it?" he asks.

I scoff. "Not particularly, since I didn't want you there."

Aaron laughs, and it's warmer than I expect. Whenever he laughed at me in the past, it was snide and cold, usually in response to a stern scolding. "I meant the history club," he says, wandering to the passenger side after we've loaded the groceries onto the back bench. He offers his hand to help me up like I'm a five-year-old and not a grown man who can now legally vote. Ignoring it, I step up and flop into the seat. Aaron grins, circles around to the driver's side, and tucks his long limbs into the seat. "Did you have fun?"

"I guess," I admit, folding my knees into my chest as we peel out of the lot. "They were nice. Amy said you're the reason I joined. Care to explain?"

Aaron shrugs. I notice then that while his limbs are lean, his shoulders are wider than I remember. I can see it in the way his shirt strains around his chest and falls looser on his waist. "You never felt like you had time to do things for yourself," he says, though I've already forgotten what we were talking about. "You like history, and I was friends with Amy, so I asked her to approach you. After months of me saying you should try it, all it took was a stranger telling you to come to a meeting, and you caved. Because you hate disappointing people you've just met."

I squirm with irritation. That does sound like me. "Amy said you came on the field trips sometimes," I say, eyeing him suspiciously. "Why?"

Aaron gives me a skeptical look as we pull into my driveway. "Why do you think? I like seeing you get excited over things. I like the look in your eyes when you learn something new. Just weeks ago we were planning a trip to Chicago so I could take you to every museum on your bucket list. Do you get it now?"

Of course not. It sounds too cutesy and romantic. Chicago is my most anticipated city to visit in the country—I can't imagine letting him ruin that experience for me.

Aaron single-handedly carries all the plastic grocery bags inside despite my disgruntlement. "You can leave now," I say as he dumps everything onto the kitchen island.

"But you have to label everything, right?" Aaron fumbles around the kitchen, clicking his tongue when he can't find the roll. "Your parents moved shit around—"

"I'll do it myself," I say, sharper. "Don't just ignore me when I tell you to leave. Why do you think disrespecting me is going to win me over?"

Aaron must hear the venom in my voice, because he stops rustling around and turns toward me. My fists are clenched, my stance is tall and combative, and my jaw is tight. "You're right," he says, his eyes finding mine, and the webs of gray in his insistent irises freeze me. "I'm sorry. I'm not trying to upset you. There's a lot you're dealing with, and . . . knowing that you're suffering through it alone . . . I just want to be here for you."

My right knee twitches. For a second I think I might collapse, but it doesn't trigger my apprehension. I'm not sure why, until a realization strikes me.

It's because I know he'll catch me.

But I *don't* know that. I have no memories of Aaron, no reason to trust him or his words. And yet . . .

"The truth is, I'm not . . ." Aaron's throat bobs with a nervous swallow, and he tears his eyes away. "Since you woke up, I haven't been doing well. I know if I give you space, everything will go back to how it was, and I can't let that happen. Please understand I'm not trying to hurt you."

"But you clearly already have," I croak, extending my palms so I can push him toward the door. He catches them, then gathers them together and strokes my fingers, pouring the warmth of his hands into mine. I don't squirm because he won't relent. Because it feels good. "I moved out to live with you and inconvenienced your entire household. I left my family in the dirt. I'm enrolled at some no-name college instead of the one I wanted. And it's all because I let you convince me we're good for each other."

"Please hear me out." He tucks my hands under his chin. At first, I think I'm trembling again, but I'm not. It's him. His eyes are beginning to water with a level of desperation I've never seen before. "You did nothing out of selfishness. You left home because it was the right move for you. My dads and I made a readjustment, yes, but it was worth it. We don't want you to be afraid of the place you're living. As for college, you started considering you might want to pursue something else, so you enrolled at a general education university to explore your options. That's all."

He says it like none of this had any negative impact. "What do you mean I left home because it was the right move?" I demand.

"For one, you were tired of getting sick. Your family isn't careful about what they touch or use or leave behind. Or they forget to be careful. Your parents especially."

"They're not hurting me on purpose," I say defensively.

"I know. Doesn't excuse anything." He works his way to my wrists, which he massages in earnest, thumbs kneading my sallow skin and purplish veins. "The bigger reason you left is because—"

Suddenly, the front door swings open. I yank my hands out of Aaron's slackened grip, but the damage is done. Logan stands in the doorframe, staring us down in angered disbelief, his backpack slung over his shoulder and his green eyes ablaze.

I blink, and suddenly, Logan has a fistful of Aaron's shirt and is heaving him against the wall with such force that one of the decorative framed pictures hits the tile, fragmenting into pieces.

"Logan!" I yell as my brother shoves his arm across Aaron's chest, pinning him to the drywall, his face warped with malevolence.

"I told you to stay away from him," he snarls.

A nasty smirk slices through Aaron's face. "You should keep him on a leash, then," he says softly. "Otherwise how will you know I'm not following him around, tainting his mind?"

Logan throws his other hand around Aaron's pale neck before I can snap at him for saying something so ridiculous. "After everything you've done, you have the nerve to show your smug fucking face back in my house . . ."

Aaron's eyes flicker with unbridled fury. "You won't like the way this ends," he says, his voice a frosted whisper. "Let go. I won't ask you again."

Logan's hair is frizzed up like an angry cat's. After a tense moment, I place my hand on the nape of his neck, hoping to inject him with calming energy. His shoulders loosen, and he sighs, backing away, his fingers uncurling from around Aaron's throat. "Get out," he breathes.

"Happily." Aaron straightens up, turning his attention to me. "Walk me out?"

"He doesn't need to do shit," Logan snaps, seizing my sweatshirt and hoisting me behind him with such force that I nearly stumble. "Leave before I give you two black eyes to go with your fit."

Even now, I'm uncomfortably lost. Logan and Aaron have never regarded each other with this much contempt. I don't want to lurk around like some voiceless damsel, so I step around Logan's extended arm. "I'll walk you out," I say, narrowing my eyes warningly. "Just don't try anything."

Laughing quietly at the chaos he's caused, Aaron walks to the front door, then winks back at Logan before stepping outside.

"Make it quick," Logan growls at me.

I wince from the ferocity in his voice. "You don't have to protect me," I mutter.

"Yes, I do."

I furrow my brow. He doesn't offer any other insight.

So I follow Aaron outside and leave him to sulk.

7

The moment I'm outside, Aaron seizes the door and swings it shut, cutting Logan away. "Alone again." He gives me a knowing smile that I want to smear off his face.

"Is the reason you guys stopped talking really because of me?" I blurt out.

Aaron scratches at his neck, peeking around my emerald-green yard as if seeking the answer in the unruly grass blades. It's been a while since someone bothered to mow it. My parents probably forgot to upkeep it after I left home. "It's complicated," he admits. "But me dating you was definitely the final straw for him. He didn't think I was a good influence." Aaron's eyes flick farther away, and I get the discomforting feeling I'm missing something. "He's going to try to keep me from you. He probably blocked my number from your phone to keep us from communicating."

"Maybe that's a sign that you should . . . I don't know. Stop communicating with me," I say, folding my arms. "Maybe he's right."

Aaron sighs with feigned misery. "If everyone thinks I'm some disgusting villain, then I should at least do something to warrant it," he drawls, and suddenly, he's seizing me around the waist and dipping me, forcing me to scramble for something to hang on to. I choose his shirt because it's the only thing nearby. Aaron leans over me with a grin, close enough that I can smell mint on his breath. He must've popped one on the way home in preparation for a dastardly move like this.

"Aaron!" I snap.

"What should I do to validate your brother's fears?" He snags the crook of my knee and tucks it around his hip, his boyish laughter ricocheting between my ears. "Kidnap you and hold you hostage in a faraway tower?"

"You should pull me up!" To my horror, I feel an inexplicable laugh rise into my throat, which I promptly and forcibly swallow. What the hell is wrong with me?

"Oh dear. Seems I've started annoying you again." Aaron clicks his tongue, I guess at himself, and draws me gently to my feet. Immediately I go to shove him, but catch the mischievous glimmer in his eyes and withdraw my wrists from snatching range.

"I said I'd walk you out and I did. Goodbye," I snarl.

"Okay, okay." Aaron lifts his hands defensively. "Can I ask you one more question, though?"

"What?" I grumble.

"Is there really nothing?"

I blink up at him.

"It seems like, in cases like this, memories come back gradually after head trauma," Aaron explains, leaning against one of the awning pillars. He's trying to sound nonchalant, but I can see his jaw working subtly with apprehension. I have the feeling he's been waiting for this moment. "It's been two days since you woke up, so I wondered if you started remembering anything. Or had flashes."

"Obviously n—" I bite the words back. *Flashes.* I think . . . right. They were brief enough that I assumed my brain made them up.

Aaron must notice my contemplation, because his face lightens with poorly concealed hope. "Tell me," he pleads.

"Um . . . it happened twice. The first was in the hospital, when you kissed me. I could smell peppermint," I explain, my eyes wandering every which way but toward his. "And I saw us. Lying on my bedroom floor. Um. Making out."

Aaron is silent for such an arduously long moment that I launch into the next one. This flash is even worse, though, and doesn't ease my hammering heartbeat.

"The next is when you offered to show me your back. I could feel your skin under my nails." I clear my throat a second time, hating my life, hating this moment. "That's all."

"Something triggered them," Aaron whispers. He doesn't sound sly—in fact, he almost seems choked up. I rear my head and notice he's procured that fidget toy again, and he's twisting the cogs and gears, his fingers moving at a taxing pace. "It's possible, then. That you might remember . . ."

He swallows the warble in his voice.

"They're barely memories," I admit, because I can feel excitement budding in the air around him.

"But it's something." Aaron steels himself with a deep breath, then scoops my hands up, peering down at me with uncomfortable intensity. I think he's obsessed with holding them, and I'm not sure how to feel about it, considering they seem to enjoy being held. "What if we start over? We could reenact our first dates, and maybe putting you in those familiar situations will bring everything back."

The thought is so ludicrous I want to bark with laughter. It's clearly a devilish ploy to lure me in, right? But when I meet his gaze, his own is so desperate, so intense, so *excited*, that I immediately feel bad for assuming negative intentions.

It's a silly idea, but I don't have any others to choose from. If I go along with this, maybe the past fifteen months *will* come back. Not just memories of Aaron, but everything in between our bizarre relationship. Maybe I'll finally understand why I made the choices I made. How I managed to completely upend my life over the course of a year and some change. Both flashes came after Aaron did or said something to trigger them, so maybe the key to remembering things rests with him.

I should know better than to let him get closer than he's already gotten with sheer persistence. Yet I can feel my hopelessness rising, because I have the feeling that the longer I go without my memories, the harder it'll be to get them back. This might be my best chance at awakening them.

I hear myself say, "Fine."

Aaron's eyes glitter so brightly that I nearly shield my face. "Really?"

"Sure, yeah, but not without ground rules," I mutter, my cheeks glowing like hot cinders.

Aaron grins and takes an exaggerated step backward. "Yes, sir."

"First, no lying," I say sharply. "When you fill me in about the past, or when we redo events, I want to know every detail. Like if we got into a fight during a date, and you conveniently don't mention that, I'll consider that lying by omission. Got it?"

Aaron is shuffling around like an eager child who can't stand still. "Got it."

"Next, you have to listen to me," I snap. "When I tell you to stop bothering me, respect me and do it. Lastly, this doesn't mean we're actually dating. This is to help me regain my memories. It's nothing more."

"I understand." Aaron's head arches sideways, and I catch sight of the narcissus flower tattoo behind his studded ear. Part of me wants to ask if it means anything, but I keep my mouth shut. "One of your flashes came because we did something physical. I kissed you. Even if your mind doesn't remember, it seems like your body might. So if we ended dates with a kiss or something, we shouldn't skip it." He offers a cheeky grin, and says, "For the sake of your memories, of course."

The proposition makes me want to kick at his excessively long shins. He's not wrong, though. The reason I briefly remember him kissing me is because I smelled peppermint while I was in the hospital bed. By rooting myself in my past actions, maybe I can unearth missing pieces. Even if it means . . . ugh. Following the physical progression of our relationship, too.

"Fine," I say, trying not to sound as rattled as I feel. I'm not blind. Aaron is attractive, even beyond his snow-prince appearance. It's the confident gait, the cocky smile, the way he stands. But he comes with several qualities that make me shudder. So the fact that I've kissed him, *slept* with him, is still something I can't comprehend.

"I draw the line at sex," I say sternly.

I figure Aaron will make a snide or flirty comment like *We'll see about that*, but there's warmth in his next smile. "No sex," he agrees. "Unless you initiate it."

"I won't," I assure him.

"But if you do." He sprawls a hand over his chest. "I will allow it."

"How selfless."

Aaron snickers and wanders off the porch. "Tonight, we'll re-create the night I asked you out. I came over around midnight, so be ready." He saunters toward his car. "Keep your window unlocked. Oh, and avoid mentioning our plans to Logan."

"I didn't say we should start immediately!" I cry out. "It hasn't even been a week since the accident. Maybe my memories will start coming back in the next few days, and then we won't have to do this ridiculous plan—"

"Too late. It's already been added to my mental calendar: *Midnight—rile Riley.*"

I think I'm about to tell him off, but then I remember why he came here in the first place. I call, "Wait—you forgot your snacks."

Aaron is circling around the driver's side of his truck when he pauses. "Keep them," he says. "You get cranky when you don't have snacks."

I can't muster a response before he's closing the door and driving off. My shoulders slump, and I say, "You didn't have to do that."

I shouldn't feel guilty—I'm going to reimburse him for the grocery list later, so he's basically making my parents pay for unnecessary snacks. Yet the fact that it was on his mind . . .

I knead my temple, the pulsing lump in my head becoming a familiar pain. Now that he's gone, it's coming back. The frailness in my legs, the soreness of my bones, the relentless fatigue. Aaron kept me so distracted, I nearly forgot that I'm falling apart.

I push inside to put away the remaining groceries. As soon as I'm through the frame, Logan has my wrist in a viselike grip, so tight that it causes a pang to shoot through my forearm. "Ow," I choke out, but he's already talking over me.

"Why did you let him in?"

I look up at Logan, astonished. The apples of his cheeks are flushed, and his eyes are frenzied, like he's seconds from detonating. "I didn't ask him to come," I say, to which his nostrils flare.

"But you let him inside," he growls.

"He's been following me around like a lapdog," I say defensively, mirroring his aggravated tea-green gaze with mine. "And he doesn't listen when I tell him to leave."

"Right, no, of course." Logan nods with a vehement smile. "How could I forget that the whole reason this bullshit started in the first place is because you're a fucking doormat who can't put your foot down or stand up for yourself? Silly me."

His words are shivs to my chest. Water glasses my eyes. I don't recognize this person. Logan has never been aggressive with me, has never shouted at me. Even as children, we rarely fought—our temperaments were mild, so when we were upset, the flames rising between us quickly sputtered out. I've never seen him succumb to emotions like this, especially not toward me.

"Do you hate me?" I whisper.

Logan's attention flits to his unforgiving grip on my arm, and he snaps his hand to his side, his eyes widening with horror. He staggers several steps backward. "I'm sorry," he breathes. "I didn't mean . . . Shit, Riley. I'm sorry. It's just . . . knowing what he's done . . . I'm sorry. Did I hurt you?"

Of course he did. My entire arm is throbbing. My chest is on fire. "No," I mumble.

Logan groans, dropping his face into his palms. "I'm sorry. I watched him poison your mind for a year, so seeing him near you makes me want to scream. Given the chance, he'll do it again. Because he hates me."

I can't even defend myself, and that makes the sinking sensation even worse. He's right. I could've put my foot down and not acknowledged Aaron. But my half-hearted attempts to keep him at bay only encouraged him to pursue me. Because of that, I'm now wrapped up in a foolish plan to regain my memories—one that involves me putting myself in the exact same scenarios that presumably ruined my life. And my family's. Logan has every right to be accusatory.

It still hurts, though.

"Sorry," I say. "I'll try not to be such a doormat."

Logan's face twists with regret. "I didn't mean that," he says, reaching for me, but I dodge his grip because it's not as kind as the other one. Seeking distraction, I work on putting the remaining groceries away, then search for the labels so I can mark my gluten-free food and put it somewhere separate. The usual cabinet I keep my items stored in has been stuffed with regular pantry products, so I have to clean it out. I fumble around for gloves and a mask—there's flour on the top shelf—then crawl onto the counter and start scrubbing, my knees shivering with strain.

Logan lingers in the kitchen. "Maybe you should just go to bed, Riley," he says.

"Can't." If I close my eyes, I'll think about his words. My horrible life decisions.

Logan must conclude he's not winning this argument, because he leaves.

I decide I'll lock my window tonight.

8

I make my dinner after my family's. Normally I prepare mine in advance so I can eat with them at the dining room table, but even though Logan's anger is justified, I don't want to see him. As they munch on the beef stroganoff and almond bacon green beans, I remain in the kitchen, combining my gluten-free ingredients, listening to them chat about their day. I don't think a lot of families do this nowadays without a TV in front of them, so it makes mine feel special.

Yet I left them like they meant nothing to me.

"How about you, Riley?" Mom calls, stabbing a sliced almond and bringing it to her mouth. "Did you get any rest?"

Not really, since I was desperate to keep busy after Aaron's departure. I could bring up the history club's surprise appearance and my trip to the ice cream shop, but I don't have the energy to get into details, so I merely say, "Yeah."

"Good meal, by the way," Dad tells me. "Your cooking is as good as we remember."

The statement is another serrated knife to my wounded heart. "Sorry," I breathe, so softly that they don't hear it. When I retreat to my room that night, I turn on my space heater to warm my frigid hands and feet, then pull on a T-shirt and sweatpants and huddle up in bed with my laptop.

I eye the curtain draped over the bedroom window. I locked it earlier.

Logan is right. I wasn't strong enough to battle Aaron's manipulation the first time, so why do I think I have the strength to do it this time? I did, at the very least, find Aaron's number to unblock it and tell him the plan is off. Then I immediately blocked him again.

When midnight passes, I think I'm in the clear.

But then it starts.

Tap. Tap. Tap.

My heart staggers over its beat. I roll out of bed, then storm to the curtain and wrench it aside. Sure enough, there's the nuisance himself, crouched like a gangly bird on the branch extending past my window. His obsidian tips sit low on his forehead, curling toward his brows, and his gray eyes are vivid enough to light up the night.

Seeing me doesn't stop his tapping, so I unlock the window and fling it open, allowing a rush of balmy air to surge into my room. "Leave me alone. I've changed my mind," I snap.

"I can fix that," he says.

"You can't." I try slamming the window shut, but he catches the frame, keeping it propped up.

"This is where it started," he says, his free hand gesturing into my room. "Fourteen months ago. April eighteenth." His default smile extends into something more teasing. "This is where you said yes."

My jaw locks with frustration. I scrutinize every inch of his handsome face, seeking deception. I don't think he's lying to grab my attention. The issue is that he has it now.

"Want to know more?" Aaron is analyzing me with a fondness that burns me to my chest. "It's not a pretty truth, but it's a truth I've promised you. So I'll be honest."

The hooked tips of his claws are cracking through the surface of my bones. Rooting themselves. "Just tell me what you know. Then you can leave," I say sharply, backing away. As soon as he has room, Aaron lurches through the open window with frustrating grace. I wish he'd look clunky and awkward for once, but every move he makes is smooth and elegant. "How did we get together? Why isn't it a *pretty* truth?"

"Well . . ." Aaron twists the black stud in his ear, and when his eyes flit to me, I realize something that nearly drops my jaw. He's *nervous*. His shoulders are hunching, like he's curling into himself for protection, and his voice is thicker—something's weighing it down.

"Don't lie," I tack on. "That was my first condition."

"I know. It's just . . . *saying* it is a little . . ." Aaron's face brightens, and he swivels on me. "Let's reenact the night. Role-play."

My brain is about to leak out of my ears. "Can't you just tell me?" I ask faintly.

"If it's in the moment, it could jog your memory."

I knew we'd revisit our previous dates if we went through this, but I didn't think we'd be role-playing our former selves. Still, maybe this *will* help me understand how the impossible came to pass. I'm hopelessly lost as to how we got from A to B.

"Okay," I say uneasily. "Then set the scene, I guess?"

Aaron is clearly on the verge of giggling. "Right. April eighteenth, it's three in the morning," he says, bracing his hands in a "picture this" pose. "I used to crawl through your window when Logan and I were friends, so—"

"You *what*?" I choke out.

"Yeah." He waves his palm dismissively. "Your alarm only monitors the ground floor, and the system logs whenever it's disabled. If Logan and I wanted to hang out, he couldn't disarm it without you all knowing he was up to something that night. So instead, I'd climb through your window and go to his room. Or he'd leave through your window."

This time, my jaw really is hanging, though I can't tell if I'm more incredulous or incensed.

"You're a heavy sleeper," Aaron continues, propping his hands on his hips. The length of his fingers makes his waist look narrower. "The issue is that it takes a while for you to actually go to sleep, so we had to wait until late before making a move. Once you're out, though, you're *out*."

"How long?" I demand. "How *often*?"

"Couple of years," Aaron says. "Usually once a week—more frequently in the summer."

I stumble back into my bed frame and collapse onto the mattress, then stare at the ceiling in dismay. Aaron Beckham used to sneak in through my window. I was Logan's first and only line of defense, and I couldn't even wake to hear the frame sliding open.

Aaron shuffles across the carpet and leans over me with a grin. "Should I go?" he asks seriously.

"No!" I snap, lurching upright to grab him. Only when I'm on my feet do I realize how close he is, and now we're practically chest-to-chest—or face-to-neck, I guess, since he's a head taller. Instinctively, I go to nudge his shoulders back.

In a flash, my hands are folded in his.

"No?" Aaron's fingers work the frigid skin between my knuckles. The moment his warmth permeates me, I sigh softly in relief. Mercifully, he doesn't hear it. "You want me to stay?"

"I want you to stop withholding information," I grumble.

One side of his mouth pulls higher than the other, and it's that crooked, devious smile that puts my heart in the most peril. I shouldn't be attracted to it, considering it's my least favorite part about him. "Then I'll keep painting the picture," he says, drawing my palms higher, until his warm breath tickles my fingers. "April eighteenth, I climbed into your room at three in the morning. For the first time in all my passes through your bedroom, something happened." His lower lip grazes my middle knuckle. "Want to guess?"

I readjust my palm to flick his nose. He blinks, startled, then laughs despite my crabbiness. "Don't make me work for it," I order.

"But I like making you work for it, sunshine." The glint in his eyes is wily. "For months, you've been a spoiled princess who gets what she wants, because you learned what makes me weak. Tragically, this knowledge is now lost to you. So I get to hold you hostage."

There's an underlying *something* in his voice that causes a shiver to scratch my spine. All I can do is sputter out, "You . . . you're treating this like a joke."

"My feelings for you have never been a joke," Aaron whispers. He thumbs through my fingers until he finds the one that flicked him—my middle. He plucks it free from my curled fist and nudges his lips against each knuckle, like they're made of precious jewels rather than flimsy bones. "That night, your light was off, so I thought I was in the clear. But when I crawled through the window . . ."

Aaron steps back, his fingers sliding away. I hate that a nonsensical part of my brain wants him to keep holding them. I haven't felt relief in my hands since . . . well, since he last held them. Annoying.

"What are you doing?" I ask crossly as he snatches a pillow off my bed.

"Recreating the moment." He nudges it into my chest, winking.

I stare down at it. "Did I . . . ?" My voice fizzles out.

"What do you think?" he prompts.

"I think I probably hit you with a pillow."

"I think you're onto something."

"Oh." I place the pillow on the bed and wait for him to continue. Aaron gives me this small exasperated smile that seems kinder than not and picks the pillow up, tucking it into my chest again.

"We're recreating the scene, right? It's not authentic if you don't smack me."

"But I know it's you, and I let you in this time, so why would I hit you?" I ask sternly. "That's not fair to you."

Aaron chews so hard on his index knuckle that he looks like he's trying to break skin. The thought that I've frustrated him to this extent plagues me with sudden guilt.

"Sorry." My fingertips curl into the pillow's fluff. "I'm not trying to be difficult—"

"No." Aaron sighs with violent force. "I just really want to kiss the fuck out of you."

Heat lashes through my face, and I brace my legs, preparing to sling my pillow at him as I apparently did once before. Aaron notices my battle stance, and his smile returns.

"Can I?" he asks, his eyebrows and fingers wiggling with evil intent.

I reel the pillow back in preparation. "Keep your horny mouth away from me!"

"Just your forehead?" He inches forward.

"I'll hit you! I mean it!"

"Behind your ear?" he pleads.

The moment he takes another half step forward, I unleash my wrath, hurling the pillow forward and thwacking him with enough force to make him stagger. "Sorry," I choke out.

"Thank God," he says, huffing with relief. "I thought I was going to have to get on my hands and knees and beg for it. That's a side of me I save for special occasions."

I try not to gag on my next breath. "Move on," I order, hugging the pillow in case I need to use it again. "You came into my room and I hit you because I thought you were an intruder. What next?"

"Right. So you assaulted me with your pillow until I"—Aaron seizes it, ripping it from my grasp—"stole it from you. It was dark, and you were disoriented, so you didn't realize it was me. What happened next?"

"I punched you in the face?" I ask flatly.

Aaron laughs again, and it's a cozy sound. "What if I say yes? Are you willing to re-create it?"

I shift my jaw with annoyance, because of course not, and he knows that.

"Actually," he says, "you tried shouting. It surprised me because I figured you'd be the type to freeze up. But you attacked me, then your mouth opened, and I panicked."

"Did you punch *me* in the face?" I ask nervously.

Aaron gasps and clutches at his nonexistent pearls. "Good heavens, Riley, do you think I'm the type to hit people half my size?"

I scoff, wanting to shove him but knowing full well he'll just trap me. "Half a foot in height doesn't mean I'm half your size," I mutter. "Also, I wouldn't be surprised. You used to start fights plenty in high school."

"With dicks who deserved it," he points out, his eyes brightening. "Either way, no, there was no punching involved. How do you think I stopped you from shouting?"

He's having way too much fun, his voice brimming with enthusiasm. "I don't know," I say in vexation. "Did you nonconsensually put your tongue in my mouth?"

Aaron makes a dissatisfied ticking noise. "Was your opinion of me always this low before we started dating?"

"Well, did you?" I ask accusingly.

"First rule of storytelling," Aaron says, his finger jutting into the air. "Show, don't tell."

I give him my fiercest glare, which must not be very fierce, because his diabolical grin doesn't falter. "Show me, then," I say.

He must've been waiting for permission, because he lunges for me and seizes my wrists in one hand, the other flying to my mouth before I can even squeak with surprise. He drives me onto the bedspread with his weight. In two seconds, I've been made useless, my hands pinned over my head and my mouth shielded by his palm.

"I said *It's just me*," Aaron tells me. "What do you think you did?"

He asks, like he doesn't have my mouth covered. I give my wrists an experimental tug, but he merely tightens his grip, pressing them deeper into the comforter. It's not threatening, but he's definitely not going to let me up. I jam my tongue out and lick his hand, hoping to disgust him into reeling backward.

Aaron's eyes widen, but then he grins and bends closer, until the only thing separating our lips is his palm. "Cute," he whispers, and then the madman kisses the back of his own hand. "But I'm used to that feeling, so it's not going to work."

He can probably feel the temperature rising in my cheeks. I must've done something else to get him off me, but my instincts are useless right now. Aaron is the last person I'd ever trust, and yet . . .

My body isn't reacting like I'm in danger.

I should be squirming with discomfort. Is it possible part of my mind recognizes that this situation is familiar? That *Aaron* is familiar?

My temple throbs with enough power to make me wince. Aaron's hand is still over my mouth, firm, tight, but I'm standing. My fingertips are dragging against rough wood, and his teeth are sharp but gentle around my earlobe.

Shh. Do you want them to know you're here?

I blink, and the moment folds away, but it was a *moment*. A memory! I squirm again, and Aaron must sense the urgency, because he draws away and peels his hand off my mouth. "What's wrong?" he asks, stepping back when I lunge off the bed.

"I remembered something," I blurt out.

Aaron stops in his tracks. I hear him exhale faintly—shaky, violent—before he's closing the distance and nestling his warm palms on my shoulders. "It worked?" he asks. His eyes are glazed with tears, sparkling the way fresh snow does on a suburban lawn. "Tell me."

"I think we were hiding somewhere," I admit, uncomfortably aware of his fingertips grazing my neck. "There was a wooden door in front of me. Your hand was over my mouth, and you were telling me to be quiet or I'd get caught."

Aaron rakes his memories in silence. Eventually, he murmurs, "My closet."

"Your what?"

His grin returns suspiciously quickly. I guess he's back to being amused at my expense. "My dads grounded me, so you weren't allowed over. You came anyway because they were supposed to be at an all-day repair job. But they stopped home in the middle of the day for lunch, so you hid in my closet."

"But you were in there with me," I protest, lamenting that I disrespected his parents like that.

"Yes, I joined you eventually. We were in the middle of something when my dads came home, which left you in a predicament. I felt bad, so while they were eating, I joined you to . . . well." He clears his throat. "Help?"

Scarlet heat explodes through my body, and I actually cry out with rage, then slam my palms into his chest and shove. He catches them and draws me closer, his smile like sugary candy.

"What did you think we were doing?" he asks, kissing my fingertips as I try valiantly to hide my face in my shoulder. "In what other situation would I tell you to keep it down while hiding?"

"I don't know!" I snap, wanting to melt onto my knees. "I'd never let you do something like that while your dads were home!"

"Oh, but you see, love," Aaron says, thumbs kneading the pale skin of my wrists, "you're forgetting my horrible, no good, very bad influence on your delicate maiden spirit."

I wrench out of Aaron's grip, then collapse onto my knees, seize the pillow on the floor, shove my face into it, and groan while he laughs at my misery. I can't believe this. I have more willpower than to just allow him to do what he wants, right? Unless . . .

You're a fucking doormat who can't put your foot down.

I scowl into the fluff. Right. Aaron is naggy, persistent, and I was the carpet under his shoes. It's my fault for letting things escalate to that point. Maybe I should let these memories rot in oblivion so I don't have to confront my mistakes. But if I want to keep myself from repeating these lapses in judgment, shouldn't *being aware of them* be the first step to correcting them? Running away without acknowledging everything I did wrong is just continuing the cycle of selfishness.

I won't stop here just because I'm uncomfortable.

"Okay, fine, whatever," I say shortly, muscling back to my feet. It takes more strength than I realize—I'm exhausted beyond repair, my joints and bones aching, my hands losing warmth the longer I go without Aaron's grip. I wish my body would hurry up and fully heal so these irritating issues can go back to being background noise. Still present (always present) but less difficult to bury with distractions. "We're offtrack. Let's get back into position."

I lie on the mattress and yank Aaron to where he was before—his knee leaning on the comforter between my legs, his hand sealing my mouth. Once it's secured, I cross my wrists over my head and give him an approving nod so he can take them.

If the words *utterly bamboozled* had a face, it would be Aaron's. He's staring at me like I just asked him to rail me here and now, his mouth parted comedically. He clears his throat and leans over me, reclaiming his grip around my arms, fastening them to the comforter.

"Okay, so, I told you it was me," he says, his voice dropping lower. "What happened next?"

I consider the options, but I'm not sure how I escaped this situation if not by licking or biting his hand. I'm not strong enough to squirm out of his grip. I give him a clueless look, to which he smirks, and says, "Left leg."

My eyes slide down to observe. It's resting flat on the bed between his braced thighs.

"Think," he encourages. "Someone crawled through your window in the middle of the night. Even if you know that person is me, you're still operating on instinct. So . . ."

My eyes widen with understanding. I try to protest, but Aaron's palm presses more firmly into my lips, silencing me.

"Go ahead," he says, like his manhood isn't in imminent danger.

I shake my head insistently.

"Should I inspire you?" He lowers himself over me, his nose drawing precariously close to mine, clearly trying to fluster me into relenting. "You're too nice, Riley. I'm giving you permission to knee my sack, and you won't, even though I've been insufferable all day."

When I merely uphold my stern stare, he groans, draping his head forward so his curled black tips are grazing my chin.

"Sometimes I want to eat you alive," he says, like that's a normal thing to say to another human being. "Fine. We'll skip the knee-to-balls part. But for the record, it worked." He draws back so he can dramatically cup his pants and whimper at the nonexistent damage. He sniffles with just enough theatrics that I have to forcibly wipe the smile from my face as I stand.

"What next?" I ask.

"Seeing me after the whole"—Aaron clears his throat, struggling with the words—"trespassing incident with Logan pissed you off. I tried explaining that I was only here to talk to Logan, but you yelled at me." Aaron rolls his hand toward me with a wink. "Care to guess what you said?"

The mention of the arrest raises my blood temperature. "I probably told you to stay away from my brother," I assume.

"So tell me to stay away from your brother." Aaron's smile is annoyingly cheeky, and once more, it's clear he's enjoying the role-playing thing a little too much.

"Stay away from my brother," I say with a dreary sigh.

"How about with enthusiasm? You were furious."

I don't doubt it, but I'm depleted of strength. "Stay away from Logan," I try again with more bite. He still doesn't look satisfied, so I jam my index finger into his chest. "Quit ruining his life. You've done enough damage."

Aaron's eyes glow with eagerness. "Or what?"

I try to envision what I might've said in this situation. "I'll snitch to your dads," I suggest.

"They already know I go out at night," he admits. "They don't like it, but they've given up on leashing me. So, anything else?"

What else is there? I can't threaten bodily harm, and he doesn't care about consequences, so I have no way of blackmailing him. "What would it take to keep you away from him?" I ask, and my heart skips, like my body is telling me I'm on the right track.

Sure enough, Aaron's grin widens with satisfaction. "What could you offer me?" he prompts.

I feel like my brain is short-circuiting and smoke is about to curl off my scalp. "I don't know anything about you to help me out."

"You know I'm single," he offers.

I give a squeaky scoff. "No way I promised my body to you," I snap.

Aaron laughs at me. *Again*. I'm getting sick of this bastard. "Then, how about this? For every date you go on with me, I'll stay away from your brother for two whole weeks. Surely that's manageable for someone as busy as you."

The blood boiling in my face drains away. "I thought you hated me," I mutter.

Aaron's smile disintegrates, but it's so brief that I'm not sure if I hallucinated it before it comes searing back. "I thought you were annoying as shit for a while, but you're cute, so I'm curious to know more about you. Does that suffice?"

I have this nagging feeling he's illuminating 90 percent of a whole truth. Like I'm missing a fragment of information that could fully interlock the puzzle pieces and pry open my world of understanding. "Is that all?" I ask dubiously.

Aaron nods.

"Fine." I sharpen my voice. Maybe I can endure this just long enough that Logan will break all communication with Aaron. They're already on the rocks after the arrest. Spending a few hours with Aaron a month seems like a tolerable exchange for ensuring he's not further screwing Logan over. I don't know if he has hidden motivations for suddenly pursuing me, but—

Wait.

I shake my head, centering myself. I was so into the thought process behind these decisions that I forgot I already made them. "This is what you meant when you said our relationship wasn't a *pretty truth*," I say, brows arching. "You figured I was desperate to protect Logan."

"Yeah," he admits. "Sorry. I ran with what I knew."

I sigh, glad that things are coming together but hating that I agreed to this. At least he's capable of acknowledging when he's done something tasteless.

Aaron inches closer to me, and it's like I can see the mischief beginning to claw into his expression, flickering in his eyes and sculpting his black brows. "What do you think happened next?" he asks softly.

I'm too exhausted to deal with whatever teasing he has planned, so I say, "You left."

"You think so?" Aaron reaches for me, and I hate that after spending one day with him, I no longer feel the need to lurch away. I hate that his touch is warm. That my body recognizes it and feels comfort in it. He sprawls his palm around my jawline and tugs, pulling my irritable face toward his. "You think we parted ways without sealing the deal?"

My scowl deepens. Aaron suggested following our relationship's physical progression, so skipping over the kissing isn't going to do my clueless brain any favors. I'll get this over with, then, and maybe I'll get a flashback out of it.

I close my eyes and pucker up.

I feel a tiny puff of air against my nose, like he laughed. He nudges my chin higher, and I brace, my heart drowning out any other sounds, waiting for the feeling of his slender lips to fall on mine. Suddenly, his amused voice is whispering in my ear.

"I never said we kissed. But I'm glad to see you're so willing."

Fiery heat tears through my body like a rip current, and I shout in frustrated disbelief, then shove his shoulders. To my surprise, he lets me push him, but it's because he's too busy clutching his stomach and laughing to seize me. "Shut up!" I growl, and catching sight of my body mirror does me no favors. My normally pasty, ashen face is rose red. "I can't believe I let you into my room! Get out, you creep!"

"Creep?" he chokes out, allowing me to usher him to the window, tears of hilarity glassing his eyes. "How could you? I'm a gentleman—"

"*Get out!*" I say in a high-pitched wheeze, and with one final laugh, he slides out of my window and nestles his weight onto the branch outside.

"Tomorrow," he says. "Keep the window unlocked. I'll take you through our first date. So get lots of sleep, okay?"

I slam the window shut and draw the shades without answering. I can still hear him snickering through the glass. "Asshole," I snarl quietly, and I storm to my bed, then throw myself beneath my covers.

Of course, I don't sleep a wink.

9

I don't let my distractions stop me from tackling my to-do list. Mom is a speech pathologist with an erratic schedule, Dad works overtime at the bank, and Logan is balancing community college summer courses with his part-time position as a student assistant, so it's my job to make sure the gears are turning.

I separate the mail and mark the most important ones, then pick up everyone's prescriptions at the pharmacy, then stop by the library to get Mom's book on hold, then buy a cake from the bakery so Dad has something to bring to his office party (I'm glad I had an emergency mask on hand for that one, since the request came on my way home).

My insomnia since the coma hasn't been helping with my "healing" process, and last night was the worst yet. Every time I closed my eyes, Aaron's smug, snide face awaited me.

And I have to see him again tonight.

It's still strange around the house. My family avoids mentioning the accident, my move-out period, and Aaron Beckham. It's as if the past year doesn't exist, and their nonchalance is making it more difficult for me to process everything. Existing is a surreal, disorienting experience, and whenever I run into some small issue—like the Tupperware is in a different cabinet than I remember—the frustration is crushing.

Aaron doesn't show up until midnight, which doesn't do my apprehension any favors. I've texted him twelve times, asking what I should wear and what the date will involve and when we'll get back, because I'm a planner. I need to know these things. He sends back a single message that reads:

You'll see 😉

To which I call him and he sends me to voicemail.

To which I call him again and leave a heated message about how the date is off because I would sooner eat an entire loaf of bread and suffer the consequences than ever see his face again.

To which he shows up anyway and pokes at my bedroom window until I rip the curtain open and spit, "*You're unbearable*," through the panes.

He taps his ear. "Can't hear," he responds, his voice muffled but perfectly audible. "There's a window in the way."

"Child," I grumble, hiking the frame up and allowing him to slink from the tree branch into my room. His curls are unkempt and his black nail polish looks new but is chipped at the tips, like he painted them this morning and then had to work with his hands all day. He looks perfectly . . .

Casual.

It's too late for me to throw myself behind my dresser and hide. He's taking me in—my slacks, button-down shirt, brushed-out honey-blond hair. He sucks his lips between his teeth to keep from bursting into laughter, and the sight chars every inch of my skin. "Don't make fun of me!" I order, and that's what gets him to hunch over and laugh manically. "You didn't give me any information, so I wanted to be prepared!"

I throw my hands against his shoulders to shove, and he immediately detains my wrists, pulling me across the carpet. He hoists my imprisoned arms behind his neck, drawing my face closer, his own distractingly luminescent and warm. Moth to a flame and all that.

"Thank you for dressing up even though you hate me," he says. "I kept you in the dark last time, so I thought I was just following the rules."

I'm hot enough to crisp bacon. "Just because I'm smaller than you doesn't give you free rein to yank me around," I snap, twisting out of his grip.

"You're right. Sorry." He gives me a playful but warm smile that quenches my fiery aggravation. "Change into a swimsuit and something comfortable."

"It's midnight!" I squeak.

"Correct."

"But swimming is dangerous in the dark," I tell him, my unease rising. "I don't know what the temperature was like last year, but it's supposed to get cold tonight, so—"

My words dissolve when I realize he's laughing again.

"Last nerve," I say flatly, and he cups his mouth, trembling with mirth. "You've found it. Congratulations. Goodbye."

"I'm sorry . . . You're just really cute . . ." He coughs through his fit and backtracks to the window, closing his eyes like the sight of me will trigger another giggle-fest. "The sooner you get changed, the sooner our date will be over."

It's a fair point, and the best one he could've made. So I scramble for a swimsuit and, after personally placing his hands over his eyes, I change into it.

"There isn't a single part of you I haven't licked, so I'm not sure why this matters," he says, which literally, actually triggers my gag reflex.

"Don't be disgusting!" I choke out, wrenching sweatpants over my thighs.

"You have a lot to relearn about yourself, sunshine."

I decide I'm better off ignoring that. "Then . . . I'm ready," I say after a moment, shuffling toward him feeling sufficiently awkward. "Let's go downstairs and—"

"And turn off your alarm so your family will know you left at 12:13 a.m.?" he asks, smirking. "Your flighty parents might not notice, but do you think Logan will let you live it down if he finds out you snuck away with me? No—we go out the window."

My heartbeat quickens as I peer into the darkness of my front yard. He's right. I'd rather avoid any confrontation with Logan. And though my parents haven't said much about Aaron, other than frowning or clicking their tongues whenever they hear his name, I'd rather they didn't know that I'm following the same steps that apparently led to my abandonment of them. "I'm not sturdy like you," I say weakly, inching away from the frame. "If I fall, I'll break my whole body—"

"You won't fall." Aaron lurches out onto the branch extending past my room, which sways under his movement. The gap between my window and the tree isn't big, but it's just wide enough that I can't scoot onto the branch with my short limbs.

"I can't," I start to say, but then Aaron's open palm is hovering in front of me. His other is latched to a branch over his head, holding it to balance himself as he leans over the gap toward me.

"I won't let you fall, Riley," he whispers. "I promise."

I have no reason to trust him, but my hand is settling into his before I can decide otherwise. Swallowing nervously, I climb into the window frame, taking the edge in one hand and letting him pull me forward with the other. The ground seems so far away, the grass tips spiky and threatening.

"Look at me," Aaron says softly.

I do. Silver moonlight twirls in his eyes like flames.

I guess the distance doesn't matter, since he promised.

"Right foot first," he encourages, and I extend my leg, planting it on the tree next to him. He gently hoists me out of the window and fully onto the branch.

"This is so unnecessary," I say, sounding as shaken as I feel.

"You're doing great." Aaron speaks so earnestly that I believe him. Slowly, never releasing my hand, he helps me ease myself down, branch by branch, until I'm close enough to the ground that a fall won't break my whole skeletal frame.

Aaron sneaks a kiss to my hand before letting it go so I can hug the trunk. He maneuvers down the rest of the tree like liquid, showing me just how often he did this in the past. Then he's on the ground, extending his arms, and saying, "Jump."

"No!" I cry out. "What if I hit my head again and forget the rest of my life or something?"

I know I'm being dramatic at this point. A drop from this height won't do much more damage than making my frail ankles throb in protest. But the thought of jumping into his arms like some princess in a tower is causing my heart to shriek with embarrassment.

Aaron is smiling in this way that tells me he knows exactly what I'm thinking, but he indulges my protest anyway. "I've never dropped you, Riley. And I never will. Ever."

Does that mean we did this regularly? The thought of enduring this torture for dates I didn't even want to go on makes me want to throw a tantrum. I merely sit on the branch, suck in a breath, and drop. My weight collides with Aaron, and he catches me around the waist with ease. Instinctively, my arms fly around his neck to anchor myself.

"Oh," he says in surprise. He's close enough that I can smell musk and . . . is that axle grease? Maybe he was under a car today. Whatever bodywash he uses isn't enough to fully scrape the metallic scent away. "You're heavier than you used to be. I guess that means the meal plans were working."

"The what?" I ask, dazed from adrenaline and his proximity. He has so many eyelashes. They're as dark as his hair. I blink out of my stupor, then wriggle out of his durable grip.

"You kept skipping meals at home," Aaron explains, wandering toward his pickup truck. There's equipment in the bed that makes me wonder if he was doing lawn work today. "You admitted you were having trouble maintaining your weight even with the iron supplements because you weren't getting nutrition anywhere else. And your family wasn't making sure you kept up with meals—"

"Why should my actions be on them?" I demand. "It's not their job to monitor me."

Aaron is quiet, maybe to let me cool off before continuing. It works. The silence forces me to sit with my thoughts and impulsive reaction.

"Sorry," I mumble.

He gives me a pained look over his shoulder, like the word is a stinging insult and not an apology for snapping. "The point is that sometimes, you wouldn't eat out of sheer paranoia that you might get sick," he explains. "When you moved in, my dads and I helped you plan out weekly meals. You were more willing to eat knowing how careful they were about maintaining a gluten-free section of the kitchen."

I purse my lips, wondering why I was worth the effort.

Aaron opens the passenger door and winks. "Shall we?"

Then we're off.

10

"Is this some kind of sick joke?"

Aaron observes me with his signature "innocent" smile, always hindered by a hint of mischief. "What do you mean?" he asks, sliding into a parking spot behind the high school. The one we've both graduated from. The one we definitely shouldn't be approaching at midnight.

"There's no way our first date is *trespassing*," I growl as Aaron unbuckles himself.

"There aren't any cameras, and this lot faces the woods, so nobody will know," Aaron says. "The boy's locker room latch has been broken since before I graduated. Don't worry your pretty blond head about it." He slings a backpack over his shoulder and circles to the passenger side, opening my door.

I glare down at him, still buckled.

"So stubborn." Aaron sighs, but there's a fond glimmer in his eyes. "They're *your* memories, sunshine. If you want to find another way to remember them, I'm happy to help you brainstorm, but this is all we've got to go on for now. Do you want to give it a try?"

Grumbling, I clamber out of the pickup truck, ignoring his offered palm because it's already touched me too many times today.

So then we're sneaking into the high school pool room with its towering, piped ceiling and silver bleachers and low golden lighting that barely illuminates the tile walkway. The pungent smell of chlorine stings my nose. The pool is the only luminescent thing in the echoing room, causing the glassy water to sparkle aquamarine.

"Ridiculous," I mutter, and Aaron smirks as he slings the backpack onto a bleacher and spreads a picnic blanket over it.

"You said that last time, too. What a coincidence."

I crinkle my nose with distaste, sitting atop the quilt. Then, to my surprise, he starts pulling out cling-wrapped food. "What's this?" I ask suspiciously as he pushes one into my hand.

"A gluten-free everything bagel with chive cream cheese, cucumber, tomato, avocado, and kale pesto," he says. "Prepared with a gluten-free counter and toaster."

Normally, I don't trust non-celiacs to make me food, but it sounds delicious, and I start salivating a grotesque amount. "Did you make these the first time?" I ask, tearing through the wrap.

"No," he admits, watching as I sink my teeth into the bagel. "I didn't have anything, and you got hangry. So I came prepared to soothe my fussy, grouchy boyfriend before he gets fussy and grouchy."

I nearly choke on a thinly sliced cucumber. "I'm not fussy!" I snap, tearing another chunk out of the bagel. It's annoyingly good—the taste, texture, and quantities are perfect. "Also, I'm not your boyfriend."

"Oh. Right. Whoops." Aaron shrugs before pulling out his own sandwich. Out of the corner of my eye, I see his expression wilt, and I have to choke back an apology so he doesn't realize I saw it.

We eat in strange but not uncomfortable silence, gazing out at the crystal-smooth pool. Every inch of me should be shuddering with revulsion at this scenario, but my body and mind are disjointed, operating on two different levels. My mind *knows* it should hate being here, but my body doesn't reflect the anxiety.

"The first time I made food for you, I glutened you," Aaron says. "I cleaned my kitchen and thought I was in the clear. But I used a silicone whisk and a cast-iron pan that I hadn't reseasoned. So we had a romantic picnic, and then I spent the night holding your suffering little body."

I lick the cream cheese from my fingers, watching him warily. He's leaned back on his palms, gazing up at the tangled mess of pipes, vents, and lights threaded along the high ceiling. His eyes are glazed, almost wistful. And sad. "Well . . . thanks for going through the trouble," I murmur.

"It's not trouble. Not for you."

I feel a flush spreading through my cheeks, and I'm suddenly glad the lighting is so low. I knew Aaron was a smooth talker, but I didn't realize how effortless it was for him to fluster me.

"Open your hand," Aaron says, and I do, frowning. He places a mint in it. "You don't let me kiss you when your mouth tastes like food, so I came prepared."

I toss the mint behind me. It clinks against the bleachers and falls into the darkness.

Aaron sighs in disapproval. "Riley, I thought we were going to reenact the physical parts of our dates, too," he whines.

My heart takes an unfortunate stagger. I forgot about that aspect of the agreement. Scowling, I open my hand again, and Aaron plops another mint into it with a shiny ear-to-ear smile that makes me want to kick him. As I'm popping it into my mouth, another realization ices my blood.

If he's giving this to me, does that mean we kissed on the first date?

I watch, dismayed, as Aaron sticks a mint in his own mouth, then pries his clothes off, leaving him in nothing but his black stud and swim trunks. The bluish lighting of the pool reflects against his pearly skin, making him look nearly ethereal as he turns to me.

"Well?" he asks softly.

I try unsuccessfully to keep my eyes above his collarbone. He's definitely firmed up over the past year, which makes sense, considering his profession forces him to perform constant manual labor. He's lean, but he's solid. I can see the stoniness of his midsection, the indent trailing between his chest and ribs. His shoulders are more squared than I realized, and the shadows of the pool cast against him emphasize elevated veins snaking along his upper arms.

"I'm . . ." I hack through a hitch in my throat, hugging my shirt. "I'll stay up here."

Aaron scoffs, framing his hips. "What am I supposed to do in there alone? Drown?"

"Find a way to entertain yourself," I say sternly.

"But I can't bully you when you're over here," he complains, shuffling closer so he takes up more of my line of sight. "Besides, the sooner you follow my lead, the sooner you get to leave."

Another good point. "Fine," I mumble, kicking off my shoes and beginning to shrug out of my clothes. I pause when I realize he's watching intently.

I swirl my finger at him.

He sniffles and turns around.

I know it doesn't matter, since he's going to see me anyway, but having him stare so unblinkingly while I'm stripping makes me squirm. "Is it cold?" I ask when I'm finished, inching toward the pool's edge. Now that I'm only in swim trunks, the air seems unusually crisp. I continue hugging my arms to conceal myself, because I don't want him to see . . . *me*. I guess. And the toll that everything has taken on my body.

Aaron hops up beside me like an excited puppy. If he had a tail, it would be wagging. "It's usually cold," he admits. "But don't worry. I'll—"

"If you say you'll *warm me up*, I'm leaving immediately."

Aaron sighs with dreariness. I must be ruining all the fun of this situation for him. "Let's jump in," he says, with a sidelong glance. "On three?"

"Whatever," I say.

"One. Two . . ."

A sudden memory swirls into my head. My reflection in the water is different. My body is thinner, my skin more sallow, my expression warped with a scowl. Then I'm flopping into the pool with a shriek of surprise, and I hear raucous laughter . . .

I blink, and I've returned to the present.

I reel sideways and miss Aaron's attempted shove by inches.

"You dick!" I cry out, my fists shivering as infuriation battles exhilaration. I *remembered* something. "The first time we came here, you shoved me into the pool and laughed! And you just tried to do it again!"

Aaron's eyes sparkle brighter. "You remembered?"

"A couple of seconds."

"So if I reenact it," he says, stepping closer, "then more of your memory may come back."

I expand the distance between us. "You know, I don't actually care to remember more details about this moment."

Aaron laughs, warm and honeyed, and my flushed face cools in spite of my desire to cling to my fury. I should hate that sound, but it's like an antidote to my tension, loosening my limbs and chilling my boiling blood. "Then we'll edit the date and jump in together," he says, ambling back to the edge. "No pushing, I promise."

I'm not sure if his promises mean anything, but I can only avoid the inevitable for so long, so I reluctantly return to his side. Maybe I shouldn't jump into a giant vat of liquid since I was in a two-day coma less than a week ago, but the lump on my head is gone now, and I admitted to Aaron during the drive here that I haven't had any issues with balance, vision, or dizziness. Besides, part of me trusts that he won't let anything happen to me.

"One," he says, toes dangling off the edge, that boyish smile stretching across his handsome face. "Two . . ."

I shouldn't. It'll make me just as bad as him. But I'm too petty to fight the abrupt thirst for revenge, so before he can get the final number out, I shove Aaron to teach him a lesson. Then I remember something crucial, and the triumph evaporates from my body.

When I push, he pulls.

He shouldn't have the time, but somehow, he manages to pivot on his heel and snatch my wrist. I shriek in protest as he drags me down with him, and the last thing I hear is mirthful laughter as I'm being swallowed by water.

Frigidity hits me like a brick wall, seizing my limbs. The warmth of Aaron's touch dissolves in the pool. I kick upward and break the surface, coughing as I drag myself away from him. "You suck!" I snarl when his face emerges, but I'm not sure he hears me, because he's laughing again.

"Predictable. You're *so* predictable. I love you."

"Shut up!" I say shrilly, grabbing the pool railing and trembling forcefully as my body readjusts to the change in temperature. "Stop saying that so carelessly. We're teenagers, so we don't have the maturity to fall in lo— What are you doing?"

"Swimming," he answers, butterfly-stroking toward me.

"Stop approaching me so ominously."

He switches to a breaststroke, like that's not worse.

"Stop approaching me in general," I say, but he's already on me, standing flat where I'm treading water, his onyx locks slicked back. He has a widow's peak. I've never noticed.

"Your hair gets darker when it's wet," he notes, though I'm already distracted by his abdomen—now sparkling more intensely under the sheen of fluorescent blue water—being a foot from mine. "How was your day?"

I'm not sure why the question startles me, but it does. I wait for the punch line, but he's merely watching me with genuine curiosity, the lighting making his irises glow. "Fine," I say, too preoccupied with the sight of him to offer anything substantial. "Why?"

Aaron reaches out, then hesitates, his fingers hovering near my forehead. When I don't protest, he plucks strands of sopping wet hair off my face. "Because this is a date, so I want to ask you things about yourself," he says. "Maybe you haven't heard, but I have a pretty big crush on you, sunshine."

The pool's iciness is melting away the longer Aaron stands beside me. "Then . . . how was your day?" I ask awkwardly.

"Fine," he says with a playful wink, before shifting his hand through the water and tapping the back of my palm—a request, I think. When I don't pull away, he carefully threads our fingers. "I was outside all day—you should've seen me before I showered. I was more grass stain and grease than human being."

Aaron heaves a weary breath and tries slumping against my shoulder, but I float backward, causing him to face-plant the water. He picks it up and continues like I didn't just dodge him.

"I spent hours chopping up yard debris, which didn't do my back any favors." He shrugs those less-narrow-than-I-thought shoulders, which still shimmer with water droplets. "I tore down a shed with Pops, which was fun. My mom rescheduled lunch with me, but that's normal. I mostly wanted the day to end so I could see you."

His sheer earnestness makes me swallow a lump of guilt. He's giving me information in such a cozy, familiar way, it's almost overwhelming. "Sounds busy," I say weakly, because I'm not sure how to respond. He seems tired but also fulfilled—he's not complaining so much as he's just talking about what he did. I can tell he enjoys his job. "I didn't know . . . um. That you were in contact with your mom. Do you have a good relationship?"

A look of raw dismay flickers across his face. It leaves as quickly as it comes, but it only heightens my shame at not remembering. "It's complicated," he admits. "Not something we need to talk about right now."

My lips furl down. I guess I won't push it. His thumbnail works the lines of my palm, like he's sketching them into his mind. His eyes wander to my neck, where an ugly yellowish tinge lingers, then lower, where a persistent purple splotch spans my elbow. The joy disintegrates in his smile.

"They don't hurt," I say, though I don't know why I care to tell him.

Aaron's palm slips away from mine so he can smooth his thumb along my cheekbone. He seems despondent suddenly, so I allow him. "How much pain are you in?" he asks.

"I just told you—"

"Come on, Riley," he pleads.

I'm fine. The words are fully formed in my mouth, but he's watching me so insistently that I can't push them out. "It's not that bad," I say, steering my attention to the water lapping against my collarbone. I wish we weren't alone in this massive room, where every sound reverberates noisily against the high ceilings and tiles. The air leaving my mouth is ice-cold, and I'm glad for the mint, otherwise I'd be preoccupied with thoughts about how I smell like pesto.

"Has it been keeping you up?" he asks softly.

I should feel annoyed that he's persisting, but his eyes are still glittering like silver sequins under moonlight, and I don't have the fortitude to focus elsewhere. "I've been sleeping," I claim.

He sees through my thinly veiled concealment of the truth and offers a small smile that twists my stomach into knots. His canines are sharper than most. More and more, he's beginning to resemble a Labrador. "You look tired, Riley," he whispers. His other hand shifts through the crystal water, and a shiver rakes my body when it spreads over the curve of my waist, tugging, guiding me closer until our chests are inches from grazing. "Please don't feel like you have to downplay your pain. The sore joints, the cold hands and feet, the headaches, the exhaustion. I promise I'm the last person you have to hide from."

I stare at Aaron in disbelief, my lips parted. With every word, I feel the pain of existence resurfacing. An acknowledgment I suffocate by busying myself with other thoughts and tasks.

It hurts.

Obviously. That's the thing about chronic pain. Even when it's quiet, subdued, it's always there. Iron supplements and special dieting don't dissolve anemia's symptoms—they only lessen the severity. My *best* days are normal people's *okay* days.

"I don't . . ." I swallow the hitch in my voice. "I don't see why it matters. Why do you need to know the exact degree of my pain?"

Water glimmers in his soft curled tips and midnight-black lashes. His palm is still fastened to my waist, his pinkie scraping the elastic of my swimsuit, stimulating enough that I hardly feel his other hand massaging my cheekbone. "It helps to know for several reasons," he says. "I watch you constantly push through your own boundaries for others. If you're having a bad day, you'd rather suffer through it than inconvenience people by shifting plans around. Knowing where you're at helps me adapt. Like, sometimes it's better to spend the day resting in bed rather than going out."

Aaron presses a lingering kiss to my forehead. I'm too stunned to have the visceral reaction I know I should give him.

"And sometimes," he says, "I just want to know because I care."

My lip is trembling, so I try to gnaw it away. What could I possibly have to offer Aaron Beckham, who could nab anyone off the street and woo them with a wink and playful grin? With all my restrictions and unpredictable pain levels and stubborn attitude . . .

"I'm too much effort," I say, and the frailty in my voice brings salty tears to my eyes. "There are so many people who don't have inconvenient conditions . . . people who have energy and exciting personalities and unbroken bodies . . ."

"Riley." His word comes with quiet breathiness, like he didn't mean to voice it. "You have no idea how effortless it is to love you."

I bite harder on my lip. Aaron draws my navel against his, and my palm reluctantly leaves the pool railing so I can flatten it on his solid chest, just in case I want to push. His other hand catches the crook of my knee and props it around his hip—a way to keep me elevated above the water. He's luring me in, literally, just like he presumably did the first time around. Not only with his touch, but his soothing words. I can't fall for it again.

But he keeps talking, and my antsy thoughts go numb.

"Your body is easily aggravated, but you're not broken," he tells me, his hand sliding from my hip to the small of my back, where it roots itself to support my weight. "Sure, there are billions of people who aren't anemic celiacs. But none of them are you."

I stare stubbornly at his dripping collarbone, but he bumps his forehead against mine.

"Other people don't glare at me like you do," he says. "Other people don't call me a jerk and then immediately apologize. Other people don't accidentally fall asleep during hand massages. Other people don't turn the color of cherries when I compliment them. Other people don't hiss like a cat when I flick them, or feel guilty for swearing, or sleep in leopard-print flannel pajamas and matching socks. Other people aren't Riley Wilson. Do you get it now?"

The water is so thick in my eyes that his very image is swimming. My next breath shudders. I've always assumed that I've been a recurring burden on my family my entire life. Aaron is making me feel like . . . like I'm . . .

Worth it.

"Sorry," I breathe.

Aaron's palm leaves my back so he can frame my face and draw it up. "Why are you apologizing?" he asks, pressing a kiss to my cheek.

"I don't . . . I'm sorry . . ." I hear a choked noise in my throat, which I try unsuccessfully to swallow. I don't need to cry, so I won't.

"Why?" he asks again, still low and gentle, moving between each cheekbone and pausing to kiss the bridge of my nose whenever he passes over it.

"B-because I just feel like . . ." I don't know what I'm blathering about or apologizing for, only that it's my defense mechanism whenever I feel cornered. I can't handle the tenderness with which he caresses my face, and my hand nudges his chest back. "Stop . . . Please stop kissing me like that . . ."

"Why?" His cool breath unfurls against my upper lip. I squeeze my eyes shut to seal the incoming waterworks. His bare skin pressed flush with mine beneath the water is disorienting. I don't remember my other leg joining the first on his opposing hip, but I'm sitting fully on his waist now, ankles crossed at his back, like my body knew it would be more comfortable here. I'm pushing at him with one hand because

I need distance before I do something I'll regret. But my legs are locked around him, hugging stubbornly.

"How can I hate someone who kisses me like that?" I whisper.

Aaron smiles with a warmth that radiates. I know because I can feel it despite my closed eyes. "You don't know how to *hate*, Riley," he says. "Even when you have every reason to."

I peek through one eye. He winks in greeting.

"My legs hurt," I mumble.

Aaron's brows rise in surprise. Then he nods thoughtfully, his other arm joining the first around my waist to hug me to him. "Tell me more," he encourages.

"My knees are sore. My shins. My knuckles. My neck and head are throbbing, but it's background pain, so it's not that bad." Every word drains the remaining energy out of me. My eyes droop and the grip of my legs around his waist slackens as I acknowledge it.

"Rate your discomfort from one to ten," he says.

"Mm . . . four, maybe?"

"So it's six?" he asks, and his index finger twists into the ridge of my spine, which instinctively makes me squirm and blush.

"I can handle it," I protest, and Aaron scrapes his index finger higher up my back, which tickles enough to make me knock my fist against his chest. "Don't do that!"

"We had a water war here the first time, which I won easily," he says. "But you're hurting, so let's call it quits."

I scrunch my nose in disbelief. "We haven't even done any swimming."

"True. But it's better to play it safe, since you're still recovering.

Besides, just sitting in the water is romantic, right?" Aaron's grin is cheeky, and he does something truly diabolical. He snaps the elastic of my swimsuit.

Blood rushes hotly through my limbs, and I squawk in protest, then plant my foot on his abdomen and push with all my strength. "Brat!" I snap. "Let go! You're supposed to listen to me!"

Aaron bursts into laughter, allowing me to thrust myself away through the water. "You're cute when you boss me around," he says, hiking himself onto the edge of the pool. "Normally you like it vice versa, so this is refreshing—"

"Shut up!" I wheeze out, and I plunge beneath the surface so I don't have to listen to him. Naturally, I last about ten seconds before my lungs burn, forcing me to resurface.

Aaron is still seated poolside, dripping with sparkly beads of water, his face propped in his hand. "You done?" he asks.

"Are you?" I shoot back.

"If I must be. Though I could go on and on about our amazing sexual chemistry—"

I throw myself back underwater, cutting him off.

He teases and torments me all the way back to my house.

11

Climbing up through my bedroom window isn't as daunting as coming down. Aaron goes first, pausing along the way to offer his hand and hoist me up. I've been shivering since the pool—once I got used to the water, the cool air became my next burden. Because I can never be comfortable, ever.

"So," he says when we're inside, and I'm panting from the strain of having climbed a whole entire tree.

"So . . . goodbye, I guess?" I say, peering awkwardly around at the sunset-orange walls and mounted pictures I still can't get used to. Aaron has good taste. Or maybe I picked them out, and he hung them for me. "Sorry the date was a bust. But at least I remembered you pushing me into the pool. I'm hoping the memories will get longer."

"Me too," Aaron says with a softer smile, and I swallow hard, twisting toward my dresser to fumble around for fuzzy pajamas. We changed out of our swimsuits in the locker room, but I still feel damp in all my nooks and crannies. "Though our first date didn't end after the pool."

I pause my rummaging. "What do you mean?"

"I said you had to spend at least three hours with me for it to qualify as a date," Aaron admits, guilt hinging on his voice. "Like, a dinner-and-a-movie length of time. So you suggested a movie to avoid talking to me. We watched it in bed on your laptop." Aaron rubs his neck sheepishly. "You must be exhausted, though, so you should just get some sleep—"

"Let's do it," I say firmly.

Aaron blinks. I match his fierce stare with mine.

"What we're doing is working, at least a little," I say, pulling free my checkered flannels (not the leopard ones. I hate how he knows about those). "Flashes are better than nothing. Let's follow our previous dates as closely as we can. What movie was it?"

Aaron glows with delight, I guess because he gets to spend more time prodding me. *"1917."*

"Really?" It's my turn to brighten. "I love that movie. Did you like it?"

Aaron gives me a fond look that warms my face. "Sure, sunshine," he says.

We both fit on my bed and each have a pillow to lean against the headboard with, but it's not a queen or anything, so we're thigh-to-thigh. I try escaping this fact by wriggling under my comforter and sheets. This doesn't seem like a *date* movie—why didn't we watch a rom-com or drama or just something not horribly traumatizing?

"Do you know any history behind this movie?" I ask, nestling into my pillow. Thankfully, Aaron hasn't tried snuggling up with me. He's just sitting there, his lanky legs stretching across the bed, his hands folded in his lap. He examines my face with a carefulness that makes me want to bury myself deeper in my comforter.

"Not much," he says.

Then I'll tell him everything I know, because he's basically my prisoner. "It's based on a real person's experiences," I say, eagerness thrumming under my skin despite the time of night. "A lance corporal who carried messages across no-man's-land. It's a great representation of trench warfare, though it has some historical inaccuracies."

"Oh?" Aaron smiles from the corner of my eye. "Like what?"

"The German trenches shouldn't be empty here," I say, gesturing to the screen.

"I see."

"And there should be more machine guns."

"That so?"

"Also—it's early for this one, but you've seen it, so it's fine—they show Sikh soldiers with the British units. But they were suffering casualties, so it's unlikely you would've seen them at this point."

My attention is glued to my laptop, but I feel the heat of his stare. Maybe he's waiting for me to shut up about things he doesn't care about. I try not to chirp too much, but it's difficult, because Aaron keeps pressing for my opinion on certain scenes, meaning I have no choice but to indulge him and info-dump.

It's a high-tension movie, but I'm beginning to doze. An hour in, Aaron's hand sneaks across the bedspread and scoops mine up, then begins to massage little circles along the joints. It's soothing, though I *humph* at him to show how I feel about him doing whatever he wants. He merely smirks in response as my head sinks deeper into my pillow.

When I blink, the lights are off, my laptop is gone, and I'm curled on my side under my blankets. Blearily, I peek over my shoulder to find Aaron sitting against the headboard, fidgeting with his gadget toy. He glances at me, his thumbs working the cogs faster. "Missed the end," he whispers. "Like last time."

I feel a pang of guilt in my stomach. "Sorry."

"Don't apologize. Go back to sleep. I'll get out of here soon. I just wanted to . . ." He fades away, his attention shifting to his fidget toy, his expression uncharacteristically flat. "Never mind."

I have a sinking feeling about what he was going to say. He probably just wants to bask in this moment—one of the few where I'm not glaring or snipping at him. When I'm asleep, things must feel normal. Like nothing has changed.

"Did you leave after I fell asleep?" I ask, drawing the comforter higher over my chin.

"You woke up, and I asked if I could cuddle with you and sleep here."

The blanket rises higher over my face so he won't see the rosiness surely blossoming through my cheeks. "What did I say?"

Aaron plucks a cog from his toy loose and rolls it along his lower lip, the puckishness returning to his smile. "What do you think?"

I can't believe I would've allowed something as intimate as cuddling after a first date. But he seems forlorn. The ghost of melancholy is etched into his grin, in the current dullness of his eyes. He's hurting. And why wouldn't he be? If we've been together for over a year . . . if he truly loves me . . .

I chew on my tongue. One date. It's been *one date,* and already my animosity is fractured. He shouldn't be able to win me over so easily. But I feel the weight of his sincerity in every word. In the intensity of his stare. In the way he cradles my hands. Even now, the fact that he's content to sit beside me in silence while I sleep, just so he can spend more time with me . . .

"Do what you want," I mumble, turning my back to him.

"Really?" Clearly astonished, Aaron peeks over my head to see my face, which I promptly bury in my pillow. "You're sure?"

"Should I change my mind?" I ask, huffing.

"No, no. I shan't allow it." He's speaking through another teasing smile. He's been touchy-feely, but I've never felt threatened by his grip. He meets my resistance with his own stubbornness, and maybe he knows I don't mind it as much as I claim I do. He's really warm, after all.

I hear rustling, and when I peek back, I see he's now wearing nothing but black boxer shorts. "I didn't say you could strip!" I croak, to which he giggles maniacally and slinks under the covers.

"I get hot." He nestles his head on my pillow. His arm creeps around my waist, his fingers purposefully grazing the hint of skin between my shirt and pants. I feel a puff of air against my ear when he notices me shiver. Laughter. I resist giving him a good kick as he fits his waist against the curve of mine. His arm sneaks between my limp ones, his fingers resting inches from my face. I can smell chlorine mingling with his musky bodywash.

I try to steady my raging heartbeat, wishing I weren't so easily flustered. It doesn't help when he tugs my shirt down, sliding my collar lower along my nape. Aaron's long exhale unfurls against my skin, as if the sight of my neck has frustrated him. Then I feel the warmth of his lips just below my hairline, and a pleasant, unexpected tingle scratches down my back.

"Go to sleep," I order, scoffing when he slides a leg between my curled ones, tangling them beneath the blankets. How are his feet warm? I guess I don't mind them touching mine, since I forgot socks.

"You first." He plants a soft kiss in the scoop between my neck and shoulder.

"So you can put your hands all over me in my sleep?" I demand.

"Harassing you is only fun when you're awake to respond to it," he protests.

"Amazing. You're a beacon of integrity."

Another puff of air in my ear, which means he's laughing again. "I like it when you get sassy," he says, his index finger tickling my hairline, which makes me squirm my neck with a hiss. "Or I like making you regret it."

Something hot scrapes at my stomach. I decide responding will only give him more ammunition, so I close my eyes. His warm breath and his thumb massaging mine is strangely relaxing—a repetition that eases my tension. I think we've been here before. His weight pressing into my back. His arm snug around me. His legs trying to heat mine. His mouth moving slowly, methodically, along my skin.

I'm startled when I feel something join Aaron's lips against my neck. A droplet that slides down my nape and melts into my flannel shirt. Then another.

He's crying.

A lump expands between the walls of my throat, thinning my air supply. I try keeping steady, but my eyes are moistening and my heart is plummeting into my stomach. "I'm sorry," I whisper.

"Don't." Aaron rolls me into his chest with such overwhelming desperation that I don't dare protest. His right hand sprawls over the back of my head, hugging it to his shoulder, and the other latches around my waist, notching me tight against his body.

I wish he were wearing a shirt so he wouldn't feel my wet lashes. "I don't mean to cause you so much pain," I say, my voice muffled in his collarbone.

He buries his lips deep into my locks. "Please sleep, Riley."

I don't know how I'm supposed to do that when he's clearly feeling so tormented. I've never seen Aaron Beckham cry. Or show any emotion aside from amusement. I want to see his face—to know what he looks like when he cries—but his hand is nearly clawing through my hair as he holds me to his shoulder. My palms are limp and smashed between our chests. They're warm there, so I don't try to move them.

"Can I help?" I ask quietly.

His lips stretch into a gentle smile against my head. "Just stay here for a bit, if you don't mind."

His grip is so unyielding, I'm not sure I could leave if I wanted to. "I'm not going anywhere," I say, relaxing until I'm fully limp in his arms. "It's my bedroom."

I hear a breathy laugh. "You're right. It's been a while since we've slept here."

He's probably referring to the fact that I was supposedly living with him before the accident. I wonder if we shared a room, or if they had a spare. I don't feel like prying, though, so I remain where I am, letting him squeeze me into unconsciousness. This hasn't jogged any memories. Maybe I'm okay with that. I'm not sure I want them to interfere with what's happening here now.

Aaron Beckham is being human. I'm not sure why he fell in love with me, but the longer I spend around him, the more I'm convinced it's not an exaggeration. And the more I believe him, the less anger I feel.

A couple of days ago, I would've shuddered with revulsion at the thought of falling asleep curled up in Aaron's arms.

Tonight, I allow his warmth to carry me into my dreams.

12

Aaron slides out of bed earlier than I expect. Something about a paint job in a fancy house that he's tackling with his dads. Which is good because it gives me time to handle my to-do list. I use Dad's account information to make his quarterly tax payment (he forgot), I book an appointment for Mom to get her license renewed at the Secretary of State (she forgot), and I take Logan's car (or technically Aunt Lydia's, since his was totaled) into the shop to repair a leaking tire, since he took mine to a late-morning study session.

Thank you!! I owe you some Ben and Jerry's ice cream, Dad texts.

You're the sweetest, honey. Love you and hope you get lots of rest today, Mom texts.

You didn't have to do that. You should be relaxing, Logan texts.

I'm in less pain today—my bones and joints aren't throbbing as offensively. But I'm lightheaded and my knees are wobbling more prominently. My body is clearly sucking on all my energy to continue healing. Anyone else's marks and bruises would've faded by this point, but I try not to annoy myself with pointless thoughts.

I cleaned the kitchen already, but I'm paranoid about the rest of it. I haven't had any side effects to indicate that I've been glutened, but I shouldn't risk extending my healing process, so I decide to do it all again. Mom apparently took an online baking class after I moved out, so there's every possibility the dust from the top shelves and living room might have flour in it. Better to be safe than sorry, so I get to work.

As I scrub every nook in the house I can find, I try to keep my thoughts from wandering. Aaron occupied my mind all of yesterday—I won't let him steal today, too.

But when I close my eyes, I can still feel his tears sliding down the back of my neck.

This "reclaiming my memories" ploy isn't a game to him. He genuinely wants to help me remember the time we've spent together. The teasing and prodding . . . it's more than personality coming into play. I think it's a defense mechanism. A way for him to cope with my inability to remember.

Though I have the feeling teasing and prodding is also a regular part of our relationship.

I wander around, throwing open drawers and cabinet doors, because the duster isn't where I remember it being. Eventually, I open the hallway closet, and I see the feathery head at the top, far out of reach. I sigh with exasperation, then drag over a kitchen chair and clamber onto it, my limbs trembling with strain.

I reach for the duster, rising to my tiptoes. I'm looking at it. It's within reach.

But then the image swirls, my weight evaporates, and the world goes black.

I only realize what's happening when my body collides with the hardwood floor. The pain is so sudden, so all-consuming, that all I can do is lie still for several seconds, agony radiating through me like electricity. I can't cry or scream or breathe.

It hurts.

Eventually, a staggering gasp enters my lungs. My ribs, hips, knees, shoulders, and neck throb at different, disorienting levels of pain that I can't distinguish. I'm not sure how long I lie immobile, wondering how many bones I've fractured. I have my phone . . . Maybe I should call an ambulance? No, God no, those things are money swallowers.

I'll ride this out until the pain recedes. Though I'm not sure I'll be able to get up. It's like the floor absorbed every fragment of my energy.

My fingers curl around my phone. I manage to draw it out and unlock the screen, then call Mom. She must be with a client, though, because there's no answer.

Dad is next. He sends me to voicemail and then shoots me a text: Everything okay? I'm about to meet with my boss. Can I call you back in a bit?

Somehow, I manage to type out and send the words Everything is fine. See you tonight.

Of all the times this could've happened, why now? I took my iron supplements and ate this morning, so why would I faint at such an inopportune moment? Logan is my last hope. It rings once. Twice. Three times.

"Hello?"

"Hey." I try steadying my voice, but it's thick and raspy with pain. My wrist clunks against the wooden floor. I don't have the strength to hold the phone up. "Just wondering if you'll be back soon?"

Logan is quiet, like he can sense something's wrong. "I was planning on studying here for the afternoon," he admits. "Are you okay?"

I'm not sure what to say. It's not fair of me to pull him from his plans because I did something ridiculous and have to pay the consequences for it. What is he supposed to do when he gets back, anyway?

Get me to the couch and then what? I shouldn't upend his whole day so he can spend ten minutes cleaning up my mess.

"I'm fine," I say. "Good luck with studying."

Logan hangs on the line, then makes a noise of uncertainty, and says, "Okay. Let me know if you need anything."

"Okay," I murmur.

I'm alone again. I keep lying on my side in the entryway, blinking slow, throbbing everywhere. My vision is blurred as I stare at my list of contacts. I can muscle through this.

"Sunshine?"

The voice startles me out of my daze. I'm in another call—the icon is a picture of Aaron Beckham grinning and licking whipped cream off his fingers. I wonder if I made that his contact photo, or if he seized my phone and did it himself. I hear two men bickering in the background, and an echoing sound, like they're all in an empty house.

"Don't tell me you miss me so much that you're calling just to hear my voice," he says. I can hear the smile in his words.

I wasn't anticipating having a conversation with Aaron. My fingers must've been operating on their own to find his name.

"Riley?" His voice is less amused. "Is everything okay?"

Everything is fine, because what am I supposed to do if it's not? He's at his literal adult job, and I can't selfishly expect him to drop everything because my body decided to be dramatic today.

But I can't hang up. My fingers won't move.

"I can hear you breathing," Aaron says, the worry rising in his voice. "Say anything. Please."

". . . Sorry."

I don't know what else to say.

"Where are you?" Aaron demands.

"Home," I whisper.

"Did you hit your head?"

I'm not sure how he knows I fainted. "No."

"Are you on the floor? Can you move?"

I don't answer.

"Ten minutes," he says, and I hear rustling and clinking sounds, like he's putting supplies down. "Stay where you are. Focus on breathing, okay?"

The pain is sharp and overwhelming. All I can do is exist on the wooden floor, half-conscious, and stare at the front door. I count the minutes, forcing myself to breathe through the aches. One minute. Two. Three. Four. Five. Six.

The door handle wriggles. It's locked. I hear a faint curse.

Seven.

There's a thud in my bedroom. Then thunderous footsteps are sprinting down the staircase, and a shadow falls over me. Aaron's pale face is flushed, and he's heaving deep breaths as he glances between me and the toppled chair. He's wearing white overalls flecked with teal paint, along with a scrappy bandanna to keep his hair off his forehead.

This is a humiliating situation, but I can only feel relief.

"I'm here," he says, collapsing onto his knees. He slides one hand delicately under my head, settling it on his thighs. "Where does it hurt?"

I blink up at him lethargically. "Don't know," I mumble.

"Everywhere?" he translates.

I don't answer.

"Do you know how long you were out?" he asks.

"Couple of seconds."

"You're sure you didn't hit your head?" His hand roves my scalp gently, feeling for any new welts before shifting to my neck and shoulders, pressing light divots into the skin. "I don't see obvious signs of broken bones, but we should go to the hospital to check—"

"No!" I say. "I'm fine. Just got jostled, I think . . . Just need to catch my breath . . ."

Aaron gives me a stern look, which I return with as much ferocity as I can muster. He says, "I'll move you. Try not to tense up." His left arm slinks beneath my shoulder blades, and my head sags as he cradles me to his chest and leans my face in the scoop of his shoulder. His right arm notches beneath my knees, and he hoists me off the ground. "You can cry," he says softly, lips brushing my forehead as he proceeds toward the staircase.

"No," I mutter. I don't need to cry, so I won't.

He climbs up to my bedroom, then shoulders me into one arm like my weight means nothing to him as he draws my sheets back. He nestles me into my mattress and pulls the blankets to my chin. "You can cry," he says again, apparently having not heard my answer the first time.

"I'm fine," I say wearily, though I'm still throbbing relentlessly. At least my voice is strengthening, and feeling is returning to my hands and feet. A blessing and a curse, since they're the coldest parts of me.

Aaron bends over me and locks eyes with my tired, drooping ones, his own full of such ardency that it stuns me. "You don't have to pretend," he says. "Not around me."

"I'm not going to cry," I snap.

He smiles with a kindness I've never seen and strokes a tear streak from my temple.

"I don't need to cry, so I won't."

He massages away another one.

"Crying doesn't help anything, so I . . ."

Both of his thumbs are working my cheekbones now, smoothing the wetness away.

Suddenly, I'm bursting into sobs.

They're ugly and pitiful. I wish I could drag my hands up over my face and conceal it, but I don't have the strength to move my arms yet. "It hurts," I cry, because it does, it really fucking *hurts*. "I hate my life. It's not fair . . ."

I don't mean that. My life is perfectly fine and privileged and secure. I have a roof over my head, a bright future, a loving family, and a mostly functional body.

But I'm so tired of pain.

"Everything hurts all the time, no matter what I do," I bawl, completely limp, pathetic, and useless. "My body hates me . . . even when I do everything I'm supposed to, something always hurts . . . The accident was a whole week ago, so why am I still so weak? I hate . . ." I choke on my breath, wishing I could dissolve into my mattress. "I hate that I can't remember the past year of my life. I hate that I have to pretend like everything is normal. I hate everything . . . all of it . . ."

I'm barely conscious of the words tumbling out of my mouth. Aaron is still nudging the tears off my face, not minding my soggy and splotchy appearance. I hate feeling like this. I'm not supposed to let my negative emotions escape in such a grotesque way, so why can Aaron draw them out of me with a few simple words?

He doesn't say anything. His thumbs find my eyelids, and he drags them closed, pushing me into darkness. His fingers shift to my neck, and he kneads the skin, his touch becoming a familiar warmth. He lingers there as I lie motionless, aside from my shuddery breaths. He journeys to my collarbone, never applying enough pressure to hurt, and then to my shoulders. His light, circular movements are soothing and ease my incessant soreness.

"You should get back to work," I breathe.

Aaron's lips find the space between my brows. "I won't leave you," he murmurs. "Don't worry about anything but your breathing."

He pulls my leg out from beneath the covers and folds my knee so he can massage my foot, which I welcome despite the ticklishness, because I'm freezing. He kneads the bones of my ankle next, then smooths his thumbs toward my shin. The pain is receding as he loosens my body's stiffness and carefully rubs away the aches. He's being so kind and patient. I don't know how to respond to it.

"Want a bath? Warm water will help," he says, fingertips gliding over my hairline.

It sounds nice. I did just clean the bathroom, so the sparkling tub is itching to be used. "Don't want to move," I say.

"I'll help."

I open my eyes to glare at him. He's playing it straight, not a hint of flirtatious mischief fracturing his concerned expression. When he notices my suspicion, he smiles, but even that isn't playful.

"I won't touch you," he says, pinching the curve of my ear and causing a surge of heat to spill through my face. "But I'm happy to get you into the tub. Want me to bring you your swimsuit?"

I consider the offer. I'm not sure I'll even be able to wriggle it on—my limbs feel like al dente fettucine. But I decide to try. "Okay," I say, and Aaron's expression brightens.

He goes to retrieve the swimsuit draped over my hamper and drops it off with me, then heads to the bathroom to fill the tub. Slowly, I muscle myself up and shove my sweatpants off, then drag the swimsuit up my waist. Every movement increases the severity of my achiness, and by the time I'm finished tugging my shirt off, I'm depleted of energy.

Aaron returns to my bedside and nestles a hand under my neck. "Can I carry you?"

The thought of making him do that again makes me squirm. Despite my overwhelming exhaustion, I manage to sneak my legs over the edge of the bed and push upright. My knees threaten to fold, and Aaron lurches out, snatching my elbows and supporting my weight.

"I'll carry you," he says pleadingly, but I shake my head.

"It's fine. I'll get over this."

"Pain isn't something you can just shove through. All you're going to do is make it a worse problem for tomorrow. Please let me help."

I hate that he's making sense but hate the thought of being schlepped around like a toddler even more. But if I do force through it, I'll worsen the pain like Aaron said, and it'll take longer to recover. I can't risk getting further behind schedule.

I don't protest, so Aaron gathers my legs out from under me and carries me into the bathroom. He settles me in the beige tub, and though my tailbone aches when I reach the bottom, the water's heat is relieving enough that I barely notice. I exhale, my head falling back against a fluffy towel. He must've put it there.

Aaron sits with his back pressed to the tub, his lanky knees tucked into his chest. He's quiet. Maybe he can sense I don't have the energy to tolerate his cheeky banter.

"Are you feeling better today?" I ask.

"Hmm?" Aaron angles his head back to offer me an amused stare over his shoulder. He's still wearing the paint-stained bandanna that contains his curls. Paired with his overalls and the dried sweat on his hairline . . . well, "handyman" is a better look on him than it should be. "Am *I* feeling better?"

"You were crying last night," I say.

"That was nothing."

My lips slant downward. "Your emotions aren't nothing," I whisper. "If you tell me not to downplay my pain, you shouldn't downplay yours, either."

Aaron blinks in astonishment. Then he twists to face the tub, folding his arms on the ledge, observing me meticulously. "Do you want me to wash your hair or anything?"

The thought induces hot redness in my face, but I indulge his obvious change of subject. "I showered this morning, so no."

"I've done it before." Aaron's smile spreads into his face, his teeth as porcelain pale as his skin. "You fall asleep on my shoulder eight times out of ten."

I'm about to steam alongside the water I'm swallowed in. "You're not lying?" I ask warily, because it doesn't sound like me. I've been uncomfortable with my appearance my whole life. Gaining weight has been an issue since birth, and my skin is always too pale or too yellow. Being in my swimsuit in a low-lit pool was almost too much to handle, so I can't imagine willingly putting myself unclothed in a bathtub with him.

"Do you want proof?"

"You took pictures of me naked in my sleep?" I squeak in horror.

"We were concealed by the water. I'm not the type to take nudes of my partner, surprising as that may sound." His eyes drift toward the ceiling in contemplation. "Well, we were both naked, technically, but—"

"Don't tell me more!" I interrupt, raising my hands and accidentally splashing him. Unfazed, he blinks it out of his magnificently long lashes.

"Can I show you the picture? It's cute."

I scrunch my face in annoyance, but I'm curious. I've scoured my phone for pictures of Aaron and me, seeking physical proof of our relationship. Either I never took any, or Logan deleted the ones that existed to help me rid myself of him. Aaron, though, probably has moments like this documented mere inches away. I haven't asked to see them because I've been anxious to witness myself in places and situations I can't remember. He hasn't offered to show me any until now, either, probably because he doesn't want to overwhelm me.

"Show me," I say, hoping I don't regret it.

Aaron draws out his phone and thumbs through his gallery. He must find what he's looking for, because his eyes sparkle brighter, like icicles caught in dawn sunlight, and he flips the screen.

There we are. I'm concealed from the neck down by swirling colors—we must've used a bath bomb—but Aaron's cryptid legs don't fit, so they're bent up, his knees poking above the surface. His left arm is draped along the ledge, and his right is elevated to take the picture. I'm nestled against his chest, seated between his legs, my head leaning in the crook of his shoulder and pressed up against his pale neck. My skin looks healthy. Even next to his. It's probably his bathroom lighting.

An unfamiliar sensation settles over me. I don't see anything, but I can feel it. A moment like this. The dampness of Aaron's smooth skin against my back. His arms wrapped around me, hands crossed over my waist, the water cooling. We've been sitting there awhile.

His voice.

"Five dollars. Hand it over, sunshine."

I hear my own disgruntled response, but it's warbled and distant. I have the feeling I bet him I wouldn't fall asleep this time. I try clinging to the memory scrap, but the harder I focus on it, the faster it slips through my fingers, until it's barely an incoherent whisper. Soon, it will be lost entirely.

No. I can't let this one get away. It's an actual memory—an *extended* one!

Suddenly, I panic.

"Get in!" I choke out, and I swat the phone from Aaron's hand, anxiety clouding my senses as I seize his overall straps and heave his weight over the side of the tub. Aaron splashes into the water on top of me with a squawking noise, and the resulting wave sloshes onto the tile floor.

"Riley?" he yelps as I wrestle him beneath me.

"Spread your legs!" I order.

"What?"

"For God's sake, Aaron, do I have to do everything myself?" I demand, and I seize his soaking wet overalls by the knees, folding them up and wrenching his legs apart. I flip so my back is to his chest and lean against his soggy clothes, angling myself like I was in the picture. I seize his wrists and wrap them around my front until we're in position, then close my eyes, letting the seconds pass in silence.

Come on. Come on, memory. Come *back*.

It doesn't. It's gone.

Which means I just dragged Aaron Beckham into the bath, fully clothed, for no reason.

"I'm so sorry," I choke out, trying to pry myself away from him, but he merely folds his arms tighter around my midsection, hugging me.

"You're trying to torture me," he says, his low voice scraping my ear and causing little bumps to spring along my neck.

"I didn't . . . I'm sorry . . . I was remembering something," I say, his breath on my skin overwhelming. I've been frigid all day, but now I feel like I'm battling a fever. "I wanted to reenact the picture and grab the memory before it disappeared. It didn't work."

Aaron's nose is grazing the divot between my earlobe and jawline. "I'm soaking wet, and there's nothing to show for it?" he asks, sighing. "A shame. What should I do now? Your clothes won't fit me."

"We'll dry yours." I try drawing away again, but his knees press inward around mine, pushing them together, locking me in place against his chest. "Aaron, I said I'm sorry . . . What are you doing?"

"Bullying you," he whispers.

"Well, don't!"

"You willingly dragged me in here." His lips ghost over my temple, and I blush down to my hairline. "Now you're paying the price."

My nostrils flare with indignation. I sit there grumpily, perfectly still, pin-drop silent. I'm glad he's clothed and I'm wearing swim trunks, because otherwise, I'd pass away from heat exhaustion.

He's being a brat by holding me where I am, which is annoying, but I simmer down after a moment. The water is hot enough to steam, and it feels nice against my achy joints. Aaron is more cushiony than the tub. His grip around me is snug, protective, and it should make me feel awkward and uncomfortable.

I can't explain why it's not, and it's frustrating.

"Do you have other pictures?" I ask.

"Naturally. You never took any yourself." Aaron's fingers fumble briefly along my bare waist as he seeks my hand, and it tickles enough to induce a full-body shiver that he probably, definitely notices. He doesn't react other than to smile wider as he scoops my hand out of the water and brings it to his mouth. He deposits soft, methodical kisses to each of my knuckles. "Want to see them?"

"How many are there?"

"Hundreds. But two-thirds are just of you. The other third is of us."

"Why would you take so many pictures of me?" I ask in mortification, twisting my head on his shoulder to glare up at him. It's a bad idea, because his face is now only an inch from mine, close enough that his exhales brush my forehead. I'm at the perfect angle to spot the intricate narcissus flower tattoo etched behind his left ear.

Aaron presses a lingering kiss to my palm, smirking. "You know the answer to that."

I purse my lips, because even now, it seems so illogical. "I don't get it," I mutter. I slink deeper into the water, sliding down his sopping overalls until my chin is nestled on the water's surface.

Aaron doesn't let me hide. He grips me beneath my arms and hoists me up, pulling me sideways into his chest, so my head is tucked under his chin. I curl my knees up to fit, and he responds by wrapping his wingspan around my body. I can tell he likes our size difference by how he's constantly going out of his way to make me feel smaller than a potato. It's annoying.

It can't be comfortable sitting in his handyman attire. Cotton and jeans are painfully itchy against wet skin. But maybe it doesn't matter to him, since he gets this moment.

"Can you handle it?" Aaron asks. "If I start listing the reasons I fell for you. Or will you stop me after the first two because you'll be too embarrassed to hear the rest?"

I clear my throat awkwardly. "Don't tell me."

Aaron bursts into laughter, which sends frustration scorching through me. I flick where I think his forehead is, catching one of his brows. "Predictable," he says, catching my index finger before it can land a second flick and massaging it. "There's one reason."

"What?" I demand.

"Your reaction to compliments." His voice is unbearably low, the vibrations strumming my muscles. I understand why it was easy for past-me to fall asleep here. "Watching you get flustered is my favorite hobby. I only wish it weren't because you don't believe the compliments could be true."

I glare up at him. His eyes are glittering with a familiar impishness I should know better than to address.

"Your face is red," he says. "Are you overheating?"

"Yes. We should get out." I start wriggling so I can stand, but he won't give me room to move. In fact, he's drawing his knees in, choking away my mobility and crushing me against him, so our noses are nearly grazing.

"But the water is cooling down." Aaron's head cocks with curiosity. "What's making an anemic like you so flushed?"

"You're being a brat again," I snap.

"Yeah?" He flutters his lashes. His eyes remind me of frosted glass. "What are you going to do about it, sunshine?"

I close my eyes and take a deep breath to settle my heartbeat, hating how strangely comfortable I feel being trapped against him. Hating that I must've told him this at some point in the past, and that's clearly why he does it. Then I feel it. His lips, warm and smooth, meeting mine. His fingertips scraping up my back, his bare arms grazing my shoulder blades, the water shifting around us . . .

Aaron Beckham is kissing me.

13

"Agh!" I shriek, and I reel my hand out instinctively, slamming it into Aaron's forehead and snapping his head back. He bangs it against the tub, and the sound echoes through the bathroom.

"Ow," he comments.

"H-how could you?" I demand, knocking my fists against his knees until he loosens them. I begin my panicky escape onto the floor towel outside the tub.

"Why did you just slam my head into your tub?" he wheezes, his eyes spinning.

"You kissed me!"

Massaging his head, Aaron frowns at the agitated bathwater, like he's recalling the last ten seconds. "I've been itching to kiss you for a while, so I'd probably remember doing it."

"But . . . but I felt . . . and your arms were . . ." I stumble through the words, trying to navigate what just happened. The quickened breaths, his arms pushing up my back, his bare chest flush with mine . . .

I look at Aaron's chest, fully concealed by his overalls.

Then the kiss was just another memory?

Which means I nearly concussed Aaron Beckham against my tub for no reason?

"Oh no," I croak, raising my hands apologetically, humiliation coursing through me in shock waves. "I'm so sorry . . . I think I had a flashback and thought it was real. I'm so sorry—"

Aaron laughs so hard that his head flies back and smashes the tub a second time.

"*Stop!*" I shriek, leaning over and seizing his lengthy arm, then giving it a vicious tug to heave him up. "You'll crack your skull, and then we'll both have amnesia! How am I supposed to regain my memories when you don't even have yours?"

Aaron is laughing so hard he's hardly making noise, his chest racked with violent shudders. He allows me to haul him into a standing position, though, and water pours off his paint-smeared clothes. His cheeks are rose pink—a contrast to his usual black-and-white scheme—and he's sparkling under the golden lighting as vibrantly as he did under the pale blue of the swimming pool. There's a fleck of teal paint on his temple, just below his bandanna, and I'm . . .

Very attracted to him.

I knew this, obviously, because I have the power of sight, and it's one of the most exasperating parts of this situation. So I don't know why this thought whacks me as hard as it does. Only that I've never seen him so gleeful, so unrestrained. So genuine. He's not even angry that I dragged him into the bathtub and then nearly shattered his skull.

"I'm . . . towel," I choke out, swiveling toward the closet and wrenching out the longest towel I can find. I thrust it at him, before claiming another and wrapping myself in it like a burrito. Aaron discards his clothes, so I rotate on my heel and start striding from the room, heart pulsing in my ears.

"You must be feeling better, since you can walk again," Aaron says brightly.

I realize then just how far my body has come over the last half hour. I was so weak mere minutes ago, but the adrenaline of the situation coupled with the lingering heat of the water helped alleviate my pain. I can still feel it—I always will—but it's more muted than earlier. Because of him.

"Thank you," I whisper, my eyes falling to the tile. "For being here."

I hear wet, heavy thuds as his soaked clothes fall to the floor. "I'll be here whenever you need me, Riley," he says softly.

"You don't have to—"

"I want to." His voice firms with resolve. "If I have to ditch bed at four in the morning, or drive through an ice storm, or fly across the country, or swim to shore, I'll be here. So call me every time. I'll find a way to you. Always." He falters, then sighs with annoyance. "I just wish I could be here to catch you before you hit the ground."

My hands tremble around my towel as I hug it to me. The longer I stand here, the more heat begins to seep from my body, and the deeper I ache. I don't notice it fully, though, because Aaron Beckham is doing that thing again where he makes me feel valuable. Like I'm a catch and not a curse.

"I want to kiss you," I breathe.

I hate that it's true. That after a couple of measly days around him, after promising myself that I wouldn't fall for his manipulation following everything he did to Logan, I have. Fast. And hard. It's pathetic. This is the same person who drove my brother away from a successful future by giving him a taste of rebellion. If not for him, Logan would be preparing to enter sophomore year in an established university, his room and board and schooling all paid for, playing his favorite sport. He wouldn't be stuck at a community college and working as a student assistant to help him pay for his classes. He would be on the golf course every day, happy.

So, why? Why am I so weak to Aaron Beckham?

"What?" Aaron steps around my front before I can escape the bathroom, twisting a finger in his ear. The towel is knotted at his waist, and despite its length, it only conceals him halfway down his shins, leaving his upper half pale, flat, and exposed. Seeing him like this knots my stomach.

"Nothing," I say quickly, closing my towel tighter around myself. It's the same length as his, but mine fits me more like a dress.

"Oh?" Aaron's eyes crinkle with a knowing smile. "Didn't sound like nothing."

I glare up into his glittery irises. "Harassment," I state.

He stares back at me. "Please elaborate."

"My breathing space. You're in it."

"How are you going to kiss me if I'm not?"

I contort my face with aggravation, and one of my palms leaves my cocoon so I can shove his chest back. I've made a mistake in my distraction and don't notice until he catches my wrist midair, then tugs me closer and bends lower so his lips are hovering above mine.

"Just trying to make things easier for you," he says.

I catch the faintest whiff of paint despite our soak in the water. "Whatever you heard, it was wrong," I snip, directing my stare at his neck.

"I heard that you want to kiss me."

"You're hallucinating."

"I don't think that's true."

"Are you sure? You hit your head twice."

"Riley Wilson, are you gaslighting me?"

Dread stiffens my limbs. "No, wait," I say squeakily. "I didn't . . . I'm not trying to gaslight . . . well, maybe I am, but—"

Aaron explodes with laughter again, the sound overtaking my crumbling sentence. I groan, wishing I couldn't feel the warmth spilling off his body and haloing mine. He looks so good when he laughs, all teeth, eyes wrinkled, cheeks red, throat working. Water dripping from his jaw, carving erratic paths toward his collarbone. He would probably look just as good if it were sweat.

Which . . . what the hell am I even thinking about?

Aaron's eyes flit around my flustered face, and his smile softens. "Sorry," he says. "I know I shouldn't tease you this much. I can't help it. You're cute." He could drop my hand, but he lowers it to my waist like it's fragile glass, then heads to the door. "What chore were you doing when you fell? I'll finish it while you nap."

I can't do this. My heart feels like it's ripping through the walls of my throat. Aaron has charmed me in the exact way I told myself I wouldn't allow. I should know better—I *do*—but those thoughts are an incoherent slur against the rush of blood in my ears.

He's nearing my bedroom door when I lurch out and catch his palm. He turns in bewilderment, and I sling my other hand around the back of his bare neck, pulling him down. I thrust myself to my tiptoes and . . .

Crush my nose against his.

"Ow," he says.

"Sorry!" I shriek, reeling away, my mortification levels soaring through the stratosphere. I rub my throbbing nose, blushing pathetically. "I didn't mean—"

"You are trying to kill me," he says flatly.

"I'm not!" Though it probably seems that way. First, I dragged him fully clothed into the bath, then shoved his head into the side of the tub, and now I've all but broken his nose. He has to be angry at this point, considering how I've met his kindness with pure, unrestrained abuse.

"You're trying to rile me up," he accuses. I think he's trying not to laugh again, because there's a tremble in his lips. I want to fling myself down the staircase and shatter my body to escape this torment. "Congratulations. I have been properly riled."

"Stop making fun of me," I plead, throwing my hands over my face. My towel drops to my feet, and cool air immediately swathes my body. "I'm not intentionally trying to hurt you. I'm sorry. This is the worst day of my life. Please assassinate me."

"You can't atone for your sins if you're dead."

I groan loudly enough for it to reverberate through the empty house. "How many times do you want me to say sorry?"

"Zero," he says, tickling the backs of my hands with his index fingers, from my knuckles to my wrists. I try to squirm away, but back myself into the hallway wall beside my bedroom. "I've heard you apologize enough to last lifetimes. I was thinking something else."

Reluctantly, I slide my fingers apart to glare daggers at him. When my eyes find his, he leans his arms against the wall on either side of my head, caging me in. All of a sudden, I wish I hadn't dropped my towel.

"Try again?" he encourages, angling his head.

"It . . . it was spur-of-the-moment," I say sharply. "You made me feel not horrible, so I wanted to thank you."

"By slamming your face against my face."

"It was an accident!"

"Meaning I still haven't been thanked," he says, drawling his voice in this way that quickens my already-panicked heartbeat. "I'm offering you the chance to make up for it. Because I'm a gentleman. And a beacon of integrity, or whatever you said."

I can't think of a witty response. His proximity and lack of clothing make it difficult for me to keep my grip on my irritation, plus the fact that I probably have no right, after everything I've put him through today. He didn't have to come here. Why am I putting up a fight? I tried taking him by surprise with a kiss, and now that he's literally consenting, I suddenly can't do it?

The answer, of course, is that I'm just being stubborn and cranky because I screwed up, and he thinks it's funny.

"If . . . if I mess up again, do you promise not to laugh?" I ask.

Aaron blinks in surprise at my sudden shift. His face warms with happiness, and his hands slide down the wall until they're nestled on my shoulders. He presses inward, rooting them gently along the sides of my neck so he can use his thumbs to tilt my chin up, guiding me closer. "I promise," he whispers.

My pulse must be ramming against his palms. My instincts whine and kick at my subconscious—somewhere deep within me, I know I'll regret this.

But he's here.

So call me every time. I'll find a way to you. Always.

I shouldn't. I know I shouldn't.

I tilt my face, having learned from my mistake. His lips twitch upward at my caution, and he leans his forehead against mine, the edge of his bandanna brushing my hairline, his eyes falling shut and freeing me from the cool steadiness of his gaze. I can hardly think straight, the position of his hands under my jaw overwhelming. The light hairs of his body brush up against my bare midsection, sending my senses reeling.

I don't know what to do with my hands other than let them dangle. If I touch him, I might jostle the towel free from around his waist, or the feeling of his damp, smooth skin might make me lose all sense of reason. The sides of our noses are brushing, both still red from the collision.

I nudge my lips against Aaron's slender pink ones, then draw back.

Immediately, I want to evaporate. His forehead is weighing against mine, and his breath is strained and slow, like he's consciously trying to control it. He's not dropping his palms—it's like he's waiting for the kiss I just gave him.

"Aaron?" I say.

"Again," he breathes, or rather pleads. He's broken into a tremble, like he's on the brink of losing himself.

I press my lips to his a second time, then linger, my eyes falling shut. His right hand slides up along the back of my neck, cradling the weight of my head and tugging me deeper into the kiss.

Something is different. His mouth is moving, his lips parting, nudging mine to do the same. I try to register what I should be doing, but I'm distracted by his other hand, which grazes the edge of my abdomen before rooting itself in the scoop of my waist.

He yanks suddenly, slamming our bodies together.

"Heh?" I say, and the moment my mouth opens, Aaron swallows me in a deep, ravenous kiss that sends warmth exploding through my limbs. My hands slip up between our slick midsections, flattening out against his chest, but I can't manage the energy to push. Or maybe I don't want to.

No, I *should*.

But the hand cupping my head pulls, angling me farther back, and every protesting thought I have dissolves into useless puddles. His other palm presses up from my waist, carving divots into my rib cage as he scratches a path to my chest, to the jut of my collarbone. His touch leaves behind a violent eruption of goose bumps, and I accidentally sigh shakily into his mouth.

It's too intense. I never got to prepare for something as desperate and consuming as this. My whole body is on fire, made worse when his touch wanders again, clawing a trail down my back, his middle fingertip digging into my spine. The feeling instinctively arches me into him, and though I haven't uttered a command, my arms move of their own volition, slinking around his neck, curling in, and locking tight. Like they know they belong there, even if I don't.

It happens then. Another memory in the form of a frustratingly quick flash. My back is pressed against this wall, and my breaths are concerningly short, my lips swollen, my arms tied behind his neck. The swimsuit is gone. So is his towel. I feel all of him pressed up against my frame.

But the memory passes, and the towel and swimsuit are back in place, and some small, twisted part of me wishes they'd disappear.

"B-breathe," I choke out, disgusted by my own sudden, inexplicable wants, and I tear my face sideways, gasping for air, eyes stinging from low oxygen. "I can't . . . This is a tenth-date kind of thing . . ."

Aaron laughs. "Feels good, doesn't it?" he asks, his hands sliding to my hips.

"That's the problem," I mutter, scrunching my eyes shut even tighter. "I've just started not hating everything about you, so I shouldn't . . ."

My sentence sputters away when Aaron begins to massage the curves of my waist.

"Shouldn't what?" he whispers.

I can't thread the words together. His breath and the deliberate, slow movement of his palms are scrambling my sense of logic again.

"Over fourteen months, I've gradually learned what makes you tick," he says, equally as softly. "What makes you laugh, cry, roll your eyes, scold me. What makes you feel safe and warm and comfortable. Most importantly, though . . ."

Aaron's tongue flicks at the divot behind my ear, and my heart just about lunges out of my mouth. I try wriggling my head away, but he takes my jaw and presses it back against the wall, pinning me.

"I know what riles you up."

The effect his voice has on me is, frankly, preposterous. Absurd. Ludicrous. *Unacceptable.* I'm responding without words, my pulse a cry for medical assistance, my skin deep-fried the color crimson, the stiffness melting out of every part of my body. Almost every part.

I don't know him—I don't *freaking know him.* Yet again, my mind and body are perplexingly disjointed to a dizzying degree. Being under his grip, under his eyes . . .

I hate how right it feels.

"I'll stop whenever you want," Aaron breathes, leaving kisses on the curve of my neck, his grip still firm on my jaw, holding me in place. "If this isn't the distraction from pain that you want, or if it's too much, tell me. Otherwise I'm going to make you hot and bothered. Is that okay?"

"I already am," I say, squeezing my useless arms even tighter around his neck, because I'm afraid I'll let them wander otherwise. "So you don't need to keep trying."

I feel Aaron's grin press against my skin. "You think *this* is 'hot and bothered Riley Wilson'?" He closes his teeth under my jawline, and I yelp, my face blistering.

"Don't just bite me!" I order, to which he nibbles me again, and I make a rabid hissing noise, seizing his hair and giving it an irritated tug. Aaron laughs for the sixteenth time today.

"Do you want me to stop?" he asks lightly.

Yes, he should definitely stop. I need to reunite with common sense. Surely, I have more willpower than this. But my resolve is as weak as the rest of my pathetic body. I say, "I want to keep kissing you." But then my pride gets in the way, so I tack on, "Because I want to find more memories."

Aaron smirks, my intentions translucent to him. Suddenly, he's scooping me up under the knees and slinging them around his waist, hoisting my weight into his chest. "Whatever helps you recover your memories," he says seriously.

"Don't just pick me up!" I cry out, to which he laughs harder and carries me into my bedroom.

"Sorry. Your legs were getting shaky, and I figured you were sore being pinned to the wall. So . . ."

He lays me out on my comforter like I'm made of expensive silk.

"I decided I should pin you to your bed instead."

14

I hate Aaron Beckham after all.

First off, he's wearing the sturdiest towel in existence, because it stays rooted to his waist despite how enthusiastically he's moving. Second, even though he just said I could stop him whenever I want, he *ignores* me.

"Don't massage my ear like that," I plead, so he does it harder.

"Stop rubbing my waist," I snap, so he does it harder.

"Quit doing whatever you want," I order, so he does whatever he wants *harder.*

I hate him.

I feel good.

I hate him.

I like it when he ignores me. He knows.

I. *Hate.* Him.

"Stop squirming, sunshine," Aaron whispers, his thumb tugging at the skin under my eye until I open them. "Your body is still recovering from fainting."

He removed his bandanna at some point, because his dark, curled tips are in full force, dangling over his forehead. I regret looking into his eyes, because his own are so fervent, warm, affectionate, eager that I want to do something I'll regret. I know I'm already going to regret *this.*

But I can't stop looking at the way he looks at me.

"I'm moving around because you're annoying me," I say stiffly. The weight of his waist between my thighs is a sensation I can't get used to, even if it's been a few minutes since he snuck it in.

Aaron smiles, the dimple poking into his cheek as he smooths out my clenched fists. He threads our fingers, pressing my palms into the bedspread over my head. I don't mind, because it means his hands are occupied, and not busy poking every sensitive spot I didn't know I had. "How am I annoying you?"

"By fiddling with me like I'm that gadget toy you carry around," I grumble.

Aaron snickers, then leans over me until the tips of our sore noses are grazing. He shifts my wrists into one of his hands so he can use the other to trace my lower lip. "Open," he says.

Blood burns in my face, and I part my lips to tell him off.

He kisses my protest away, sliding his tongue along the edge of mine. A low, quiet noise reverberates through my body and sends flames shooting from my ears. Did he just moan? Does kissing me feel that good? Even now, when my thoughts are mush, one word materializes before me with sharp clarity:

Why?

It's just me. It's one thing if he's using me for his own pleasure, but he's not. His touch is unbearably gentle. Every kiss brims with a fearsome passion I can't hope to comprehend. His weight fastens me to my mattress, but he uses his core strength to keep from leaning too heavily on my aching body. I like it. The way he's holding me, whispering to me, kissing me . . .

Somehow, it feels like home.

"How are those memories coming along?" Aaron asks amusedly,

lips nestling under my jawline. I curl my toes to keep from squirming again.

"They're not," I say, swallowing hard, because he doesn't need to know that I briefly remembered his fully naked body pressing against mine in the hallway. I've been hoping that some of the things I envisioned are exaggerated. Though his waist being pressed between my thighs has dashed that mental plea.

"A shame. Guess I need to work harder to get you to remember."

He's insufferable. But he's a very good kisser. Or I think he is. I've never had anyone to compare with—though, if there's a sensation more intense and all-consuming than this, I don't want it. This is already too much. I can't keep up. His lips slide along my neck, returning to my mouth, but I tilt my face away, and his kiss catches my cheek.

"Aaron, stop," I plead. "Please."

He must hear my urgency, because his grip around my wrists goes slack and he shifts his weight off me to hover. I resist the urge to pull him back down, along with his body heat. "Are you in pain?" he asks softly.

"I'm fine." The palpable concern in his voice is nice. "It's just a little fast. I feel strange, so . . ."

"Strange?" Aaron's open palm finds my face, and he strokes my cheek, his smile like melted chocolate. "In what way?"

"My body," I admit, giving him a cautious look. He must know me well enough to realize when I'd rather not be teased, because he doesn't make any sly quips. He merely watches me, his eyes flitting around my face like he's not sure which part is his favorite. "I feel disconnected with it. I know we've been dating over a year, but since I can't remember, my brain is telling me to run. But my body trusts you.

I feel relaxed when you touch me. It's frustrating, trying to bridge the gap. So if you could please stop . . ." I swallow with embarrassment, squeezing my eyes shut. "If you could stop trying to overstimulate me, I would appreciate it."

My muscles go taut. He's been ignoring me thus far—does he know the difference between when I'm haphazardly making requests versus genuinely making them?

His lips touch down between my brows. "I'm sorry," he whispers. "I lost control. Seeing you actually want me again . . . it was a lot. Thanks for the reminder."

I peek through one eye, my jaw clenching with uncertainty.

"Should we get dressed?" he asks.

"No," I say quickly.

His brow pops into his forehead. I want to scream with embarrassment into my comforter. Why did I say no? Isn't it better if we're clothed so I can maintain some level of focus? Half the reason I'm overstimulated is *because* he's not wearing clothes.

"Keep kissing me, but stop putting your hands everywhere," I mumble. "Kiss me like there's no history and this is the first time we're doing this and you don't know what I like. Okay?"

Aaron laughs, and I'm getting sick of that sound, because it's usually followed by crushing humiliation. "That's perfectly reasonable," he says, stooping down to kiss my nose. Then my left brow. My temple, cheekbone, jawline. By the time he makes it to my mouth, I'm groaning again.

"Doting on every inch of me isn't something you'd do if there was no history," I say irritably.

"Apologies." Aaron presses a sweet kiss to my lips, still holding his weight off me, his arms propped around my head. I keep my eyes pinned shut as he pauses, then comes in for a second, nestling his mouth against mine, letting me get used to the feeling of lingering. His tongue nudges against the curve of my lower lip, and tingles spiral up my neck.

A third kiss. He's easing my mouth open, his body shifting downward, inch by inch, until his chest is close enough to graze. I don't notice my hands are moving until I feel the smoothness of his skin beneath them, and I realize I'm sliding them along his upper arms. I can feel the tautness of his muscles threaded through his limbs. I should've known he'd be stronger than I thought, considering the ease with which he carries me around. Not that I'm particularly heavy, but the lack of strain in his quest to get me from point A to point B is, admittedly, kind of attractive.

My fingers roll over his shoulders as he plants a fourth kiss on me, his tongue sneaking little jabs against my still one, since I'm too embarrassed to move it. As my knuckles brush the curves of his neck, a faint shiver courses through him. He reacted. Maybe I found a sensitive spot?

"Can I touch you?" Aaron breathes before I can experiment with it, the words fluttering against my upper lip.

I swallow, and say, "Behave."

Laughter. *Again*. I should never speak out loud. "How could I deny you, sunshine?" he asks, and one of his palms slides under my head to cradle it, his fingertips digging gently into my scalp. The other sneaks down my waist to latch beneath the crook of my knee, and he pops it up, hugging it around his waist, my thigh leaning against his exposed skin. He's already pressed firmly against me, but the added contact makes me feel like my head is spinning.

"Can I also touch you?" I blurt. "I shouldn't have assumed . . . Sorry . . ."

Aaron smiles against my mouth, his thumb stroking the outer edge of my knee. "Do whatever you'd like," he murmurs. "I want you to relearn the feeling of me."

I peek through my eyelids, dazed. When our gazes meet, his fingers curl in around the back of my head, clinging more firmly to me.

"You said you can't bridge the gap between your mind's and body's reactions to me," he continues. "Familiarize yourself with me. My face and touch and weight. My voice. My lips. Over time, maybe your mind will feel just as safe and comfortable here as your body does."

With little more than his words, and his hand cradling me like I'm the most precious thing in his life, the disconnect is already shrinking. Slowly, my other knee rises along his narrow waist, hugging it. I don't have much strength, but I apply enough pressure to make him notice. A pink tinge flourishes through his cheeks.

"You seem to know how to . . . like, *excite* me," I say, his blush causing my own face to warm. "I want to learn how to do that. To you."

Aaron snickers, the brat, and pushes his hand up along my thigh, his fingers bunching the nylon of my swimsuit. "Excite away."

"Making fun of me again," I say.

"No, no. I would never." He's rubbing my thigh now, and it's worse than when he was massaging my hips, so I give the back of his leg a good kick to stop him. He grins and obediently returns his wandering hand to my knee, holding it against him. "Then I'm going to kiss you senseless."

He starts closing the distance between us. My mind works in overdrive, wondering what I should do. Does he have any other spots that might give me a reaction? Maybe I should run my hands over his shoulder blades, or rub his ear like he rubbed mine, or—

A door slams so violently downstairs that it shakes the house. Aaron flings himself off my bed, and I swing upright, short of breath as quick footsteps storm up the staircase.

Logan is walking in on us again. Only this time, the situation is far more damning.

"Where is he?" he growls, shoving through my cracked bedroom door with such force that the knob dents the sunset-orange drywall. His tan face is flushed with anger, and his schoolbag is hanging over his shoulder. "I saw his fucking truck outside again."

His eyes tear across the room and find Aaron, who's standing nearby in nothing but a fluffy towel that does—pardon me—*absolutely fuck all* to conceal what we were just doing. I immediately begin to word vomit as I hike my knees into my chest.

"It's not what you . . . We weren't . . . I was just trying to . . ."

The attempt to excuse my actions doesn't last. The moment Aaron sees Logan, he's flying across the room, his eyes searing with icy, vengeful flames. *"You piece of shit!"* Aaron snarls, seizing my brother by the neck so he can spit words in his face. *"He said he called you! There's no way you couldn't hear the pain in his voice! You knew he needed help, and you ignored it!"*

Logan gags under Aaron's grip. "The hell are you talking about?" he gasps out, grabbing Aaron's wrist, the veins popping in his arms. He manages to loosen Aaron's choke hold and shove him away.

"Riley fainted!" Aaron yells, his face gnarled with such visceral anger that the blood drains out of my body. *"He needed help! He was lying on the fucking ground when I showed up, because you couldn't be assed to be there!"*

Logan's face pales.

"Wait," I choke out, scrambling off the bed. "Stop, it's not Logan's fault—"

"You think I would've stayed out if I'd known?" Logan breathes. His attention snaps to me, and frustration mingles with his fury. "Why didn't you tell me?"

I squeeze my fingers tight to keep them from shivering. "You . . . you were studying, so . . ."

Logan's lips are so thin they've nearly disappeared from his face. His fists quake at his sides. "If you'd told me, I would've come home," he says, his nostrils flaring. "But you didn't, so you . . . what? You wanted to get revenge on me by inviting Aaron here? By ignoring my warnings about the kind of shit person he is?"

His words are sharp and molten hot, cutting through my wobbly confidence like a knife through gelatin. "It has nothing to do with revenge," I say. "My experience with him is different than I thought it would be. Um. Positive. And kind."

Aaron's tight posture slowly loosens, like my voice is an antidote to his anger. Logan, though, does something I don't expect. He laughs. Harshly. Bitterly. "Yeah?" he asks, grinning, but there's no merriment behind his eyes—only a frigid rage I've never seen before. "I'm sure he was a ray of sunshine while he waited for you to spread your legs. Hey, did he ever tell you why he asked you out? Or were you too busy fucking to ask?"

These words are nothing more than sound cutting through air, so they shouldn't knock me off balance. They do anyway. I stumble back, and my tired knee folds under me, striking the bedroom carpet. Tears singe my eyes. I want to demand where this is coming from, why he's treating me like this, what he's talking about. I don't get the chance.

Aaron punches Logan across the face.

It happens so fast that I barely catch it. Aaron's fist is a blur, veins are bulging in his temples, and his pale face is ruby red. His knuckles collide with Logan's cheek, snapping his head sideways and causing him to crash into the wall. Logan gasps for breath, like the impact stole the air from his lungs.

Suddenly, I'm the one who's livid.

"What's wrong with you?" I shout, forcing my feet under me and throwing myself between them. I plant one palm on Aaron's bare chest and shove, and for once, he allows himself to stagger back, the wrath bleeding out of his face. *"Is this how you're still solving your problems? By punching through them?"*

Aaron takes a shuddering breath, his fists bone-white.

"Get out," I snap.

Aaron gives Logan one more scathing glare, then storms into the hallway, throwing the towel onto the floor and basically flash-banging me with his junk before scooping up his wet clothes and heading downstairs, staggering into them along the way. He pauses on the third step, his shoulders deflating.

"I'm sorry, Riley," he whispers.

Then he's gone.

15

"Are you okay?" I ask, tugging Logan's arm. His hand is nursing his face, and he's still leaning against my bedroom wall beside my calendar, which has been corrected to the current month and is filling up with tasks.

"It's fine . . . He didn't use full force," Logan says, which startles me.

"Are you sure? It looks like he got you pretty good."

A smirk slices through Logan's face, and he batters my frantic hands away. "You haven't seen him in a real fight," he says, his voice softening. He hoists himself off the wall with a dreary sigh. "I'm sorry for what I said. And for not coming home when you needed help. I've been treating you like shit lately—"

"Don't apologize," I say, waving my palms awkwardly. "You couldn't have known that I called you because I fainted. I would've felt horrible if you left for that."

Logan gives me this pained look, and I have the feeling I've said something to frustrate him. "How are you feeling?" he asks quietly.

"Better." I don't tell him it's because of Aaron. Because he carried me to bed, and drew a warm, soothing bath for me, and kissed away my thoughts, distracting me from discomfort. Now that he's gone, though, the pain is starting to come back. I didn't break any bones, but I jostled them well enough to know I'll be aching and frail for a while.

"You . . ." Logan fizzles off, and his fingers scrunch up at his sides. "You don't have to do a million chores all at once. Give yourself time to breathe. Move slower."

"I don't like falling behind," I say, beelining for my dresser when I realize I'm still in my swim trunks. "The backyard and flower beds are a mess. None of you know how to properly clean, either. Or cook. If I don't do it, everyone else will forget to."

"Teach me," Logan says desperately. "I'll help. And maybe then you won't go running back to him and falling for all his tricks."

I give him a sidelong skeptical glance as I pull out sweatpants and a T-shirt. "I tried teaching you when I was first diagnosed with celiac disease. And Mom. And Dad. You were all so useless I decided it was better to handle everything myself."

Logan's throat bobs with a swallow. I get changed while he's focused on the towel Aaron threw on the staircase. "I wish you'd been up front on the phone. I could tell you weren't saying something. If I'd known, I swear I would've come home."

He speaks with such force, it's almost like he's trying to convince himself, too.

"It's fine. Really," I say, ambling toward him and scrutinizing the swelling skin around his cheekbone. I start toward the staircase so I can wrap ice in a bag for him. "Sorry for not being clear. Aaron just sort of figured it out and came over before I could tell him not to."

I'm halfway down the staircase when I realize Logan isn't following. He's still hovering in my doorframe, like he wants to say something else.

"You should put ice on your eye," I say, gesturing to him. "Come on."

"And you should be resting," he mumbles.

I huff with annoyance. I'm starting to think people enjoy me more when I'm unconscious. "I have to prep dinner."

Logan shuffles between his feet, his jaw squared like he's clenching his teeth.

"Why would he hit you?" I ask.

Logan's pale green eyes sharpen. "What?"

"You were best friends, so . . ." I clear my throat, knowing I'm approaching touchy territory. Maybe he'll be more receptive now, though. "You guys were together more often than you were apart. What happened that it got to this point? What am I missing?"

Apparently, I'm off base in my assumption, because Logan's expression hardens. "I did something he didn't like," he says coolly. "He did something worse in retaliation. It showed me how shitty he is, so we stopped being friends."

"What *something* are you talking about?" I ask tentatively.

Logan gnaws on his nubbed thumbnail. "It's nothing," he says. "Just know that he's a waste of your time."

Days ago, I would've believed him without question. I *did* believe him. "He showed up for me, though," I whisper, partially hoping he won't hear me. "He's been kind. And considerate."

"Because he wants something from you," Logan snaps. "Which—judging by the state you were both in when I came home—is something you're willing to give him."

My cheeks turn flaming hot. "We didn't do anything."

"Right." Finally, Logan tromps out of my room, then blows past me down the stairs, his lips set in a thin, unfriendly line. "You deserve better, but if you want to keep making all the same mistakes you did last year, I can't stop you."

I swallow with difficulty, watching his retreating back. Aaron obviously doesn't just want sex—it's clear we had some kind of emotional connection, since our relationship lasted over a year. And after everything he's done . . . I can't imagine he'd go through all this effort just to sleep with me. Contacting the history club, buying me gluten-free snacks, rushing here from work to take care of me, trying to help me jog my memories.

But he also just hit my brother in his anger. He used to get into the occasional fight around school—he has a smart mouth and runs it frequently. It seems like he's matured, but has he really, if he's still willing to throw his fists when he's emotional?

Logan is about to turn the corner when he pauses and sighs. "He's a master manipulator who knows how to get what he wants, Riley. Keep that in mind."

He walks away, one palm still framing his swelling eye.

That night, when I should be having a peaceful slumber after an exhausting day, I find myself tossing, turning, and waiting for a familiar tapping noise on the window that doesn't come. When I'm not annoyed, I'm flustered. Why did I let him kiss me for so long in nothing but a towel? It's ridiculous, immature behavior.

But then I hear his voice. Soft, earnest, low.

Familiarize yourself with me. My face and touch and weight. My voice. My lips. Over time, maybe your mind will feel just as safe and comfortable here as your body does.

Then I think about his hands. How one of them was big enough to hold both of my wrists. How carefully, deliberately, his long fingers grazed my skin. I don't fantasize often about intimacy, because I figured any potential partner would be deterred by my appearance. My skin is sallow and pasty more frequently than not, and the scoops beneath my eyes are plagued by constant violet crescents. I look brittle, like one gust of wind could make me lose my balance. Touching me can't possibly be a pleasant experience, considering how ice-cold I am and how my skeleton likes to jut through my body.

But Aaron makes me feel desirable.

I don't feel well the next day, either. Shocker. I wake with a familiar throbbing in my temple and stiffness in my neck and chronic ache in my rib cage and legs and whatever. I have errands to run, so I decide to get those out of the way.

I pick up a pair of earrings so Dad has something to give Mom for their anniversary, then a leather wallet so she has something to give him (they forget every year unless I remind them by physically entering it into their phone calendars). I drop by the post office to mail a couple of graduation checks to the children of extended family who live too far to visit. I make clothing returns for Mom, since I know she'll probably forget the return deadline despite telling me she'll handle it, and as I'm heading out the door, my phone chimes. I stop in the parking lot to open it, my heart sneaking up into my throat.

It's just an email from the local university I'm enrolled at. Ugh.

I read the orientation letter, eyeing the logo and wondering what swayed me to apply to a random no-name college instead of the one I've been planning on attending for years. Having enough money to support myself during a health crisis has always been important. After research, I determined computer science was a good profession to pursue. Aaron mentioned that I apparently wanted to "explore my options," but why? For what reason did I allow my long-term plans to be disrupted?

I want to understand what changed my mind.

The campus is twenty minutes from here, so I decide to check it out. I find public parking on the edge of the campus, set a timer for thirty minutes so I don't get too offtrack, and wander.

It's small but scenic, with meandering walkways framed in forestry, expanses of lawn, and gardens where people can linger on benches or at grated tables. There aren't many students around, probably because it's summer, but those that are look perfectly content. Some swing in hammocks between trees, enjoying the early warmth of the day, or sit propped against trunks with laptops on their knees.

The library is an enormous glass-paneled building with towering ceilings, and the sight makes me want to twirl around with glittery eyes like a Disney princess. There's a farmers market on the edge of campus. The atmosphere is intimate. Cozy. I can see why I was drawn to it, though I'm not sure it's mind-blowing enough to change my career path.

"Riley?"

Hearing my name behind me is so startling that I actually yelp. I swivel and find someone passing by on a pathway intersecting my own, wearing a tank top and shorts, her black hair parted into two braids draped over her shoulders. It's Amy Choi—the previous president of the history club. "Oh," I say, instantly flustered for some reason, like I've been caught red-handed. "Hi. What are you doing here?"

"Summer class. I'm heading to the library to meet up for a group project. What are *you* doing here?" Her dark eyes glitter with eagerness. "Coming to scope the place out again before fall semester?"

"I guess." I glance around at the neatly placed buildings. They're all relatively small, which leads me to believe the admission rate is smaller here than most colleges.

"You probably don't remember me giving you the tour a few months ago," she says with a knowing smile. "Beckham came with you. You were really unsure about the place until he convinced you to come look around."

My cheeks warm with embarrassment. "Thanks for going to the trouble."

"What trouble?" Amy smirks, adjusting her shoulder bag. "I got to watch you geek out over the campus and history program. It was great."

History program? My lips curl down with confusion. "There's not much I could do with a history degree other than be a teacher," I say weakly. "And I'm awkward around kids. I don't like talking in front of groups, either, so it's not for me."

Amy cocks her head, looking a mixture of amused and bewildered. "Who said you have to be a teacher? You could get involved with museum culture. Collection management. Preservation. Archiving as a librarian. So on."

My heart rate quickens. I discarded the idea of pursuing history because I thought I'd get cornered into teaching. I'd rather be indifferent toward a profession (like computer science) than repulsed by it, so I never took the idea seriously. These options probably don't pay as well, but . . .

My phone alarm screeches, giving me another good jolt. "Ah, sorry, I have to go," I say. "Good luck with your class."

"Good luck with your memories," she responds.

I stride back to the parking lot, ignoring the tenderness in my knees. As I crawl into my car, I cast one last lingering look at the campus.

It really is sort of nice.

I take off for my next errand.

16

I don't notice until I'm heading to the front door that Aaron's truck is parked at my curb. I pause mid-step, pursing my lips. How could he show up unannounced without so much as an apology text? Though maybe he doesn't think he owes me one after everything he did yesterday.

And maybe he would be right.

I scowl as I peek through the windows of his truck. He's not there, so he must've climbed through my window and is waiting in my bedroom. I don't want to see him, so I storm back to my car and grab the driver's-side handle, yanking the door open.

A hand suddenly falls against the frame, shutting it before I can climb in. I squeak in terror, then annoyance, whirling around. I'm not sure where Aaron was standing that he could teleport behind me like this. He's wearing a short-sleeved black button-down and shorts, glistening with sunscreen, his eyes concealed by rounded shades.

"Hey, sunshine," he says, sliding his sunglasses down to wink. "Fancy seeing you here."

"At my house?" I demand, fumbling for the handle again. Aaron steps closer, though, crowding me against the vehicle so my back is pressed flat to the door, pinning it shut.

"How are you feeling? You're driving, so hopefully *better*?"

"Yes," I say, though I offer nothing else. "Why are you here?"

He folds his lanky arm up against the car, to my left, effectively cornering me. His favorite thing to do, apparently. "I came to see my future fiancé," he says, twirling strands of my hair between his fingers. Always fiddling with me like I'm his favorite toy.

"Who's that?" I ask coolly, and Aaron grins wide enough to show the entire top row of his teeth.

"Probably the guy I kissed silly yesterday."

The reminder causes my face to swelter with heat. "That was just for memory purposes," I choke out unconvincingly. "What do you want?"

"To take you on our next date."

I stare at him incredulously. He stares back, committed.

"It's the middle of a Friday. Shouldn't you be working?" I ask huffily. "And I have chores. And I'm not happy with you."

"I have the day off. And you can do them tomorrow. And I know you're not. So let me make it up to you." He slides his hands down my arms, then finds the gaps between my fingers, curling his with mine when I don't wrench away. "This wasn't our second date, but it only comes around once a year, so I wanted to take advantage of it before it goes away again."

"What are you talking about?" I ask, scowling when he lifts my palms to kiss my knuckles. If he thinks he's getting brownie points for being sweet, he's mistaken. Or that's what I'm telling myself in spite of the way my stomach flutters.

"The carnival." He massages my joints, his smile rivaling the brightness of the sun. "I'm booked this weekend with repair projects, so today is my only free day. I was going to come later, but my mom ghosted me for lunch, so I decided to come straight here instead of going home."

Another mention of his mom. Didn't she just cancel lunch with him two days ago? Part of me wants to ask, but he's already moving on, his eager expression not betraying his true thoughts.

"Anyway, I meant to ask you about this yesterday, but then I fucked up. A little."

"Just a little," I say coldly.

"Precisely. So?" Aaron leans in close. "May I have the honor of bothering you today, Riley Wilson?"

As if he hasn't been bothering me since he first appeared. "No thanks," I say. Because I'm still upset. He hasn't even properly apologized for punching my brother. Besides . . .

He's a master manipulator who knows how to get what he wants.

Logan's former words are discomforting. I know I can come to my own conclusions with the information I have. But he's never led me astray before, so it's difficult for me to say he must be wrong about this one thing—that being *Aaron Beckham.* I guess it's the first time I've seen him heavily biased toward something, and that's reason enough not to thoughtlessly trust his claim that Aaron is a monster. Even if I once believed the same thing because I saw the effect Aaron had on him from a distance.

Regardless, my walls shouldn't come down this quickly. I should put space between us so I can think clearly without Aaron's smile, gentle touch, and soft lips infiltrating my logic, like yesterday.

"I'll buy you whatever you want," he says.

That makes me scoff. "There's nothing I could get there that won't make me sick."

"They have more than food," he points out. "They have vendors who sell pottery. Ceramics. Two of your paintings were from the fair last year. And this time, I'm going to win you a giant stuffed duck no matter how long it takes."

His final line is so unexpected that I nearly laugh, but manage to swallow it. "You failed last time?" I ask, popping my brow.

"Do you have a giant stuffed duck in your room?" he asks bitterly.

"No."

"Well."

Admittedly, I'm enticed. I've never seen Aaron Beckham be bad at anything, so the thought of watching him lose money to a silly carnival game gives me a guilty pleasure I resist the urge to apologize for.

"I'll also be your personal servant for a day," he tries again.

I give him a weary look. "So you'd do anything I ask?"

"Yes!" he says, his eyes sparkling with excitement. "I'll be your bitch!"

"So if I said *Go home*, you'd go home?"

He opens his mouth. Closes it.

"And if I said *Don't come over unless I give you permission*, you'd listen?"

He chews on his lips.

"And if I said *Apologize to Logan for the black eye*, you would?"

His gaze averts mine.

"Interesting that you've suddenly lost the ability to speak," I say frostily.

"Because I'm your bitch now," he says, his eyes giant and round and wet and desperate and, ugh, I can't hold out much longer. "But sure, go to the carnival with me and I won't trespass on your property again until next week."

"Do you even hear yourself?" I mutter, and Aaron wiggles his fingers hopefully. When I realize what he wants, I sigh, stepping between them and allowing him to frame my face in his palms. I'm not sure why I give him the satisfaction, considering my cheeks are hot enough *without* his grip.

But I'm also learning that physical touch is one of his love languages, or whatever they're called. And I don't mind it. His hands. The way they make me feel.

"Can I kiss you?" he asks softly, and I nearly reel away from him.

"What?" I squeak. "Why so suddenly?"

My response must bewilder him, because his brows scrunch together. "Because I want to?" he tries, and I snatch his wrists, groaning with embarrassment. "You can say no."

"I know that!"

He smiles again, his pearly whites gleaming under the summer sun. "Then," he whispers, drawing me in until he's inches from my lips, "you're considering it?"

Instinctively, my palms flatten against his chest, preparing. Aaron glances down at them, then gives me a skeptical smirk that sets my face ablaze, because I know exactly what he's saying without words. "You can have *one*," I sputter out, needing any excuse to get him to look away.

I close my eyes, bracing, waiting for his mouth to meet mine.

He kisses the crown of my head before drawing away.

Oh.

"I'm sorry for losing my temper yesterday," he says, his thumbs stroking my temples. It feels nice—I forgot the left one has been in a constant state of mild throbbing. "I'm sorry for hitting Logan. When he insulted you, everything went white and I lost control of myself."

I peek through one eye to offer my fiercest glare. I guess it's not that fierce, because the sight makes him smile warmly.

"Are you angry with me?" he asks.

"Yes," I snap.

"But you let me kiss you anyway?"

I uphold my glare.

"Is it because I showed up unannounced?" he guesses. "In the past, we negotiated that I could come over without warning, because otherwise you'd find excuses to stay in and do chores and homework. You wanted life to be more spontaneous, so I got used to popping over whenever I felt like you were cooping yourself up. I won't do it if it upsets you."

It's getting more difficult to glare.

"I'm sorry for not apologizing sooner," he continues, apparently knowing exactly what he's done wrong. "I wanted us both to cool down before talking. An apology should've been the first thing out of my mouth, but I saw you and got distracted. Excited. Thinking about spending the day with you. I'm sorry it took so long to hear it."

A master manipulator.

Logan's voice is starting to grate at my ears. Aaron speaks to me and holds my face so genuinely. But if we've been dating over a year, he probably knows what it takes to cool me down. Is he saying this because he means it or because he knows what I want to hear?

My brain hurts too much to contemplate it any longer. "Thank you for your apology," I say stiffly. "Please allow three to five business days for a response."

I try to duck under his arm so I can head inside, but he slings his arm around my waist and draws me back into his chest with that impish grin. "But I *can't* allow three to five business days," he says. "Not when I'm about to kidnap you."

"Excuse me?" I snap.

"Only for an hour. Just one." His eyes are sparkly and earnest and irresistible.

"You'll buy me whatever I want?" I ask coldly.

"Whatever you want," he repeats.

"And you'll be my personal servant for the day?"

"Your bitch," he corrects.

He sounds so enthusiastic, I feel my mouth betraying me by furling upward. "Why is that so appealing to you?" I ask, straightening my face so he won't see that he's lightening my mood.

Aaron shrugs those sinewy shoulders, his merriment palpable. "I've always wanted you to leash me and make me walk on my knees. Besides, you never ask for anything, ever, even when you clearly want it. Do you know how frustrating that is for a service top, even outside the bedroom? I want to see what it's like when you boss me around."

By the time he's fallen quiet, I'm radiating heat from every pore and regretting all my life choices. "Don't just nonchalantly bring up sex things with me!" I croak.

He throws his palms over his mouth with an apologetic look. "I guess I'm spoiling our physical relationship. Sorry."

"That's not the problem here."

His eyes are crinkled up, so I know he's still grinning. He shuffles a few steps closer, eyeing me hopefully. "One hour?"

An evil part of me wants to make him regret upending my day without notice. Surely, I can drain his wallet in that amount of time. "Just . . . just an hour," I say with a scowl.

"Excellent!" To my disgruntlement, he sweeps my legs out from under me and hurtles toward his pickup truck, kidnapping me in broad daylight. Someone might as well stitch the word *welcome* onto my forehead, because I'm exactly what my brother said I am.

A doormat.

17

The carnival is more crowded than I expect—maybe people have the day off or don't work Fridays in the summers, because the lines are staggering for food, rides, and vendors selling personalized goods.

As I clamber out of Aaron's truck, he reaches into the back seat, procuring a floppy straw sun hat with a white ribbon. He nestles it over my hair, flattening my dark blond locks to my forehead.

"I already lathered myself in your SPF 50," I say.

"So? Extra protection." He bops my nose, smirking when I scrunch it. "And you look extra cute, which is a bonus for me, your beloved."

"You, my bitch," I correct.

Aaron laughs, and I'd be lying if I said the sound didn't make me want to smile. "Spicy. I'm into it." Aaron locks the vehicle and offers his palm, grinning. "Then, my lord—"

"Do not."

"—shall we make the most of this hour?"

I wonder if we held hands last time. The local carnival comes around in June for a few weeks, so at this point last year, Aaron and I would've been dating for two months. Would we have graduated to hand-holding? Maybe I shouldn't overthink it, considering I just made out with him yesterday. But making out in a fit of sudden horniness is different from knowingly holding hands as if we're a couple.

Whatever. Reenacting the physical aspects of our dates has been providing me flashbacks, so I'll tolerate it. "This means nothing," I say sharply, placing my hand in his.

Immediately, he invades the gaps between my fingers with his own, then draws up, flattening his lips against the back of my hand. He lingers just long enough to make me blush before winking and whispering, "Absolutely nothing."

He tugs me to the carnival entry gates.

They handle things the old-fashioned way with printed tickets, each game or ride costing a different amount. Aaron gets a bundle for us both, and when I tell him we won't have time to spend them all, he smirks like I've said something cute.

I'm glad he's holding on to me, because otherwise I'd lose him in the beehive of people swarming around. At one point, we're so crammed together on a walkway heading toward the street vendors that I have to hug Aaron's arm to avoid getting jostled. I expect a flirtatious comment that'll make me want to snap my teeth, but when I peer up at him, his normally marble-white cheeks are shaded pink. Sometimes I think it's the simple things that fluster him.

It's getting hot. I'm glad I have the ridiculous sun hat to keep my forehead from frying. I'm wearing a tank top beneath my sweater, but I'm still bruised and my skin isn't a healthy tinge today, so I suffer through the heat. Until Aaron says, "Nobody is looking at you but me. You can take it off if you want, babe."

I nearly choke with disgust. "Don't call me that," I plead.

He tightens his grip on my palm. "Sorry, sunshine."

I should tell him that nickname isn't better, but it is, and I'm not sure why. He used to call me that out of spite when I scolded him for taking up Logan's time, and for being a general brat. He'd say things like *Ease up, sunshine* or *You're just a little ray of sunshine today, aren't you?*

I wonder when he started saying it genuinely versus mockingly.

Regardless, he's probably right—there are so many people I doubt I'll stand out, so I pry my sweater off and knot it around my waist, exposing my bare arms to the sun. The heat soaks into my skin, and it's the dry type, not the humid type, so I don't suffocate.

The shops are my favorite part of local fairs, even if I don't spend money. I like seeing people's passions and creativity, which is why I demand we go there first.

I lose myself quickly among the shops, particularly the handcrafted goods tents. I don't wear jewelry, but I like shiny things, so I take my time eyeing the assortment of necklaces, bracelets, and rings. As I examine a black earring shaped like a dagger, I gasp, whirling toward Aaron. He's not inspecting the jewelry, but he seems content to be here, a small smile lighting his face.

"You have a stud!" I say, gesturing to his tiny black earring.

"I have a stud," he confirms.

"Would you wear this?" I point at the dagger with poorly concealed enthusiasm. "It seems like your style, yeah?"

He follows my finger and smiles wider. "Absolutely," he says lightly. "Should I get it?"

My instinct is to say yes, but I bite my tongue, because he might just be trying to appease me. "If you like it," I say stiffly, and he shields his mouth to laugh. He snatches the dagger earring off the counter and hands it to the merchant. She examines him a few seconds too long as she swipes his card before offering him a baggie and thanking him for returning to support her business.

He removes the stud from his ear and drops it into a pocket on his shorts, then hands me the bag. "Would you put it on me?"

It's a simple enough request, but it makes me blush. Still, I convinced him to get it, so I can do this much. I pluck the earring out, and Aaron bends low enough that I can see his ice-gray eyes teeming with mischief over his sunglasses. As I slide the post of the dagger through his earlobe, my eyes wander to the narcissus flower in the divot behind it. It's pretty. Neatly shaded and elegant despite its size. It's even got a stem and a few slender leaves.

Suddenly, the tattoo is gone, and I'm still fumbling with the dagger earring, but my fingers are skinnier. Gaunt.

I scrunch my eyes shut, then reopen them warily. The tattoo is back. My hands are fuller, my skin healthier. The only thing that doesn't change is the earring.

"I . . . I made you buy this last year!" I cry out, reeling away from him with mortification. "The same exact earring! You made me put it on you!"

Aaron sucks his lips between his teeth, clearly wanting to laugh but noticing my skyrocketing frustration levels. "Congratulations on another found memory," he says, to which I groan and smack my hands over my face.

"Why wouldn't you tell me? I can't believe I made you buy this twice! I bet you don't even like it, since you've never worn it."

"You didn't make me do anything." He twists his fingers into the backs of my hands, tickling until I drop them. "You're experiencing today for the first time. I don't want to ruin that. And the reason I stopped wearing it is because I accidentally stabbed you with it once while I was giving you a hickey."

"You shouldn't waste your money," I say, ignoring that last part.

"It's not a waste. You saw something and thought of me." He smiles and pokes at the dagger. "It's worth everything."

Oh no. I want to kiss him again.

I shake my head of my flustered bewilderment and scan rapidly for the next shop to dart to. "Let's go there!" I choke out, hauling him to a tent diagonal from us and nearly ramming the shoulder of an elderly woman in my desperation to escape. Aaron follows after me as I plunge into a ceramics and pottery tent that makes my eyes glisten. I don't need any of it, but then I spot a ceramic bowl with a design clearly influenced by Ming dynasty porcelain.

"Gah," I say, gesturing at the cobalt and white coloring and intricate floral design.

"Tell me more," Aaron encourages.

"Ming porcelain became really popular after the Yuan dynasty, when China regained control after Mongol rule. It was a huge export for places like Japan and Europe. The designs sometimes took influence from Tibetan art—I'll show you comparisons later. Anyway, this pottery has the same colors and common designs from that time period." I realize I'm rambling and clear my throat, tearing my eyes away. "Watched a documentary."

Aaron examines the bowl in great detail, placating my enthusiasm. Then, he scoops it up and brings it to the cashier.

"Put it back!" I squeak, snatching his elbow.

"I said I'd buy you anything you want."

"It's expensive, though!"

Aaron offers another smirk that fries my face. "I have a big-boy job, sunshine. It's fine. This artist wasn't here last time, so it's not even a duplicate purchase."

So he buys it, then gets it wrapped and boxed so it won't shatter. My overwhelming guiltiness isn't worth the satisfaction of draining his pockets, so I decide not to indicate interest in anything else. Though, I'm still not ready to leave the tents, and I feel safer out here where there's less food to poison me, so I continue meandering with Aaron at my elbow. He's not particularly interested in the shops, but he seems happy anyway. Maybe because I'm letting him hold my sweaty hand.

We're passing a wood figurine tent when his stride hitches just enough to notice.

"Want to go in?" I ask.

His jaw flexes. "Nah. I have their business card and can check their stuff online."

That pops my brows. If he has their card, this place has caught his eye before. He's been tolerating my wandering, so why shouldn't I indulge his? Besides, I don't know anything about his hobbies—mostly, he's just been letting me pursue mine. "Let's look," I urge, drawing him through the entryway.

The shop is overflowing with carved knickknacks, decorations, figurines, and woodworking tools. Aaron's trying to play it cool, but his eyes are sparkling, and he can't keep from lingering near pieces he likes. When he glances at me for the third time next to an intricately painted carving, I shuffle closer.

"A nativity scene?" I ask. Prompting him.

As I expect, an explanation spills from his mouth. "Yes, but rather than having several mix-and-match pieces, it's carved into one slab of wood. It's called a deep relief carving. It requires a high level of craftsmanship—see the way the layers create these shadows?" He leans over it, admiration pouring from his gaze. "They probably used every specialty gouge under the sun to get it this detailed."

I want to insist he should buy it, since he's been wasting his money on me. On second glance, though, I don't think he cares about it as a decoration. Rather, he's focused on the craftsmanship. He wants to learn from it—not necessarily purchase it for display. "Have you done one?" I ask, nestling into the gap beside him. "A deep relief carving?"

He laughs, but it's gentle, not cynical. "No, I just started working on bas-relief—or, like, low relief carvings," he corrects when he notices my blank look. "They're shallower, usually less than a half inch. I started practicing last year. Though I've been whittling longer."

I suddenly remember my bedside drawer. I was so overwhelmed by . . . all the nonsense . . . that I forgot about the figurine of unknown origins. "The wooden duck in my drawer," I say. "Did you make that?"

Aaron rubs his neck like it's something to be embarrassed about. "Yeah. You said ducks were your favorite animal. I could make a better one now, but it was the first one I ever made you, so you kept it."

I don't know how to respond to something so sweet. I merely turn to the nearest wooden sculpture, and say, "Thoughts on that thing?"

I feel something light settle atop my sun hat, but when I whirl back to him, he's retreated and pretending to be innocent. I think he just kissed me. "That's a chip carving," he explains. "This one is free-form. Basically, they drew a pattern onto the wood and carved it out with a knife blade."

We explore the entire shop, and he explains all the varying forms of wood carving to me. I'm more a fan of paintings and pottery, but his passion is intense enough to make me care about what I'm seeing. I wonder if he ever feels similarly when I start rambling about history. If so, maybe I'm less annoying than I think I am.

In the end, I convince him to buy a new pair of wood carving gloves he's been eyeing. For no reason at all, I notice they're extra large.

Eventually, we move back to the actual carnival. The mingling smells of hot dogs, burgers, and fried everything reel back into my nose. With impeccable timing, my stomach growls, and though Aaron doesn't hear it, I foolishly react by self-consciously grabbing my abdomen with my free hand.

He zeroes in on the movement. "Want something to eat?"

"No," I say quickly. "There's nothing I could get."

He stops in the middle of the walkway, to the disgruntlement of dozens of people filtering through. His eyes wander from a stand selling funnel cakes to one offering meaty sandwiches and fries. "There," he says, pointing diagonal to us. "Kettle corn. Looks like it has its own stand, so there shouldn't be cross-contamination. Also there." He swings his index finger toward another stand, beaming. "Pre-bagged cotton candy."

Sometimes I think Aaron is more knowledgeable about what I can and can't eat than I am. It's a silly reason to be more attracted to him.

Knowing that doesn't undo the damage.

As we wander, I stuff my face with kettle corn, enjoying the energetic atmosphere. I wonder what I would be doing right now, if not for Aaron. Maybe I'd be trying to tackle the lawn work or getting a head start on dinner. Maybe I'd be organizing the basement or washing the carpets or polishing the wood. Being useful.

We pause to sit on a germy metal bench and watch the dunk tank so I can let tufts of cotton candy melt in my mouth. This and the kettle corn aren't enough to satiate me, but Aaron has some of my favorite gluten-free protein bars to get us by.

His mood noticeably sours when we approach the red-and-white-striped game tents, where people are attempting to land rings on milk bottles or basketballs in misshapen hoops or water blasters in targets. I don't realize why his demeanor has changed until his stride screeches to a halt next to one tent. We're at the balloon darts station. Hanging on the racks behind the vendor . . .

A giant stuffed yellow duck.

"Hold this," he commands, placing our bag of newly acquired belongings in my hand.

"Sounds like you humiliated yourself last year," I say. "Fortunately for you, I can't remember your crushing defeat. You're willing to go through that again?"

Aaron catches my chin between his fingers so he can match my stare. "I'm winning you that motherfucking duck," he whispers heatedly. "No matter the cost."

"Good thing for that big-boy job, then," I respond.

He swivels toward the game operator, slapping five dollars down since we can't use the tickets here. She snags it and places three darts on the red counter, then gestures to the massive board behind her, fit with dozens of colorful pinned balloons. Some of them are bigger, easier to hit, while others are tiny and fastened by themselves with gaps between them.

"Two balloons get you a consolation prize, and three balloons win a small plush," she says, gesturing to the rows of tiny stuffed animals. No ducks, but the pandas are cute. "If you hit three of the smallest balloons in the top row, you win a major prize." She points overhead to the stuffed duck, like she knows exactly why we're here.

"First try," Aaron says, scooping up the first dart, closing one eye to aim, then letting loose.

It hits the cork between four balloons, missing all of them.

I clap politely.

"Hang me," Aaron says.

"Just win a little prize," I encourage, so entertained that my willpower isn't enough to keep a smile from cracking my face. "I like pandas."

"You want the duck, so you're getting that bitch-ass *duck,*" he says bitingly, slapping more money onto the table. He ignores his remaining two darts in favor of starting fresh with the next three. His tongue juts from his mouth as he hurls the first forward.

It hits the wall beside the corkboard and clatters to the ground.

I burst into laughter, staggering back and hugging my abdomen, made worse when Aaron purposefully bends over to slam his head against the edge of the counter. Even the game operator is shielding her mouth, like she's trying to keep from joining me.

"It's rigged," Aaron says.

"Y-you didn't even . . . hit the board . . ."

"Rigged!" He whirls to scold me, but his annoyance dissolves. There are tears in my eyes, and I'm giggling so hard that my stomach aches.

"Sorry," I wheeze out. "I'm not trying to be mean."

Aaron blinks a few times like his brain is lagging. The tension between his shoulders melts apart, and I'm not sure why until he says, "I haven't seen you laugh since the accident."

My body tightens with shock. He's looking at me with such abrupt earnestness that my ears itch with heat. "Well," I say unsteadily, "just be bad at things more often, I guess."

He smiles at me, so soft and genuinely sweet that I have to break my gaze away. He returns his attention to the counter, and says, "I'm not giving up."

He smacks more money down, then hits the corkboard three times in row.

"Just take the duck," the operator says, unhooking it from the ceiling and thrusting it over the counter. "You've basically paid for it in full."

"Finally, a win for gay people," Aaron says, snatching it. He hugs it in his broad wingspan, documenting her pity as a victory. "For you, my beloved."

He shoves it into my arms, and I nearly collapse under its weight. "Can we come back for it later?" I ask the operator.

"Sure," she says. "Please leave."

So I prop it on the counter and take Aaron's hand, drawing him away before he can have any second thoughts about whether or not he's earned it.

"Later?" Aaron squirms his palm so he can knot our fingers. "So you want to stay longer?"

"I promised you an hour," I say simply.

"Well . . . yes." He glances around the carnival—the congested pathways and endless tents and whirring rides and agitated lines—clearly knowing what I do.

"I left my phone in the car, so I can't check," I say, steering my eyes to the asphalt baking under our feet. "I think we probably have . . . what, like a half hour left? That should be enough time for us to spend our tickets on rides."

Aaron is silent for an arduously long moment. Then he's pulling me out of the throng of moving bodies and steering me around the back of a game station, so we're hidden between the tent and a looming wire fence that peeks into the parking lot.

"What's your problem?" I snip.

"I'm not kissing you," he says, sliding my floppy sun hat back. "Mind if I fix it?"

My heart smashes so violently against my rib cage that it's about to burst through the bones. How can he be so smooth so effortlessly? And why is he constantly so pretty? His hair is always lightly tousled and shiny, his eyes are always glittering like silver coins in marble fountains, and his dimple is always annoyingly pokable.

I shouldn't, but he got me out of my house and bought us tickets for carnival rides and has a bag filled with items he noticed I liked and spent way too much time, effort, and money on a massive stuffed duck because it's my favorite animal.

And he smiles so gently at me.

"You can fix it," I mumble.

Aaron exhales with a shakiness that worsens the ever-present warmth in my face. Like he's been desperate for this moment but concealing it well until now. He seizes my scalding upper arms and hoists me against him, arcing down to close his lips fiercely over mine. I squeak in surprise—a sound he promptly devours. He smells like body-wash tangling with the sting of metal. He tastes like melted chocolate and spun sugar. Both gluten-free, so I don't have to worry.

Not having to worry isn't something I'm used to.

He presses himself against me with such ardency that my back is arching under his weight, nearly grazing the red-and-white-striped tent behind me. He slides one palm over my sun hat, cupping it to my head so it won't topple off, while the other hooks around my waist, dragging it up against his hips. I'm angled so far back that if he lets go, I'll fall.

He won't, though. He's made it pretty clear at this point.

My hands find his chest because I'm not sure where else to put them. It's mortifying enough to do this in a public space where someone could walk around the tent or head in from the parking lot and see Aaron's tongue in my mouth. I can't use this opportunity to explore him, even if I want to. The image of him in nothing but a towel has been carved into my memories, and I don't hate it.

It lasts ten seconds. In that minuscule amount of time, the sheen of moisture on his forehead has found its way to mine, and my knees are shivering harder than they have been all day.

"Problem solved," Aaron says with his signature smile, and then he's drawing me around the tent and merging us with the crowd.

My body is so hot that my tongue has melted along the floor of my jaw, incapable of forming words. I'm not sure what I'd say. My pain is distant, barely noticeable, but not because it's improved over the past suspiciously long hour. It's because I'm with him. He's distracting me, drawing my focus away from the things that occupy my mind day and night.

I come to an unfortunate conclusion. In spite of my best efforts, and the warnings from my brother, and my attempts to be steadfast . . .

I'm starting to like Aaron Beckham.

18

"So you failed once more to show off your dart skills," I say, flexing my ankles while I sit on a grated bench beside a clown twisting balloons into hats. "And I made you buy the dagger earring twice. Anything else we did?"

Aaron leans back on his hands, considering, and I can't help but stare at the way his collarbone juts through his open buttons. He's been reapplying sunscreen religiously, but his nose and the ridges of his cheekbones are starting to crisp. "We're a couple of queers at a carnival. What do you think?" he asks, hanging his head sideways. The tips of his loose curls are slick against his skin.

"I think we probably went on the Ferris wheel," I say.

"What a fresh and ingenious idea." Aaron bends over and scoops my legs up, slinging them into his lap. To my embarrassment, he begins to knead his thumbs into my ankles, then works his way up my calves to try to ease the ache.

"I don't need special attention in the middle of a carnival," I protest. "I'm not your pregnant wife."

He sighs. "One day, maybe."

I gag at him, and he laughs, his fingers working my skin more intensely. His thumb catches the cuff of my jeans, and he tugs it up, exposing my ankle. To my mortification, he lifts my leg to plant a gentle kiss to my skin, before continuing on with his massage.

"Don't do that in public!" I plead.

"How else will people know you're mine?" he asks with a casual shrug, and I thump his head.

"We're not boyfriends." Even if we've kissed and cuddled and are currently on a literal, actual date. It's all to reclaim my memories and not because I'm falling for him.

"Ah, right." Aaron nods, suddenly solemn. "I'm but a tool for your desires. Apologies for forgetting my place, my lord."

"Don't call me that."

"But it's the only time I get to feel like your bitch," he whines. "You haven't bossed me around at all today. Why can't you be more toxic, Riley?"

I give him an exasperated glare, and he laughs again, unveiling those abnormally pointy canines. I wonder how easily they could break skin. Which is a frankly ridiculous thing to wonder, and worsens my flustered state, so I wrench my legs out of his grasp and hurl myself to my feet, seizing his palm. "Let's get this over with," I say, dragging him toward the Ferris wheel.

Evening is upon the town, and carnival lights are flickering to life, supplementing the warm orange glow of the horizon beyond the distant cityscape. The carousel twinkles with golden bulbs, and fairy lights sparkle above the walkways, threaded between lamps like bedazzled spiderwebs. The food stands come ablaze, their windows framed in ice-white string lights. Then there's the wheel itself, the legs and spindles an amalgam of flickering rainbow colors.

As we stand in line, me leaning heavily against the metal poles leading to the ride entrance, Aaron points up at the shifting rainbow on the wheel. "Ally," he says confidently.

The color shifts to royal blue.

"You were so annoying it became homophobic," I tell him. "Like the balloon lady."

"What? She gave me that stuffed duck out of the goodness of her heart!" he cries out.

"And then whispered a slur as we left."

Aaron gasps. "She did?"

"Probably. Though that might've also been me."

Aaron laughs, his head arching back under the force and nearly ramming into someone's arm behind us. I can't maintain my neutral expression, so I twist away to keep him from spotting my grin. He notices and catches my jaw, pulling my face forward. "Don't hide it," he says. "It's been so rare lately."

I don't have time to think of a response, because the line shifts, and the ride operator shepherds us and two bickering guys behind us into one of the large, rounded booths. I'm a teeny bit disappointed we're not by ourselves, but the line is egregiously long, so I don't blame them for trying to cram multiple couples onto one gondola. Thankfully, it's big enough that we're not knee-to-knee with them, and we can probably chat quietly without them overhearing. Still, seeing other people nearby makes me inch away, because I don't know how these guys feel about sharing a cabin with—

"They're holding hands, too," Aaron says.

I glance across to the other corner of the booth and realize he's right. I haven't properly looked at the two until now, nor have I been listening to their agitated conversation, but they're clearly a couple. I pin them to be in their early twenties.

"I'll crush it," the smaller one on the right is saying, and though they're technically holding hands, it's more hostile than it should be. He's applying all his strength to squeezing his partner's palm, his face contorted in a scowl. "I'll crush all your fucking fingers and then you'll apologize through your sobs of agony."

"Apologize for what?" the taller one drawls, leaning against the gondola railing as the attendant closes the door and sends us climbing into the air. "I drove you two hours here because your impatient ass couldn't wait another month for the Delridge fair. What reason could you possibly have to fracture my hand?"

"You called me a weak little bitch in front of your brother!"

"Yeah? That's not new information for anyone."

"Get *dicked*." The first boy squeezes the other's hand even harder, teeth clenching. The second boy clearly isn't swayed by this physical violence.

I glance at Aaron in bewilderment, feeling like we've intruded on something. He's wearing an entertained grin, his arms spread along the back of the bench, his left draped subtly over my shoulder. "Is it a domestic dispute?" I breathe. "It's like they hate—"

"You can't tell?" Aaron asks, smirking down at me.

"Tell what?"

"That they're in love."

I scrunch my brows with skepticism, glancing at the two. They're discussing something else, and the first boy is now nearly huddled up in the second boy's lap. His giant gray eyes are flitting around with unease as the wheel climbs toward its peak. With his hair in disarray and his shaky limbs, he looks a bit like a small feral animal.

"Fuck this," he wheezes out, giving up his conquest to crush his partner's hand into dust. He slings his arms around the other's bicep, hugging it fiercely. "Why did you let me do this? Fuck you."

The second boy massages his brows with a weary sigh but looks admittedly pleased to be clung to. He leans his head sideways, bumping it against his partner's. "Your exact words were *We're not gay if we don't ride the Ferris wheel.*"

"There's no way I would ever say something so biphobic."

The taller one smirks and uses his free arm to scoop his partner's legs up into his lap. "Cranky as ever," he mumbles, and suddenly, what I feared was an altercation has melted into something soft and intimate and, oh God, why am I watching this like it's a movie? I whip toward Aaron, hoping he can't see my flushed cheeks with all the varying lights splashing across our faces.

"What do we do?" I choke out.

"We should make out in retaliation," he says flatly.

"Aaron."

He snickers, closing his arm around my shoulders and sliding me against his side. "If you need a distraction, let's talk about something," he suggests, cocking his head, giving me yet another look at his black dagger earring and narcissus flower.

I blurt my question before I can deliberate it. "Does your tattoo mean anything?"

Aaron blinks in surprise. His gaze detaches from mine, and he peeks down at the carnival beneath us, focusing on the spinning rides and flickering lights and meandering groups.

"Sorry if that's too invasive," I say, but he merely shakes his head.

"It's not." He says it softly, but there's an underlying hint of strain.

"You've spent the past year helping me feel more comfortable talking about these things, but it's still not easy."

I incline my head, wondering how I've supposedly helped him.

"It's my mother's birth flower," he says. "I got it when I turned eighteen so I would see it every day and think about her."

Yet another reference to his mother. Until now, all I've known about him is that he was adopted fairly young, when he was only a few years old. "You have a strong connection to her?" I ask.

"No." He shrugs, though his posture is tense. "I just admire her."

"You meet up with her sometimes, right?"

"When she's in a good place." He leans his head back against the bench, peering up at the gondola's ceiling. I have the nagging suspicion he's not used to talking about himself—or maybe he just feels like this is a waste of my time. As if learning more about the boy who apparently made me fall for him would be a waste.

"What do you mean?" I prompt.

"Like . . . I don't know. It's basically up to me to stay connected, otherwise she holes up and forgets about me. She's got some issues." His eyes fall shut. "I was a teenage pregnancy. I wouldn't blame her if the reason she bails on me constantly is because I remind her of . . . yeah."

I watch him, fascinated. I've never seen him so uneasy—it's a stark contrast from his suave persona. His fingers are tensing on my shoulder, so I pluck them off and nestle his hand in my lap, working his knuckles like he's always doing to mine. "You said you admire her," I whisper, knowing he won't persist unless I ask him to. "Because she was brave for getting through it?"

"I guess." As I knead his fingers, his taut muscles slowly relax. I hope I haven't always been the one on the receiving end of massages. "Though she doesn't like that word. Life forcing you to tackle something you're not prepared for, where the choices are *deal with it* or *die* . . . it feels wrong to shave it down to bravery." His throat bobs with a swallow. "She was fifteen in a low-income family with a barely functional support system tainted by addiction. She didn't get to choose bravery. It was forced on her. So I think when people say things like *Wow, you're so brave, I could never do what you did*, it leaves a bad taste in her mouth."

He steadies himself with a deep breath. Knowing I somehow make him feel comfortable enough to divulge this sensitive information . . . it's more proof that what we had was real.

That for as much as he changed me, maybe I've also been changing him.

"I admire her because she found the willpower to let me go," he says. "She told me once that she only gave birth to me so she could raise me at home out of bitterness. Vengeance. Like punishing me because she couldn't punish the person who put her in that situation. She thought, *Why should this kid I don't even want have a better life than me?*"

He pauses, peering down at me as if to make sure I haven't fallen asleep. I'm very much awake—though I'm so caught up in his voice, I've forgotten to continue massaging his hand. Quickly, I try picking the motion back up, but Aaron merely slides our fingers together, squeezing. Using me as an anchor, I think.

"Anyway, she let her cousin and his husband adopt me," he says, waving his other hand. "When they found out how bad her situation was, they dragged us both across the country to live with them. I don't remember any of it. But my dads say she finished school and started looking for jobs. I think I was six when she left? She stayed in the area, but she didn't want anything to do with me."

"But something changed," I say. We're descending from the peak of the Ferris wheel for the second time—I doubt we'll get a third go-around, so I'll make the most of these minutes. Thankfully, the couple across from us is locked in conversation as well, so I don't fear them overhearing.

"When I got old enough, my dads gave me her contact information," Aaron says. "She didn't respond to my texts until I was a teenager, and we've made it to a point where we meet up occasionally. It wasn't a great feeling, being ignored." His eyes settle on my lap. "I spent a long time feeling guilty for being born. I still do sometimes. But whatever."

"It's not whatever," I murmur.

"All you did was ask about the tattoo. I shouldn't have rambled."

"I want to know." My voice sharpens. "You know everything about me, apparently, so why shouldn't I know everything about you?"

Aaron's lips furl into a brief smile. "So it's not that you want to know because you're falling for me," he says with a melancholic sigh. "It's just that you think I have an unfair advantage and you're trying to level the playing field."

I squawk in horror, ripping my hands away so I can shake them defensively. "That's not true! I really do want to know more about you!"

"Mm." Aaron huffs, looking away stubbornly. "Don't believe you."

He's being a brat, trying to lighten the mood by teasing me. Maybe it's a defense mechanism. An attempt to move the subject along so we're not sitting in seriousness anymore. I won't allow it.

I reach up, splaying my palm across his cheek and tugging until his gaze is level with my fierce one. "Thank you for telling me," I say. "I know it's not easy to explain everything again. I had no idea you were in contact with your mother. Or that you knew who she was."

I falter, wondering if I should stop here. My instincts tell me to draw away—to not let this moment get deeper than it already is. I ignore them.

"You've always been a big question mark," I admit, my own nerves rising to the surface. My fingertips tremble against his sunburned cheekbone. "All I've known about you is that you like getting into bad situations and letting your impulses run wild. Part of me still wants to blame you for ruining Logan's future."

I fizzle off again, my jaw grinding through the apprehension.

"But I don't think that's fair," I say. "Logan makes his own decisions. It was easy to pin the blame when I saw you as this one-dimensional villain, but now it's more than that. *You're* more than that. After a few days, all the anger I feel for you has been . . . melted away, I guess. It's frustrating because I was so sure I could avoid you the second time. I thought you were a mistake I could erase."

Hesitantly, I bring my other hand up to cup his slender face, my pinkies latching under his jaw. He watches dazedly, like he fears this might be a dream. A shimmering sheen of water glasses his eyes. I want him to blink and let them trickle down his face, so I can brush them away like he brushes mine. But I guess we're similar in that regard.

I don't have to cry, so I won't.

He told me I don't have to hide my emotions. But he has a wall of his own. It's different from mine, built from feigned confidence rather than feigned apathy. Whereas I stubbornly bury things with a level face and flat voice, he brushes them away with a grin and an airy wave. We're the same.

Have I ever told him he doesn't have to hide in front of me?

"There are some things I'm not sure about—like moving in with you, leaving my family, enrolling at some random college. But I'm starting to understand how this . . . how *we* . . ." Embarrassment rushes through me, but I maintain eye contact, my grip firming around his face. "The point is that I'm rediscovering you. Nobody has ever put me first before, and it feels strange. But good. I thought you were trying to lure me in, but I think that's just who you are."

He's barely blinking, and his familiar intensity is causing my head to spin.

"Um. So. Basically, I just like learning these things about you, and not because I'm irritated that you know more about me," I blurt, because I can't stop halfway. "I said there's a gap between my mind's reaction to you and my body's. Spending time with you like this is closing the gap. I feel more comfortable. Maybe even safer. It's just nice to know that if something happens, there's someone I can call for help."

Aaron finally moves. Only so he can spread one hand over mine, hugging it to his face. He leans into my grip like it's his safe place.

"It's wrong to hold you accountable for my bad decisions in the past," I say. "I made them myself, just like Logan made his. So yeah. Just assume that when you're talking about yourself, I want to know all the nitty-gritty details, okay? And . . . one more thing, while I have you."

He waits. I swallow nervously, and say:

"I'm glad you were born, Aaron Beckham."

Aaron exhales with a kind of force that makes me wonder just how long he's been holding it. "Riley," he breathes, tilting his face to press his lips into the base of my palm. "Thank you."

"I haven't done anything," I say, finally able to rip my eyes away. The Ferris wheel is rolling to a stop—the attendant is waiting to unlock our gondola door.

Aaron doesn't give me reprieve, taking my chin and guiding it to face him. "Thank you," he says, his thumb drifting up to graze my lips, "for making this the best hour of my life."

I feel scarlet searing through my limbs. The moment our gate swings open, I'm flying to my feet and stumbling out of the gondola, tripping over the taller boy across from us.

"Watch it!" the feral one snaps. "Honestly, kids these days . . ."

"Sorry," I squeak. "I didn't mean to step on your boyfriend."

"Fiancé!" he says shrilly, and I wince from his volume. *"He's my perfectly hot and sexy fiancé, thank you!"*

My eyes are rolling in my head at that point, anxiety rippling through me. "Sorry."

"Don't worry about it," the taller one says, slapping a palm over his partner's rapidly moving mouth. Only then do I notice they're wearing a matching set of rings. "Sorry about him. He's not normally this much of a dick. It's just the adrenaline from being suspended off the ground, so he's wailing a bit—"

"I don't wail!" the feral one wails, his voice shoving through his partner's cupped palm. *"Remove your hand or I'll break off this engagement!"*

"Do what you want. You'll just have to propose a second time." The taller boy nods a farewell at Aaron and me. I flee, hurling myself through the exit gates while Aaron follows at my heels, giggling.

"Hope that's us one day," he says brightly.

"Seriously?" I demand, still shaken. "All they did was argue and bicker."

Aaron's arms slink around my shoulders, and he crowds up against me from behind, arching my neck back so I have to look up. He grins and presses a fleeting kiss to my forehead. "And we don't?"

I give him a skeptical glare, which he returns with a wink.

"Shall we continue on?" he asks. "I think we have a few minutes left in the hour."

The sun has been completely swallowed by the horizon, leaving the glittering neon lights of the carnival to lead the way. I know I've wasted half a day coming here, but I can't find the energy to be upset. Maybe it'll hit me tonight at home where Aaron can't distract me.

But I'm not home, and Aaron's irises are shimmering all kinds of colors under the lights radiating from the rides, walkways, and food stands.

"Just a few more minutes," I say quietly.

He smiles, bending lower so he can brush a kiss against my lips. "Just a few," he promises.

So we wander off. Faintly, I can hear the irritable voice of that boy behind us, telling his partner off while the other snickers at his disgruntlement.

Suddenly, I have the feeling they'll be okay.

19

Four days. Apparently, that's all it takes for me to lose my resolve.

The first day, Aaron followed me around, pestering me until I agreed to re-create our dates and then admitting I only went out with him so he'd stay away from Logan. The next night, he forced me to trespass at the high school and go for a swim. The day after, I fainted, and he came over, made out with me, then punched my brother. Today, he kidnapped me from my schedule and brought me to a hot, sweaty carnival.

On paper, it sounds ridiculous.

Yet Aaron Beckham is the only reason I've been able to cope with everything. Around him, I don't feel lost. Until now, I feel like I've been wandering aimlessly in a cavernous black tunnel, in which his light is the only one—faint, ominous, blood-red. But a light nonetheless.

The closer I get to it, the more I realize the shade is more like roses. Sunburned cheeks. Freshly cut strawberries and romance-red lipstick and cardinals against a winter-white snowscape. An exit sign guiding the way out from a shadowy nightmare.

When I think about the past few days, I linger less on unpleasant moments and more on the things that made my stomach tingle. Aaron bringing me gluten-free ice cream so I could enjoy myself more with the history club. Teasing me into thwacking him with the pillow because it was truer to the memory. Making me a delicious snack so I wouldn't get cranky at the pool. Encouraging me to open up about my discomfort and then falling asleep curled around me, his tears melting into my shirt. Rushing to me from work so he could carry me to a warm bath. Kissing me . . . like that. Spoiling me at the carnival. Opening up about his mother.

It's been four days, so why does it feel like months have passed?

When Aaron pulls up to the curb of my house, the subdivision is glowing under warm golden porch lights, and a balmy breeze whishes past his cracked windows, fluttering my hair. I'm properly full, since we ate at a restaurant on the brink of the city that apparently has a perfect track record of not poisoning me. It's one of our go-to places, I guess, even though I don't ever remember being there.

The salad and gluten-free pasta eased my hunger aches, and I learned more about Aaron's mom. She works in a chain restaurant, and though she never reaches out to Aaron first, she does accept every third or fourth invite he sends to get lunch. He talks. She listens. That's the extent. He doesn't seem to mind, appreciating that she's willing to see him at all.

Still, his mother is a dicey subject, and her situation clearly gnaws at him.

I stare at my knobby knees in the darkness of his car, swirling a mint around my tongue. Being home is a good thing. I can refocus. My family was left to their own devices for dinner, which is something I despise doing, because it's like, really? Can't I follow through on such a simple thing? But there are leftovers in the fridge, so that's the only reason I didn't fret.

I'm fretting anyway because I can almost feel the disappointment radiating off my house. I haven't checked my texts, and the fact that I willingly made myself unavailable so I could, put bluntly, *dick around* makes me feel . . .

"Selfish," I whisper.

Aaron crunches through his own mint, tilting his head sideways. "What?"

I'm not sure why my mouth betrayed me like that. I huff, leaning against the car door, watching the trees sway in the breeze. "Being around you makes me want to be selfish," I mumble. "Logan says hanging around you will twist me into someone I'm not. And . . ." I swallow hard, my eyes burning with frustration. "I think he's right."

Aaron doesn't respond at first. I don't dare to glance over. I just told him I'll stop holding him accountable for my own actions, and I've basically implied he's the reason I'm letting my egoism take over. I don't mean it like that, but I can't articulate it in any other way.

He asks, "Is it being selfish, or wanting to live your life for once?"

Hesitantly, I peer over at him. He's folded his arms over his steering wheel and nestled his head into them.

"Is it being selfish, or giving yourself time to be happy?" he continues, watching me curiously. "Is it being selfish, or taking a break so you don't burn out?"

The lump in my throat expands, thinning my airway. "Is there a difference?" I ask.

He smiles in that gentle way I can't stomach. "You don't exist to serve your family."

"I know," I say sharply. "I'm not Cinderella. I'm not being forced to do anything. But they're all busy, and I have nothing to do, so I'm worthless if I can't support them."

"Recuperating from a car crash that obliterated a year of your memories and left you with a dozen bruises isn't nothing," he points out. "And when did your worth become tied to how many chores you can do in a day?"

His voice is infuriatingly calm. "It's not," I say. "But I've put them through a lot, so I'm making it up to them. I can't even remember the crash, so I'm not traumatized. My anemia is just worse. The memory loss sucks, but that's *all* I lost, so I'm lucky. My mind is just a little stressed trying to fill the gaps. That's why I need to get back on a regular schedule. That's why things like this"—I gesture violently around us—"are hurtful."

Aaron observes me in silence, processing my defensive ramble. Finally, he peels away from the wheel. He slides his seat back until there's a sizable gap between him and the dashboard, then pats his thighs, and says, "Come here."

I scowl deeply. "Why?"

"So you can't hide your face."

"Who does that help but you?" I demand. "I'm not going to sit in your lap."

"Why not?" He smiles again, this one sickly sweet. "It's one of your favorite places."

I'm only in a tank top, but I start sweating like I'm in winter layers. "I told you not to make sexual jokes," I squeak out, reaching out to shove his shoulder. He smoothly threads his fingers through my extended ones, then pulls, tugging me out of my seat and over the middle compartment.

"I wasn't talking about sex," he says with an insufferable laugh, settling my weight in his lap. Infuriated but knowing it's not a battle I can win, I part my knees on the driver's seat around his thighs, straddling him.

"Happy?" I snap.

"Exhilarated," he says. I'm propped up enough to be at eye level with him, so I can pierce him with my glare more easily. I fumble with my fingers, but he captures my hands and draws them behind his neck, thrusting them through the gap between his seat and headrest. Casually, he pushes the headrest down, and it clicks over my wrists, essentially cuffing me.

"Sometimes you treat me like a hostage," I grumble, wanting to bite the smugness off his handsome face. The dagger stud in his ear catches in the yellow light trickling around the window curtains in my house. His hands fall to the curves of my waist and settle. "If you try anything weird—"

"I love you, Riley Wilson," he whispers.

I stare at him in bemusement. Then another surge of warmth floods my face, and I try to veer my head away so he won't see, but I have nowhere to hide. Not with my wrists trapped under the headrest behind his neck.

"I love you," he repeats. "But I wish you would love yourself more. You treat your time like it's worth less than others'. No matter where you are in life, you make excuses to take more responsibilities. Right now, it's because it's summer break. During school, it's because you don't have a job. You're always making justifications."

I'm starting to understand why he wants me here. My instincts are telling me to curl into fetal position so he won't see my face. I'm trapped, though, in full view of his ruthless stare, unable to duck around its hypnotic pull. My brain works furiously to defend me. I'm at a disadvantage, though—we've clearly had this conversation before, if he managed to sway me into moving in. His arguments are practiced, whereas I'm scrounging mine together from scratch.

"It's nice that you want to help your family," Aaron says, his fingertips sliding under the gap between my shirt and waist, crawling along my skin. "But you don't exist to be a helping hand. You have things you like, even if you crush them down and call them distractions. Exploring. Learning. Having fun. There's nothing wrong with wanting to live."

He's aggravating me even more, heartlessly nailing me with these points I don't have the mental energy to combat. "Pull the headrest up," I mutter.

Aaron's smile widens with mischief. His arms curl in around my waist, hugging my abdomen to his. "No," he says. "I think I'll keep you here all night."

"I order you to. Because you're my servant today," I remind him.

Aaron clicks his tongue. "But you haven't been ordering me around. You wouldn't even let me call you *my lord*. This isn't good for you. Since you've been letting me do what I want, and I know you're too nice to punish me, I've become unruly and rebellious."

I scoff as he sticks his palms up the back of my tank top again, fingertips scratching slow, deliberate trails up my spine, clearly indifferent to the day's grime probably caking my skin. He finds a spot of tension between my shoulder blades and kneads.

"It took you a long time to realize you were living your life for others instead of yourself," he says, pressing my chest against his. We're close enough now that our lips graze with every word, and being this near his searing ice-gray stare ruptures my skin with goose bumps. "I'll do everything I can to bring you back to that moment. To help you talk through these feelings toward yourself. I know you love your family, but that doesn't mean they're not hurting you."

My jaw flexes with annoyance. "They aren't hurting me," I mumble.

"But they are." His index knuckle grinds into the nape of my neck, and I hate how nice it feels. "Your family isn't helpless, Riley. But you've volunteered to take over the cooking and cleaning repeatedly, and they got used to letting you. I'm not saying they intentionally put the burden on you. I know your parents are a little . . . clueless sometimes. But guess what. When we were living together, they managed to survive."

His hand moves fully up and out the back of my tank top to grasp my neck and nudge my forehead against his.

"When you came home, things were probably a little more disorganized, but still fine," he murmurs. "Right? With the way you've convinced yourself that your family can't run their own house, you'd think your absence would've meant it would be a total disaster. But it wasn't."

My blood is cooling. He's not wrong. When I returned from the hospital, it was clear nobody had cleaned it to my extent, but it was still clean. There were some things out of place—some dishes in the sink, some dusty surfaces, the yard in disarray—but nothing unmanageable.

"But I volunteer to do these chores for a reason," I say, my lower lip beginning to wobble. "I've caused problems with the medical stuff . . . It's fine . . . I don't want to be high-maintenance, so it's better to do things myself, like cleaning and cooking . . . I'll be less worried about getting sick . . ."

My voice trembles around the words. I'm not sure why I'm getting emotional. There's no reason to be upset, because the situation is too nuanced for him to shave it down to this extent.

"It's not fine," Aaron whispers. "You don't owe your family just because you've had a history of illness. It's your parents' job to keep you healthy. They seem willing to put in more effort to stop you from getting sick, so why not let them? Why do you still feel like you need to make two meals every night when they've said they don't mind eating gluten-free?"

If I open my mouth, I'll start crying, so I keep it shut.

"You came to this realization once, and you can do it again," he continues. "If you decide to try getting some space, you're still welcome to stay with us. You don't remember meeting my dads, but they're big fans. I think they like you more than me."

I don't expect that last part, and I laugh. It's quick and frail, but something about it triggers a sudden yearning in Aaron's eyes. He draws me in, meeting my lips. I should probably yell at him for daring to do this with my wrists trapped, but for all my whining and squirming, I don't actually mind having a valid reason to be close to him.

The kiss is short. It's a test—he wants to know how receptive I am. When I don't scowl or bonk his head in protest, he comes in for a second, this one slower. His thumbs massage my jawline, working my mouth open so he can taste the lingering mint. I feel sticky and germy, but sitting in his lap, my knees braced around his thighs, I can't find it in me to care. The engine's hum is a pleasant white noise—the only sound cutting through our quiet breaths.

One of his hands traces the strap of my tank top as I try valiantly to match his intensity. It's my second time making out, but my body reacts like it's been through this scenario countless times. I'm instinctively inclining my head and leaving pecks around his mouth. I grow used to my upper lip being licked in light flits and my lower being nipped. I'm feeling less like I'm swallowing his mouth at the tail end of a lingering kiss.

Part of me wishes I could move my hands so I can put them wherever I want. Another part of me likes that I can't.

Aaron's fingers curl into my hair and tug, arching my head, exposing the curve of my shoulder. He plants a kiss under my jawline, then drags his lips down, leaving another lower on my neck. The feeling is electric—each kiss sizzles my skin, and it's intense enough that I nearly flinch. When I feel a long, slow sweep of his tongue, I bite on my lips to keep from gasping theatrically.

"Too much?" he asks.

"I . . . I probably taste like salty sweat," I complain.

"All I taste is sugar." He bites my tank top strap and drags it down until it's dangling off my shoulder. "A bit of spice, too." He closes his teeth around the arch of my neck, just enough to send shivers squirming up my spine, then tacks on, "Ah. There's the pinch of salt."

"You talk too much," I snip, and Aaron laughs, his breath unfurling against my skin. Then he's *really* kissing my neck, using every feature of his mouth—lips, tongue, teeth—and the sheer deliberateness of his movements is almost more intoxicating than the actual kissing. My eyes flutter shut, and my fingers curl up against the back of the headrest. I don't have any other flashbacks, but I also don't mind.

Aaron kisses me for a while, but even after my energy peters out, I'm reluctant to leave. I stay rooted in his lap, curled up sideways against his chest, my head resting in the scoop of his neck. I tell him I stopped by the university I'm enrolled at, where I ran into Amy Choi, and that I was pleasantly surprised by how cozy and bright it was. He tells me his dads are going out of town for a weekend next month, and that he wants to re-create our first "sleepover" date.

"You already slept at my place," I point out.

"But we'll be truly alone," he responds, grabbing my wrist—now freed from its containment under the headrest—and pulling it into my lap. I don't realize until then that I've been nibbling on my finger. "No parents or siblings to walk in on us. And it'll be planned, rather than a spur-of-the-moment decision."

The idea of intentionally spending the night alone with him causes my heart to lurch.

Eventually, he walks me to my door with my belongings (including my giant stuffed duck), apologizes for the hickeys layering my neck, kisses me once more, and heads home. By the time I make it inside, my hair is suspiciously frazzled, my lips are swollen, and my clothes are in disarray. I'm in higher spirits than usual, because today was fun. I guess.

I don't anticipate anyone will still be awake, what with it being after eleven o'clock.

But they're all sitting here, waiting for me.

The first thing I notice is that this place is a mess. Paper plates, crumpled napkins, and Solo cups litter the countertops, which are stained with liquid and food crumbs. Foldout tables and chairs are propped around the living room, each adorned with playing cards, and empty beer bottles are stacked behind the kitchen sink. Dad is shoving them into a white garbage bag while Mom is sprawled on the couch, massaging her temples. Logan haphazardly wipes the kitchen table, his eye swollen, splattered an ugly violet.

As the door swings shut, they whip toward me. Mom heaves a deep breath of relief. I look between them in confusion, my heart plunging into the bottoms of my feet, the stuffed duck falling from my arm and squeaking against the floor.

"Ah, Riley! There you are." Dad smiles with a hint of strain. "We were getting worried."

I fumble for my phone and unlock it for the first time. Notifications flood across the screen, paling my skin.

"We hosted euchre tonight," Dad says, shoving another few bottles into his garbage bag. "You weren't responding to our messages, so we hoped you were okay. It's a bit unlike you."

My attention is glued to my screen.

> Mind bringing up the folding tables and chairs for euchre tonight? Unless you're tired.
>
> Hope you're feeling better baby. You think you could make a quick bean dip for euchre? It's a potluck and I completely forgot to make something!!
>
> If you have time, could you set up the liquor on the island? Thanks kid.
>
> Just got home. Where are you? You shouldn't be pushing yourself.

Can you respond sweetie?

You didn't pass out somewhere, did you?

I blink, and Mom is suddenly cradling my face. "We're glad to see you," she says, kissing my forehead. "Don't worry about the texts. It's our fault for waiting until the last minute to get everything together. Where have you been?"

"Seriously?" Logan asks from across the room, his face twisting with a scowl. "Look at him. He's obviously been fucking around with Beckham."

"Logan!" Mom snaps at him, but then her eyes slide to my neck, and she stiffens. I don't know what it looks like, but I feel several areas pulsing, so I'm sure numerous hickeys are fully exposed by my tank top. I should've put my sweater back on before coming inside.

"I'm sorry."

It's all I can think to whisper. I'm a horrible liar and the evidence is in plain sight. Logan wipes the table with renewed vigor, his jaw squared, and Dad is kneading his forehead, a vein lancing through his temple. Mom snaps her hands to her side like I've poisoned her.

"Ah," she says lightly. "Sorry. Were you on a date with that boy, maybe? I hope he's treating you well and not taking advantage of you. Did he at least apologize for what he did to Logan's face?"

I want to scrounge together an excuse. Something to explain away my actions. But I don't have one, other than that I went along with Aaron's whims to get him off my back. "I'm sorry," I repeat numbly, the words thick in my throat. I'm trembling with embarrassment. "I should've kept my phone on me . . . We stopped by the carnival . . . I shouldn't have gone . . . I'll clean everything up . . ."

"You don't have to do that," Mom says, tapping the tip of my nose. "You must be frustrated. What you're going through isn't easy. But you don't need to run to him every time you're upset, okay? You can come to us, too. We'll be here for you."

For the first time, a spark of annoyance flickers in my chest. It's a common broken promise I hear from them, and it's only gotten worse with time as I've aged and learned how to take care of my issues. "Aaron is the only one who's been actively trying to help me remember the past year," I say, my voice as shaky as the rest of me. "He's the only one who's been *there for me* since I got home. I know you're all busy with work and school, and I know you're trying to pretend like everything is normal so I don't get overwhelmed, but I need a little more than that."

My parents exchange a hesitant look, and I know immediately they've spoken about this. "We're sorry, Riley," Dad says softly. "We thought we were obeying the doctor's orders by keeping our distance and following our routines."

"All you're doing is leaving me in the dark," I say. Something dribbles down my middle finger, and I realize I've dug my nail so deeply into my skin that I've broken it. "You're all pretending like nothing happened. You're vague when I ask questions. I didn't know I joined a history club or that I moved out. Do you have pictures of me from the past year? Did I go to prom? Where were we for Christmas? What was my grad ceremony like? Did you come with me to look at campuses? Why . . ."

I steer my watery eyes to Logan.

"Why wasn't I wearing my seat belt?"

Logan's face drains of color, causing it to look like a ghostly white sheet. My mom's eyes are glassy with tears. When nobody answers right away, all of them clearly weighing how to respond or how much they should say, the frustration mounts in my body. My temperature rises with it, and suddenly, I feel my blood simmering. Not boiling. Not yet.

"I'm sorry for making bad decisions, but you aren't helping," I croak. "I'm sorry I missed your texts. I'll do better. I'll clean the rest of this up as an apology. But Aaron is the only one who—"

"Riley, come on," Logan mutters. "Can't you read the room a little? The reason nobody's saying much is because we don't want you to reexperience all the bad decisions you made over the past year. Because all of them involve *him*."

"Leave it alone, Logan," Dad snaps at him, to which he shrugs.

"I'm just telling him the truth, like he wants. He literally let that piece of shit convince him to move out, so—"

"Enough," Mom says, her voice firming in a way I haven't heard in years. She turns back to me with a frail smile, and says, "I'm sorry we haven't been there for you as much as we should be, honey. It's all a bit new to us. We haven't been sure how to handle the situation. Now that we know how you feel, we'll be better. Okay?"

Just like that, the conversation is over. Mostly because I'm too sapped of physical and mental energy to pursue it beyond this point. I guess I should be grateful they're listening to me, but they've always struggled on follow-through, and I'm too nauseous from Logan's words to point that out to them.

All the bad decisions you made . . .

"Okay," I say flatly. "Sorry."

Mom pokes my nose. Dad comes over to ruffle my hair. They try to continue cleaning up, but I shoo them away, because finishing is the least I can do to make up for my absence. They can tell I'm not in the mood to argue, so they reluctantly bid me good night and head upstairs to bed, until it's just Logan and me. We eye each other for a moment before he says, "You had fun?"

He doesn't ask it bitingly, but it stings anyway. I drop my gaze to the floor.

"I'm sorry if it felt like I was cornering you," he says. "I think I'm just still bitter about . . . this." He gestures vaguely at his black eye. "Want to do something tomorrow? It'll be Saturday, so no classes or work."

He doesn't want me to see Aaron again. I wasn't planning on it, since Aaron is booked up with projects. I shrug, and that's that.

I spend the next hour cleaning up mindlessly, and I don't realize I'm ungloved and unmasked until the tail end of my counter scrubbing. Maybe it's fine. Maybe it doesn't matter that I've been gnawing on my index finger with the hand I was just using to sweep cake crumbs into the trash can.

Naturally, I wake up in the middle of the night racked with tremors, my stomach in knots, my body pulsing like it did when I fell off the chair. My joints hurt. I can't focus on anything, like I'm looking at the world through a disorienting haze. My head is on fire.

I'm sick.

I spend Saturday in bed curled up, falling in and out of sleep while my family hangs around the house. Mom checks on me a few times, sitting on my bed and brushing my hair, clearly attempting to follow through on her wish to be there for me more often. I can't find the energy to hold a conversation, but she doesn't seem to mind. Logan comes to refill my water every so often, which is nice, and Dad brings me a warm compress for my aching abdomen.

I've had hours to think about last night, and I'm realizing I feel more annoyed than guilty. They should've told me they needed these things done in advance. Do I always need to be at their beck and call? Why do they constantly wait until the last minute to text me their needs? I mean, I know why, and it's not intentional, but why can't they try a little harder not to be so scattered?

I get a selfie from Aaron in the middle of the day. He's in his overalls and a pair of safety glasses and gloves. He's holding a trowel up against a wall smeared with plaster and he's captioned it Filling the holes in my heart with your love.

It's so pathetic that I snort with laughter, and briefly, my unyielding pain becomes a distant hum. Wrong number, I respond.

He answers with a picture of a gaping hole in the drywall.

I laugh, then clutch my stomach, wincing. Go back to filling that hole, hole-filler, I order.

Your old catchphrase, he replies.

The reflection of my face in my phone screen is a pitifully vibrant red. Can we not have one nice moment without you reminding the world you're a top? I demand.

Clever, since you are my world, he shoots back. We have our first sleepover in a couple of weeks. You should be prepared.

I told you I draw the line at sex, I text, scowling.

> And I agreed, unless you initiate it. You'll be so infatuated with me by then that you'll be begging for my body, guaranteed.

All you've guaranteed is that I'm never touching any part of you ever again.

I can almost hear him fake sniffling as he types his next message out. Gutting. Anyway, save that second picture. You have more in common with it than you think.

I retch and nearly launch my phone at the wall. I hate Aaron Beckham with a righteous fury.

That doesn't stop me from texting him through the day, our gaps in conversation led by his work or my accidental gluten naps that leave me even more fatigued after I wake from them. I don't tell him I'm sick and in an even worse state now than when I fell. The last thing I need is for him to abandon work again and come flying over while my family is around.

A few days ago, a confrontation with my family would've left me determined to never speak to Aaron again. But things are different. For one, my own actions caused the problem—I willingly went to the carnival. It's not his fault I allowed his persistence to win. And second . . .

I don't feel *that* guilty.

My conversation with Aaron has been nagging me. Despite countering every point he made, certain snippets of conversation keep circulating my ears. My family didn't complain that the party was ruined. Which means that, though they were under a time crunch, they got things done without me. Mom made that dip. Logan brought the chairs and tables up from the basement. Dad organized the liquor. They managed.

It's always been about feeling indebted. But Aaron is implying that I'm not. That whatever is outside my control isn't something I need to make up for. If I ask my parents their thoughts, they'll tell me I'm not a burden and that I owe them nothing. But if that's the case, why do they let me shoulder everything?

I'm starting to see through the bramble cluttering the pathway that led to me moving in with Aaron. I'm not going to willingly abandon my family.

But things are beginning to make more sense.

20

Summers are busy for the Beckhams, so I don't see Aaron nearly as much as I want to over the next couple of weeks. We manage to sneak in two more dates. One is at the aquarium, where I intently read every placard while Aaron presses his face to the glass tanks in awe. We attend a baseball game in the city and eat a hearty lunch beforehand so I'll be too stuffed to feel jealous of everyone eating stadium food. Neither of us cares about sports, but the thing about baseball stadiums is that the vibes are great, and it's overcast, so the sun doesn't cook us alive.

I'm steadily recovering more memories, though they're coming in exasperatingly short flashes. We walk through an underwater glass tunnel at the aquarium, and I have a sudden memory of being here completely alone with him, in which he kissed me vigorously. He can't do that this time—a family of four is behind us, and we don't want to scar them.

At the stadium, I close my eyes and lean against Aaron's shoulder, when I feel heavy rain crashing down around us. I hear screams of delight and shock, the wet sound of sneakers slapping against concrete as people rush for cover, and the crinkling of ponchos. Aaron laughs wildly while I seize his wrist and yank so we can find space under the canopy.

When I open my eyes, the itchy feeling of wet clothes disappears, the clouds are puffy, and the shouting evaporates.

It's not just memories with Aaron that are trickling back. As I wake one morning, I have a hazy vision of being at the American Innovation Museum, where I hear Amy's muffled voice behind me while I study a steam engine lubricator. The next day, I remember peering out at a golf course in late summer from the passenger seat of a cart while my family battles a par 5. Later, I have a memory of sitting at a massive table at Aunt Lydia's, an empty plate in front of me during a holiday dinner.

Most of the memories involve him, though. Quiet, casual moments. His head is in my lap, and he's napping, his hand clutching my knee. He's washing my hair in the shower and teasing me for nodding off while standing up. We're having a picnic in the backyard and battling flies. His tongue is trailing up my thigh, and his excessively long fingers are ringing my knees, holding them open around his shoulders. If we're ever speaking in the flashes, our voices are warbled, like I'm hearing them through a brick wall.

I feel better as the days pass. Sort of. Sometimes my paranoia or exhaustion overtakes me, and I find myself postponing eating until I skip a meal altogether. My bruises from the car accident finally fade, and my unending frailness follows suit. My parents have been making an effort to expand on some of the memories coming back to me, filling in missing details or giving me context so I don't feel as disoriented. Their work hours haven't changed, but they've been in contact with me more frequently about how I'm feeling, and the number of errands they ask me to run has nearly halved.

Aaron's busy schedule doesn't stop him from coming over to harass me every other night by playing the drums against my window. Eventually, I just leave it unlocked so he can invade whenever he wants. His first step is to always pretend like he's my personal masseuse. He starts at my fingers, and I ramble about this or that because I can't stand lying there quietly and letting him massage me like I'm royalty. Sometimes he responds. Sometimes he's evil and sits in silence, smirking at my attempt to disturb the air.

The night always devolves into kissing. I'm coming to understand his preferences. Apparently, he likes to . . . um. Do the work? As in, he prefers when I'm lying there, my legs around his hips and my arms around his neck. Whenever I start feeling bad about how much more he's moving than me, I try rolling him over to take the weight off his arms. He resists every time. If I'm stubborn, he grabs my hands and pins them over my head. Sometimes I pretend I want to roll him just so he'll stop me.

It's sick. *I'm* sick.

Aaron is unbearably mindful. Even when he restrains my hands, he rubs them lightly, keeping the blood and warmth circulating. Even when I don't speak, he can tell when I'm overstimulated because he's so tuned in to the tightness of my muscles. He adjusts his strength to match my level of energy—if I'm lethargic or lightheaded, he's gentler, and keeps more weight off my body. If I'm having a good day, he's faster, more unforgiving with all his fiddling.

I can't resist the intensity of his eyes. The heat of his touch. The smoothness of his skin. He's a handyman—shouldn't he be more rugged and hairy and rough around the edges? His jaw is so clean I can barely feel stubble, and his arms, back, and chest are silky smooth. The only indications of his profession are the calluses on his palms from working with tools and wood.

After kissing, we lie in my bed, talking. At that point, I'm usually too drained to offer much substance, so he spends time catching me up on the past several months. Sometimes he's wrapped fully around me like a blanket. Sometimes he pulls me over him, pressing my cheek to his collarbone so I can hear his elevated heartbeat. Sometimes he settles for facing me on the same pillow, close enough to toy with my hair.

I don't have my memories, but I'm so comfortable around him that it feels like we've picked up where we left off. I'm not stubbornly denying his advances or convincing myself I'm better off without him anymore. It feels nice to be wanted. To be looked at. Prioritized. Held. More than that, though . . .

I like him.

He's funny. He's always fidgeting with his hands like he doesn't know what to do with them when he's not holding tools. He has a different smile for every emotion. He mumbles in his sleep. He looks unfairly good in overalls and bandannas. His hair is soft. And his lips. He knows what he wants. He's spontaneous. Impulsive. Everything I'm not.

Aaron playfully asks me to be his boyfriend every time he comes over, but something keeps me from offering a valid answer. I know it might sound selfish, like I'm stringing him along, but he's made it clear that he doesn't mind my hesitation. In fact, he's giving me time to grow into my feelings. Besides, I can't help but be antsy. Maybe it's

Logan's warnings mixed with my own fear of selfishness—like the moment I say yes, I'll revert to being someone who only looks out for himself.

I blink, and suddenly, my "sleepover date" with Aaron is here. Apparently, his dads go to this annual event at one of the casinos downtown—their single night a year where they splurge and pretend they're rich. They spend one weekend there before returning to their middle-class lives, which means Aaron and I get their house to ourselves. We've been dating for weeks now, but I haven't seen the place. Or I don't remember seeing it.

I'm on edge all day. I weed in the backyard and whack bushes and water the hanging plants. I prepare myself a fiber-rich, gluten-free lunch, because I'm not willing to get sick tonight when I'm preparing for the possibility of maybe saying yes if he asks me to be his boyfriend again. And the thought of being alone with him without prying eyes is enticing. I know we've been intimate. My bedside drawer is proof. I want to ask him what it was like and see if he'll tell me.

Or show me.

The sun is starting to hang more heavily in the sky as I pack my clothes and toiletries into an overnight bag. Logan happens to be walking by and pauses in the doorframe, his brow furrowing. "Where are you off to?" he asks.

"A friend's," I say.

He stays rooted, knowing full well who I'm referring to. "You won't be here for family movie night?"

I frown at him. "What?"

"The second Saturday of every month. We missed the last one

because of the accident, but . . ." He sighs, scratching at his light brown scruff. "I guess that's a more recent thing we started last year, so you wouldn't know."

"Oh," I say, neatly folding a T-shirt into the suitcase.

"We order pizza and have drinks," he adds. "Dad's loosened up over the past year."

"Oh," I repeat, closing the flap and zipping it.

"It's . . ." Logan clears his throat before continuing. "It's fun, hanging with the family without worrying about work. I spiraled pretty hard after what happened last year. I guess you don't remember me hitting rock bottom. I wouldn't come out of my room for days, or eat, or shower. You suggested the movie nights to remind me that my family would always be there for me. It helped. We made it a recurring thing. Though you weren't there the last few months."

I purse my lips, lowering my suitcase from the bed. "Are you trying to make me feel guilty?"

"No. You said you were frustrated because nobody's talking about the past with you. So . . ." Logan scratches at the chipped paint outside my room. "I wanted to tell you."

A rush of shame swirls through me, washing away my annoyance. "You're right," I whisper. "Sorry. That's good to know, genuinely. Thank you."

"You're still picking him, though, yeah?" he mutters.

The annoyance comes reeling back. "We've had plans for weeks," I say sternly. "Movie night wasn't on any calendars. Nobody told me about it before now. I can't drop plans last minute."

To my surprise, Logan nods. "Yeah. I get it. Maybe you can make it to the next one."

He wanders away without another word. I thought he'd take the opportunity to tell me that Aaron only wants me for my undernourished celiac body or something, but maybe he's finally maturing about the whole situation.

Aaron's house is within walking distance, and it's a cool summer evening, and my nerves are on overload, so I decide to take the walk to calm myself. Because Aaron Beckham certainly has *bullying* on his agenda.

And I might have *being bullied* on mine.

21

My brain says I've never been here, but a warm, cozy feeling settles over me as I approach the maroon door of the little ranch house. Like my body is telling me I'm coming home for the first time in a while.

I knock hesitantly, and before I'm finished, it's swinging open. There stands the beefiest, roundest, hairiest man I've ever seen. He's fully bald, but his earthy-brown jaw, neck, arms, and legs are swathed in curly black hair, and his brows are two fuzzy masses.

"Wrong house," I choke out.

"Riley!" His eyes sparkle with excitement, and suddenly, he's seizing my face, wrenching me to my tiptoes, and planting a hefty kiss between my brows. He scoops me up around the shoulders and hauls me and my suitcase inside with one arm, then calls out, "Greg—the favorite is back!"

"What?" a booming voice replies. Squeezing through a distant doorway is the beefiest, roundest, hairiest man I've ever seen. He's not bald, though, and has a full set of highlighted brown hair that blends into his bushy sideburns and scraggly beard.

I'm in a bewildered daze, made worse when he hurries toward us and does the exact same thing the first man did by grabbing my face and kissing my forehead. "Good to see you, angel," he says, clapping my shoulder gently. "How've you been feeling? Aaron been treating you right?"

I don't know how to respond. Aaron's fathers have always been a blurred smear in my mind—blank faces, vague outlines. I figured they'd look like regular suburban dads, not two of the world's most intimidating bears.

"Look at that dead stare," the first guy says, patting my hair, his hand the size of my entire head. "He's terrified."

"What?" I squeak, snapping out of my stupor. "No, I'm sorry, I'm just a little . . ."

"It's okay," the second man says. "We won't beat you up and take your lunch money."

"Not with Aaron right around the corner."

"I'm Greg, or *Dad*," says the bigger, paler one, shaking my limp hand.

"And I'm Antony, or *Pops*," says the bald one, shaking my other limp hand.

"We've been trying to get you to call us by name, but you still only call us *Mr. Beckham*." Greg clicks his tongue in that teasing disappointed way I've seen Aaron mimic. "So formal and polite. Aaron could learn a thing."

"And he has," Antony claims. "That boy was a wildfire. Now he's a semi-responsible adult. Who knew all he needed was a pretty blond boy with a mother's glare to stop acting up?"

I feel like the world is tilting. They're chatting about Aaron so casually, and it's overwhelming, considering my mind is saying this is our first meeting. Still, my brain manages to find space to process their words. Are they really implying Aaron has matured from his troublemaking ways because of me? The thought flushes my cheeks with satisfaction.

"Are you talking shit?" comes another voice, and a head pokes around the drywall from where I assume the kitchen is. Aaron is sporting a gray bandanna that matches his irises and the black dagger earring from the carnival, wagging a kitchen knife around. The sight of it brings back my sense of smell, and I realize the house is permeated with the scent of seasoned meat.

His irritable gaze meets mine, and I swear his entire face starts sparkling. "Sunshine," he says, far more brightly than whatever sunniness he thinks I radiate. "You're early. That excited to see me?"

That earns an eye roll. "I'm punctual," I say shortly, and all of them laugh like I'm joking.

"We'll be out of here in a few minutes," Antony tells us. "Wouldn't want to ruin your romantic evening."

"That taco bar is going to ruin it, if anything," Greg says, massaging his scruffy gray-flecked beard. "Shouldn't you know better than to eat greasy red meat before a night of intimacy?"

"We're not having penetrative sex!" Aaron says, a bit shrilly, and hearing him so frazzled is funny enough to snap me out of my embarrassment.

"We're not?" I ask in mock disappointment, shuffling toward the kitchen, where Aaron is dicing onions. "You mean I don't get to rail you?"

His dads burst into laughter, and in my head, I know talking about this in front of strangers, let alone his family, should be mortifying. But I can feel the house's warmth permeating me, sinking me into a sense of familiar comfort I've never felt before. I'm not sure why—it's not like my family is cold and distant. Maybe it's just the fact that

Aaron told me they've taken extra precautions to keep me from getting sick, like crafting a mini pantry solely for my products and setting aside a counter space dedicated to me. Or because I know they don't want anything out of me.

"I mean, you tried once," Aaron says with a skeptical smile. "You gave up because you kept laughing hysterically. You're welcome to try railing me again if you desire."

That's what gets the flames of humiliation rising. I want to claim he's lying, but envisioning myself absolutely *giving it* to Aaron Beckham makes me instantly giggly, so he's probably not.

Aaron's dads finish packing their suitcases and take off. On their way out, Antony rumples my hair, bends down, and speaks softly so only I can hear him.

"You can come home whenever you want, Riley. Anytime, any day, no questions asked."

The kindness in his voice wells up my eyes with tears, and I have to frantically blink them away. "Thanks," I mumble.

Then they're gone, and it's just Aaron and me. I re-familiarize myself with the house—it's cute in this purposefully archaic way, with lots of wood paneling on the floors, walls, and ceiling beams. The windows are gaping, allowing sunlight to streak and vein through the house, warming the floorboards. They have a cobblestone fireplace that would make everything extra cozy in the winter. There are three bedrooms—a primary suite, Aaron's room (judging by the worktable cluttered with wooden blocks and tools), and a guest room equipped with a twin bed, nightstand, and desk.

"Yours," Aaron's voice says in my ear.

I arch my head back, and he responds with a kiss to my brow. "I didn't stay in your room?"

"You like your space. Though you never let me hang up decor and paint it. You kept insisting it was short-term—that staying here was an experiment to see what life was like outside of your family. You tried to avoid getting too comfortable." He smirks. "My dads still made you a desk anyway, so you'd have someplace to study for freshman year."

"That's very sweet. And totally unnecessary." I offer a small, teasing smile, and say, "I guess I'll be in here tonight, then?"

I expect he'll make a quip demanding how we'll both fit on that bed, but he merely says, "If that's what you'd like."

He didn't take the bait. I try again, because the "flirting" thing is new to me, but sort of fun. "I'll probably get too cold in here," I protest. "Might have to find somewhere else to sleep."

He should respond with something like *My arms are always available* or *I happen to have some room in my bed*. He says, "Wherever you'll be comfortable."

Hmm. I take the straightforward route. "I want to sleep in your bed." Because I do. He's warm and always knows how to position himself to maximize our skin contact so I won't get cold.

He says, "I'm glad."

Okay, then.

His arms slink around my waist from behind, and I want to snippily ask why he thinks he can be so handsy off the bat. Now that we're this close, though, something feels different. Off. He's sagging against me, like he's struggling to hold up his weight. His arms hug me more desperately than sensually. The corners of his eyes are tinted pink.

I turn into his chest to properly see him. His arms remain rooted around me, hands locking at the small of my back. "What's wrong?" I ask.

Aaron blinks in bewilderment, his eyes flitting between mine before he abruptly turns his back to me. "Nothing," he says. "The taco bar is done—want to eat now? We watched *Dunkirk* during our first sleepover, so I have it pulled up."

"Another historical movie?" I ask skeptically, following him to the kitchen. I won't push yet.

"I was really into you," Aaron says, grinning sheepishly.

"You must still be, if you're willing to watch it twice and let me ramble about historical accuracies."

"I just like the sound of your voice," he admits, and I get this soft, fuzzy feeling in my stomach. I approach the counter, where Aaron has prepared a slew of toppings—onions, tomatoes, lettuce, cilantro, salsa, and sour cream. "All gluten-free," he says, slapping a corn tortilla onto my plate.

"I know," I say, spooning ground beef into my taco. "I trust you."

Aaron watches me make up a plate before creating his own. The sun is low enough that golden light shoots sideways through the window, bathing the house in an ethereal glow. Aaron has layered blankets in front of their mounted TV, so I take my place to his right, leaning back against the couch cushions.

As we watch, Aaron starts slumping, and his eyes are glazing, like his thoughts are drifting away. He's clearly bothered, and knowing this distracts me through the end of the movie.

"Next we played board games while drinking wine," he says. He's working the cogs and wheels of his gadget toy, his fingers quivering. "I won most of them, but maybe you'll get lucky. Oh, but you don't have to drink if you're not comfortable. Then we baked gluten-free brownies and iced them. Afterward, I'll start the firepit—"

"Aaron?"

He stops, peeking down at me. I push on his folded knees until his legs are stretched out flat, then sling myself over them and center my weight on his thighs. I hold his face steady in my palms—a method he uses against me when he doesn't want me to look away. My stern expression startles him. "What?" he asks.

"Something's bothering you," I tell him. "You shouldn't push through this night and pretend everything is okay because you don't want to disappoint me."

Aaron looks utterly baffled. His blank stare might normally make me laugh, but he's clearly hurting. "Getting your memories back . . . that's the priority," he says, his voice small and weak. The sound of it makes me want to curl him up and tuck him into my chest. "I won't ruin that because I'm in a bad mood."

"My memories aren't a priority," I say sharply. "This moment is. Here. Now. A relationship should be balanced—you can't go above and beyond for me when I'm hurting, then keep me from doing the same when you're hurting."

Aaron studies me in that meticulous, intense way I can't stand, but this isn't a conversation I'm willing to duck my head for. His lips twitch up at the corners. "Relationship?" he whispers.

I open my mouth but close it just as quickly. Shoot. I wasn't planning on springing that on him. "I'm just saying this is a two-way street, so if I can't hide how I'm feeling, you shouldn't hide how you're feeling," I snap. "Just because I'm dealing with things doesn't mean your pain hurts any less."

Aaron doesn't respond for a while. It's torturous. I'm not sure if he's thinking intently or if he's doing this to embarrass me. If he likes anything about me, it's how I look when I'm flustered, so I wouldn't be surprised.

Finally, he grasps my chin. "Despite how much you've changed, you're still the same," he says softly. "You're so relentlessly kind and considerate of others. You make me want to be better."

"You're already a good person," I try to say, but he shakes his head.

"I was a selfish brat for years. Borderline cruel. Whenever I met with my mother, I'd leave feeling so guilty that I would act out and make myself everyone else's problem. I wanted people to be angry with me. Especially my dads. Because then there was a reason. A logical explanation for why she didn't want me."

His palms spread over the backs of mine. He lowers them from his face so he can fiddle with my cold fingertips instead of his gadget toy.

"You've helped me learn how not to take my mother's disinterest so personally," he says, quietly enough that I strain to hear him. "That it must've taken all her strength to put me in this situation—this better, kinder, more loving situation—and that acting out in bitterness was disrespecting everything she went through to get me here."

His eyelids are sagging. I keep silent, letting him stroke my fingers.

"I really was . . . not good, Riley." He draws another long, winded breath. "I'm in a better place now than last year. Sometimes I have bad thoughts. Sometimes I still get frustrated and want to cave to it. To get into trouble and see what I can get away with. Or even better—get caught and piss people off. Before you, someone pandered to me. They made me feel like my actions were justified."

My heart sinks into the bottom of my stomach. "Logan?"

He nods. "I excited him. I had a crush on him, too, and wanted to impress him. I think he just tried to make me feel seen and heard, so he never argued with my thought processes or actions. He was in a sort of 'let him do what he wants, so long as I'm there to stop him from going too far' mindset. That's how it was at first, anyway. Until . . ."

Aaron pauses. His jaw grinds, like he's crunching up words in his mouth.

"Anyway." He smirks, his eyes falling fully shut. "Then things fell apart, and suddenly, there was someone else. They didn't sit and watch while I self-destructed. They put up roadblocks. They made me *think*. I wasn't used to it. It irritated me."

"I bet you regretted making me date you early on, huh?" I ask with an apologetic smile he doesn't see.

"Maybe," he says with a short laugh. "I wasn't used to being challenged. I should've expected it. You were always in the background, wagging your finger around. Your parents didn't like me, but the furthest they went in keeping me away was getting that alarm system installed to make sure Logan wasn't sneaking out. Otherwise, you were the only person who actively tried getting in my way. Naturally, that didn't stop just because we started dating."

I lean against his shoulder so my nose is buried in the crook of his neck. He smells faintly of cologne. And wood. Predictable. "Did something happen, Aaron?" I ask.

Aaron slings his arms around my waist, squeezing me into his chest, crushing my palms between us. "Saw my mom last night," he whispers. "She was . . . not good. I'm not sure if she was high, but she clearly wasn't all there. She asked me more about myself than she ever has before, though, and there was this sick part of me . . ."

He chokes on the words, his arms firming around me.

"I wished I could see her like that more often. But her sudden interest and energy wasn't from getting better. Her face was so sunken. She was jittery. I didn't know what to do. I'm not sure what to tell my dads, if it's even their business. So when I got home last night, I just laid in bed spiraling and feeling guilty."

"Did you sleep at all?" I ask.

"No."

"I'm sorry, Aaron."

"It's okay."

"It's not. It's okay that it's not."

"Mm."

"Do you want to talk about your options?"

"No. Not tonight." Something wet rolls off his jawline and onto my forehead. I don't bother opening my eyes or brushing it away. "Sorry for ruining the mood."

"Don't say something like that," I murmur, fingers curling into his shirt. "A date is meant for two people to spend time together. That's what we're doing, isn't it?"

"I wanted this to be as fun and romantic as the first night you spent here," he says, frustration bleeding into his voice. "It was the first time I ever saw you laugh hard enough to cry. I was going to shove gluten-free flour in your face during the baking, like last time, and then it was going to turn into a war. And then kissing. I was going to turn on music so we could drunkenly slow dance to it. Then we were going to wash the flour off each other and enjoy the firepit. Then go to bed together."

"Well, we can do all that when we're in higher spirits," I say, pulling my face out of his neck to lean my forehead against his. When he feels the skin contact, his tired, wet eyes reluctantly open to meet mine. "Why don't we skip to the *go to bed* part?"

"It's eight o'clock," he protests.

"And you're falling asleep on the floor."

"What would you even do?"

"Stare at you while you sleep," I say seriously.

He huffs. "You'll get bored."

"Your face is too pretty to bore me," I counter, smiling.

He returns my smile, his own fragile. "Then let's go brush our teeth. Just in case I want to kiss you."

"But we're just going to bed," I say scoldingly as I follow him into the bathroom, bringing my toiletry bag with me. I smear my toothbrush with mint paste, wet it, and jam it into my mouth, glaring up at him. "Right?"

"Right, which is why you're currently scrubbing every crevice in your mouth with extreme violence," he says.

I scowl, spit the toothpaste out, then storm away, only 80 percent minty fresh.

I think he'll kiss me anyway.

22

I showered before coming over, and apparently Aaron did shortly before cooking dinner, so we don't need to wash before getting into bed. I change into a crewneck and stretchy pants, while Aaron flops on his back, removing nothing but his bandanna. "Too tired to change?" I ask, propping myself on the mattress's edge beside him, then swirling my fingers through his soft black hair.

Aaron smirks and catches my wrist, then hoists me over him, until his lips are brushing mine. "I don't change," he says. "I just take my clothes off. But I was kind of hoping you'd do that."

His proximity and words are a double whammy to my heart, which thrums faster. "Getting handsy requires stamina," I say coolly. "Which you clearly don't have right now. Go to sleep."

His eyes brighten. "You're saying we could get handsy if I had the stamina?"

"I'm saying you should sleep, brat."

Aaron grins, though I can already see exhaustion overcoming him, glazing his eyes. "Sleep on me?" he whispers, pulling more firmly on my wrist, until I'm nearly splayed out over him.

"I won't be too heavy?" I ask nervously.

He snickers in response. Sighing, I maneuver myself on top of him, trying to distribute my weight so I'm not crushing any part of him. I pull the blankets over us and nestle my head sideways under his chin. His arms slide around me, one fumbling under my shirt to trace my back, the other scratching through my hair. The sensation is relaxing, pleasant, but . . .

"I should be doing this for you," I say amusedly, my eyes fluttering shut.

"Doing what?"

"Rubbing your back, combing your hair . . . I'm not the one needing comfort."

"This is comforting," he says gently, his fingertips toying with the nape of my neck. "Having your weight on me. Making you feel safe and relaxed makes me feel the same way."

I'm quiet for a moment, digesting this. It seems wrong. I've probably told him that before. "You said it's that way for other things, too," I mumble.

"Yeah. Providing makes me feel good. The problem is that you don't like to receive. Or you do, but you feel guilty about it. Like right now."

I wince, but cover it by nuzzling deeper into his chest.

"You've always felt like you're never enough," Aaron says, fingers rolling over the bumps rising along my neck. "You don't need to earn anything from me. I want you to accept it because I want to give it. Not because I need something in return. That was an issue between us for a while."

I pop my brows. "How so?"

"You accused me of love bombing," he admits, sounding sheepish. "You weren't used to being put first, so you figured I had bad intentions. It was around the time I told you some criticisms I had about your family, and you thought I was trying to isolate you."

I lift my head to look more properly at him, uncertainty gnawing at me. I can't say I haven't considered that. He tells me he loves me repeatedly, he bought me everything I wanted at the carnival, he's interrupted my schedule to spend time with me, and he's been trying to convince me to distance myself from my family. On paper, they're red flags. And I'm the perfect prey for that behavior because I'm an awkward people pleaser with low self-esteem.

But Aaron has never made me feel like I owe him. He's never tried to win an argument by telling me how much he's done for me. His compliments are sometimes sweeping and overwhelming, but he's gotten over a year to know me, and I don't want to hold his affections against him just because I don't remember how we got here. He texts me a lot, but he's not accusatory if I forget to respond. He's never tried rushing me into my feelings. I'm not nervous or scared around him.

"I don't think you're love bombing me," I say out loud in case he needs to hear it. "I'm not sure why I felt that way. I'm sorry."

"Don't apologize." Aaron reaches up, stroking my cheek with the backs of his fingers. "Your body's comfort around me probably helps the *current* you feel this way. At the time, you still didn't fully trust me, and you didn't understand why I was so eager to be there for you. I couldn't understand why you wouldn't accept anything I offered. We were frustrated. It's the closest we came to breaking up."

I listen to this in fascination and bewilderment. "How did we fix it?" I ask.

"I started *actually* love bombing you so you could see the difference—"

"Shut up," I say with a grin, flicking his nose.

He sighs, like the remembrance is taxing. "You needed space, so I gave you space. While you were dealing with that, I was trying to figure out if we were in a good enough mindset to be in a relationship. Because we're both sort of . . ." He screeches to a stop.

"Careful," I warn, and then it's his turn to flick my nose.

"Let's go with *emotionally wounded*," he decides.

I shrug. "Dramatic for my situation, but I'll give you a pass."

He gives me a smile that brinks on exasperation. "I determined my life was better with you in it," he whispers. "That so long as we weren't hurting each other, we could be a healthy couple. We're both the self-destructive type. You block yourself off. I get reckless. In that time apart, we realized how well we balance each other."

"Did we, now?" I ask, eyeing him with feigned suspicion.

"When you'd hole up, I'd drag you out scratching and clawing," he says. "When I tried running off and being irresponsible, you threw a leash out and clotheslined me. You see? Balance."

"I guess," I say, sounding dubious.

He grins a bit hungrily and draws me fully down to press a minty kiss to my mouth. "Why are you provoking me when you're the one who said I should sleep?" he breathes.

"You're the one holding me prisoner," I say huffily.

He kisses me again, lingering longer before tugging me up by the hair. "We came away from it stronger," he says, redirecting the subject, and the fact that he didn't take the opportunity to change it warms my chest. "I know it's weird hearing me talk about it without your memories. But I hope you know . . . or maybe feel in your heart . . . that I won't ever intentionally hurt you. That I *do* love you. That . . ." Aaron pauses, then says, "That it's not an act."

I initiate the kiss this time. I squeeze his strong jaw between my fingers and lean down, lips parted, to meet his. He exhales slow through his nose, his lashes fluttering like he's been starved of these moments. "It's strange hearing my thoughts and reactions from someone else," I admit. "But my heart trusts you, so I'm letting my mind follow."

"And the rest of you?" His fingers carve another trail down the back of my neck.

I roll my eyes, but my pulse quickens anyway. "Didn't you scream at your dads that we weren't having sex?"

"Penetrative," he tacks on. "There are other kinds. But I'd understand if it feels too soon."

The issue is that it doesn't. It seems so ludicrous that I'd willingly take this step when my brain says I haven't known him personally longer than a month. But I'm attracted to him in this carnal way I can't comprehend. "You said you're a service top." I swallow, hating how consistently hot my face is around him. "That means you take charge or something?"

Aaron's eyes sparkle at my willingness to discuss it. I can't stand how pretty they are. I want to be swallowed up by his stare. "I do," he says, "but I use that term because I focus more on how my partner feels than myself. Like, I only feel good if I know you feel good."

He sounds so earnest, not at all teasing. I shift my jaw, wondering if I should cut the conversation. But it's fine, right? Two people in a sort-of relationship talking about intimacy? "What about me makes you want to be like that?" I ask weakly.

"I wasn't sure at first," he says, still stroking my back. "You were just so unsure of yourself and wouldn't take initiative. You clearly wanted intimacy, but you were so shy and wishy-washy about it. It was funny to me." He takes a moment to collect his memories. "Eventually, I started to understand how your mind worked."

"Meaning?"

"Through trial and error, I realized that you like being taken care of. Nobody's done that for you, so I think the idea was attractive to you. You wouldn't admit it, though, because you have a phobia of doing anything that might possibly be considered selfish."

I scoff, steering my eyes away. "Receiving without giving *is* selfish," I mutter.

"That's where the misunderstanding is," Aaron says calmly. "You're satisfying me by letting yourself be satisfied, sunshine. That was hard for you to wrap your head around. At some point, getting you to feel anything other than guilt was such an accomplishment that the thought of it started turning me on. I wanted to do everything I could to see that rare side of you that was too distracted to worry about being selfish."

The casualness of this conversation is making me sweat. Aaron's hand cups the back of my neck and pulls me in closer.

"Are you uncomfortable?" he whispers. "I don't mean to pressure you."

"No, I'm fine," I squeak, burying my face into his shirt. "It's just weird, not remembering."

"I know." His hand on my spine creeps low enough to tickle my waistband, before drawing up again. He's been following the same trail up and down my back for a while. "Is there anything you want to know about the past fifteen months? About me?"

I consider it, lulled by the steady rise and fall of his chest. I might fall asleep before he does. "What do you want your life to look like in ten years?" I ask, with just enough of a job-interview intonation that he laughs.

"I'm living in the countryside with a massive lawn where I can let my golden retriever and black Lab run loose," he says, and suddenly, he's rolling. I make a disgruntled noise of surprise as he sprawls me on my back, then braces his arms around me, hovering, his face inches away. "The house is big with lots of natural light. It's an old fixer-upper. The kind that'll keep me busy. I have a Harley in the garage and take my partner for rides when the sky is clear. I cook him dinner every night and give him massages and whittle him wooden ducks. I let him fall asleep on me in the bathtub and make him pay for it later. I'm financially stable and still hot."

He's given it a lot of thought. Maybe discovering that he's planned a future for us after a year of dating should be concerning, but I'm mostly stirred from the fact that he sees one with me at all. "You'll need a room just for the wooden ducks to live in," I say.

"I'll build one."

I smile skeptically. He eases down, allowing part of his weight to lean against me.

"What about your next ten years?" he asks softly.

I try to envision it. Last month, I would've said I'd have a computer science degree and be making big money in cybersecurity or something. I'd be living in a house close enough to my parents that I could be nearby to help when needed.

Is that what I really want, though?

"I hope I'm living somewhere quiet," I murmur. "In a big house with a lot of wood and windows, where the sun rises in the bedroom and sets in the living room. It has a big couch I could cuddle with a cat on. Or my boyfriend. Someone who will take me to all my bucket list museums in Chicago and listen to me talk about dull things. Someone who cooks me dinner if I'm too tired and gives me massages if he's not busy and whittles me wooden ducks until he gets bored of it. He lets me fall asleep on him in the bathtub and doesn't harass me about it later. I'm financially stable and my body is stronger."

It's difficult to resist his stare when he's inches from me, his dark hair tickling my forehead. The tips of his black lashes are glittering. "I'll make it happen," he whispers. "Because I want to. Because I love you."

My lip shivers, so I chomp down on it. "Thank you," I say quietly. "For bothering to love me."

He kisses the tremor away. When his hands rise along my rib cage, pushing up the edges of my crewneck so it bunches around my chest, a familiar self-consciousness settles over me. I don't want him to see.

But he's staring at me like I'm unblemished marble.

Reluctantly, I allow him to slide the crewneck off, exposing my upper half fully. He takes me in for a moment, like he's never seen my thin skin and poke-y rib cage before, then nestles down into the crook of my neck, kissing me slowly beneath my ear. I'm not sure how a sensation can be both cozy and stimulating, but it is. The longer his lips linger, the safer I feel, and the quicker my heart thrums.

I find the top button of his shirt and fumble with it, my apprehension heightening. I spend ten seconds on it before Aaron's hands come up over mine, guiding them through the motion. The first button pops. The second. The third. Soon, they're all undone, and by then, his mouth is at the hollow of my throat, which he works lightly with his tongue. The feeling is too much, so I scrunch my hands into the bedspread, trying to center myself.

"You can touch, you know," Aaron says. "And—by the way—I like when you scratch, so don't think it's a problem."

The blood in my head and neck boils hot. "Why would I scratch you?" I squeak.

"You get overstimulated quickly. You use your stubby nails to deal with it."

I grind my jaw. "I won't hurt you."

"I'm telling you it's okay. I like it." He pauses to unfurl my fists in the bedspread, which I've been clinging to for dear life, and pulls up, spreading my hands beneath the edges of his open shirt. Instinctively, I push the sides back, and it flutters off his shoulders, sliding down his arms and off his wrists. "See? Not so hard, right?" he asks with a knowing wink.

I grimace, my hands rooted on his warm, solid collarbone. I'm not sure why today feels different, or why the thought of touching him freely is more intimidating than before. Maybe because I knew there were limits I wasn't willing to pass. Mental boundaries. Today, though, I only have one.

"I don't want to do the insertion stuff," I blurt.

Aaron lifts his head and blinks at me. My face steams hotter.

"Sorry," I choke out. "I just. Um. I'm not sure how often we do that, but I . . . I don't think I'm prepared for that . . . mentally or physically . . ."

"It's okay," Aaron says with a small, understanding smile that eases my sudden tension. "That type of sex is rare for us, anyway."

"It is?" My eyes widen. "Why?"

He shrugs. "You're a nervous person."

"So?"

"So you tend to get in your head about things."

"Like what?"

"You often worry you're not going to . . . do a good job," he says, picking his words carefully. "Or that something might go wrong bodily function–wise. You usually initiate it, but when it starts happening, you have a hard time relaxing. Knowing you're struggling to get comfortable turns me off, so we don't always go all the way."

"I initiate?" I ask faintly. "Does that mean you don't like it?"

Aaron laughs, and even though it's not at my expense, it solidifies my humiliation. "I'm a fan," he admits. "But all I care about is you, so I don't suggest it unless you do. Sometimes it works out. More often it doesn't. I don't mind either way—it's not the only avenue, you know?"

I think I'm going to explode. I grab the pillow beside me and slam it over my face, cooling myself on its surface. "Oh," I say, voice muffled.

"Then, since you brought it up again, can you tell me what you do want?" Aaron asks, sounding unbearably amused. "Or if there's something else you want to avoid?"

"Do whatever," I mutter, because I can't continue with this conversation.

"What? Can't hear you."

"Yes, you can, asshole."

"Ooh. A swear." Aaron returns to kissing my collarbone. I can feel his lingering grin. "Then, since you've given me permission, I'll do whatever."

He hooks his finger around the waistband of my stretchy pants and drags downward, slow enough that I could stop him. I don't, though I keep the pillow secured snugly over my face. I don't expect to feel his lips to follow, grazing my navel, leaving soft pecks around my waist. His hands massage the outsides of my thighs, and I claw desperately into the pillow to avoid squirming.

He toys with the elastic of my boxers as he kisses back up the center of my abdomen, my chest, my collarbone, until he's nipping under my chin. I breathe out with relief, but the feeling doesn't last, because then he's fitting his waist between my legs, and I realize he's only wearing boxers. "Do you need to hide your face?" he asks.

"Deal with it," I snip.

His hands ring around my knees, and he folds them up, deliberately slow. I feel his mouth work along my thighs, and I reach down to straighten the edges of my boxer shorts, but he catches my wrist. Without a word, he slides my palm through his hair and roots it on the back of his head.

That night, I learn that even the deepest layers of physical and emotional fatigue can't stop Aaron Beckham from getting what he wants.

And I learn that I don't really mind.

Aaron wears me out and then collapses like a sack of bricks into his pillow, falling into a deep, fitful slumber. I'm still short of breath, racked with tremors, and crimson in the face as I lay snug under his arm, listening to his slow exhales against the top of my head. I wonder how often we slept like this before the accident. I had my own room, but how frequently did I sleep in my bed? Did I used to sneak over here and curl up with him?

I like this place. Being here feels right. It's warm and comfortable, and my anxiety is a faraway echo. I don't think I'd get sick here. I'm not worrying about whether someone moved something in the pantry and kicked up flour onto my gluten-free ingredients. I'm not worried that my food might've been made with the wrong utensils and frying pans. Aaron's dads have clearly been treating me like a second son.

You can come home whenever you want, Riley. Anytime, any day, no questions asked.

His father's words have been reverberating in my head and stirring my stomach. I don't know that I'd so readily move back in after visiting this place once, but it's nice not having to worry. It's nice not to be thinking about errands.

As I cool down, I maneuver Aaron's arm so I can grab my phone on the nightstand and find the family group chat. He curls more tightly around me. His legs slide between mine, and his inhale is deep, like he enjoys the scent of my shampoo. "Stay," he mumbles in his sleep.

I snuggle deeper into his chest. Maybe a conversation is worth having with my family. Maybe I could start with sleeping over here once a week or something. To recharge. To get some of that "space" Aaron keeps saying I need. So I type out a message.

> Hi! Can you guys be available to talk after dinner? I'll make something good. Thanks!

I hit send.

Logan reads it immediately and doesn't respond.

I tuck my phone away and fall asleep.

23

"You're really considering it?" Aaron's gray eyes are bright enough to blind me.

"Don't get carried away," I warn, munching on a gluten-free waffle as I pull my shirt over my head and wrench a new pair of boxers and shorts to my waist. "Last night, I was thinking about what you said. How these house responsibilities have just sort of fallen to me. I still think it's justified, but I also think maybe they could help in the fall when I go to school. You know?"

"Right." Aaron practically skips over to me to plant a wet kiss on my forehead. He's not good at hiding his excitement. Clearly, he's hoping this is the first step of many that will lead me to his front door with all my belongings.

I have things to do, so I pack up and get going before I can feel too cozy and spend another day in laziness. It's muggy and gray outside—storm clouds swirl overhead, sagging but not buckling.

"I'll drive you home," Aaron says, but I shake my head.

"It's a ten-minute walk. I've been trying to strengthen my legs, so I'll be fine. And my suitcase is waterproof."

He gives me a frustrated look. "I'll walk with you, then."

"That's a waste of time."

"It's not, since I get to spend it with you."

I roll my eyes and decide not to tell him I'd rather my family doesn't see him with me when I'm coming up the sidewalk. "Thanks for the taco bar and letting me spend the night," I say. "And for conversations. Even if I was awkward."

"You're always awkward," he says with a pleasant smile, to which I scowl and push his shoulders. He snags my wrists and hoists them up around his neck, pulling me onto my tiptoes. "You're welcome. Thank you for not letting me bury my feelings."

"You should tell me when you're having a bad day," I say sternly.

"Why waste the time when you seem to know immediately?" he asks.

I glare at him. His smile widens, and he kisses my nose.

"I'm working on it, okay?" he says, softer. "Good luck with your family meeting. Text me when it's done so I know how . . ."

His attention wanders over my head, and his gentle expression hardens into stone. His eyes flash with rage and his jaw juts through his pale skin. Frowning, I turn around.

Logan is at the foot of the driveway, leaning against his borrowed car, arms folded over his wide chest. He's watching us, but he's not glaring or seething. Rather, he looks exhausted. His eyes are carved with purple bags, and his skin is as unhealthily pale as mine typically is.

"The hell do you want?" Aaron demands.

I slide my arms away from his neck and give him a warning look, to which he huffs but stays put on the front step. I take a few steps toward Logan's car, but he startles me by beelining forward, his fists clenched. Immediately, Aaron abandons his position to slide in front of me protectively.

"I'm here to talk to Riley," Logan says coolly.

"You can't show up on my doorstep with your fists out," Aaron snaps, though he allows me to nudge him aside.

"What's so important that you couldn't call?" I ask, furrowing my brow. "I was about to come home. How long have you been out here?"

"Your message." He draws his phone out and shakes it, lips pursed. "You're moving back in with him. You want to meet so you can tell us, right?"

"That's not true," I say, but he's already talking over me.

"This is my fault for not being honest." Logan takes another step forward, and Aaron's muscles snap tight. Logan notices and stays put, about eight feet from us. "I'm not sure why I thought warnings were enough. I just didn't think it would all be this *fast*. I thought I had more time to come up with a way to convince you not to damn yourself."

His words used to make me twinge with guilt. Now, a few measly weeks later, they do nothing but aggravate me. "Just because you have a grudge doesn't mean Aaron is a horrible person," I say sharply. "We can all change. He clearly has."

"Then has he told you the truth?" Logan asks.

"About what?"

"Your relationship."

I stare at him in frustrated bewilderment. In my periphery, Aaron's face drains of whatever little color he has. He curls his fingertips into his thighs, like he wants to scratch through his jeans.

"I've been quiet because Aaron's got dirt on me, too," Logan says, shooting Aaron a fearsome look before returning his attention to me. The sight causes my heart to pump faster.

"What *dirt*?" I demand.

"The trespassing arrest was my fault," Logan says flatly. "I convinced Aaron to break us into the theater so I could get you gluten-free candy without buying it. And times before that when we got in trouble . . . the last year or so before our friendship died. Aaron was leveling out. Drawing back because his dads got him into counseling. At that point, I was enjoying the fact that Mom and Dad were looking at me, so I didn't *want* him to change."

I feel like the world is blurring. I don't know how to react. I can barely process one sentence before he's flying into the next.

"You know how hard it is to get Mom and Dad to slow down and look at us," Logan says, his stare unblinking. "At the end of the day, they might have ten minutes to offer us. Do you know where those ten minutes go between the two of us, Riley?"

"I . . . I don't under—"

"You," he snaps. "It's you. Because of your health issues. If Mom and Dad have ten minutes, you get nine of them. They want to make sure you're feeling okay. They want to thank you for running their errands and for gluing the house together. It's been that way for *years*. I was . . . I am . . . invisible." Logan swallows loudly. "I was getting sick of it. I wanted to make them look at me. For fucking *once* before college, I wanted attention. I knew Aaron liked me at that point and used it to my advantage. When he wanted to hang out, I'd convince him to steal his dad's bike so we could take a joyride, or sneak us into the school so we could cause problems . . . or break into a theater."

Every word makes me feel a little more ill. I'm gnawing hard enough on my index finger to make it throb. "That's horrible," I whisper.

Logan winces. He inhales shakily through his nose before continuing. "I held on to this because I knew you had a certain image of me," he says. "Straight-A student. Full-ride scholarship to a good university. An athlete. You thought Aaron corrupted me. You didn't blame me for anything because you had such a high opinion of me. When we were arrested, it was worse than anything that had happened in the past. I got scared that you would find out I was behind it. And you'd hate me."

Logan grinds his jaw, scrunching his eyes shut like he's seeking the will to continue. Aaron just stands there. Silent. Stiff. His face is uncharacteristically stoic.

"So I blamed Aaron," Logan says breathily. "I let you believe he was the reason I lost my full ride. I smeared his name. Told everyone that he tainted me and that we should've never been friends. He got pissed."

There's this raw aching expanding through my stomach. My heart has been throbbing fiercely in my ears, but suddenly, it's slowing down. Like it wants to stop time to keep Logan from continuing.

"Aaron hated you," Logan snaps, his voice rising. "We used to bitch about how you'd always nag us and get between us. He knew I was protective of you, though, even when I found you irritating. He knew how important my image was. That you saw me as this perfect brother who got caught up with the wrong person. So he decided to use you to get revenge."

"Stop," I try to say, but the word lodges in my throat.

"He knew you were attracted to him, the same way I knew he was attracted to me," Logan says. His eyes are becoming bloodshot and desperate. "He decided he'd seduce you. Make you feel special and wanted. And then, when you fell for him, he'd shatter your heart and dump you in the trash for me to find and pick up the pieces. When he crawled through your window and you agreed to date him to keep him off my back, he told me his plans. He said if I warned you, he'd spill everything about the past year to you. How I'm the one who fucked my future, how I manipulated him to get us into bad situations for attention. I didn't want your image of me to crack. So I . . ."

Logan breaks into a tremble. I stare at Aaron.

"I tried telling you," he says. "We were coming home after helping Aunt Lydia move some furniture around. I explained everything in the car, because I thought you'd walk away from the conversation if we were somewhere else. We were in our neighborhood. You were angry and wanted to hear Aaron's side. You took off your seat belt and tried unlocking the door so you could get out and walk to his place. I was so distracted trying to calm you down that I . . . I didn't see the stop sign."

Logan pauses to breathe. I stare at Aaron.

"I should've immediately re-explained things when you woke up. But I thought maybe all I had to do was try to keep you away from him. Obviously, it didn't work. He's got his claws in you again. Maybe his intentions changed, but he obviously still emotionally manipulated you into leaving us so he could have you to himself. So I . . ."

He lowers his head, his lashes wet with tears.

"I wanted to tell you the truth before you tried to leave again," he chokes out. "I'm sorry."

I'm still staring at Aaron. Waiting. He won't look at me, but his face is a sickly gray, and the sparkle in his eyes is dead. I know the answer, but I ask anyway.

"It's true?"

A muscle twinges in his locked jaw. Silence hangs in the air for several seconds as he finds his voice. It's drizzling now, matting his hair to his forehead. He whispers, "I wasn't a good person, Riley."

I nod, my thoughts fuzzy, my mind echoing. I taste blood, and I realize I've chewed open my index finger again. "When were you going to tell me?" I ask.

"Riley—"

"Never?"

He falls silent, his eyes sliding shut.

"So, then." I twist toward Logan, whose face is flushed. "You decided I was better off broken than thinking negatively about you?"

He rips his stare away from mine. The gray asphalt is darkening under the fattening raindrops.

"You decided," I try again, "as my 'protective' older brother, to let me get my heart shattered so you wouldn't have to fess up? Is that right?"

Suddenly, tears are grating down his tan cheeks. "I'm sorry," he breathes.

I return my eyes to Aaron. "So you felt bad for me somewhere along the way." My voice is thick and stilted—I can't find the air in my lungs. I can't hear myself think. "I looked so pitiful to you that you realized you'd feel guilty for breaking me."

"No," Aaron says, his face contorting with desperation. "That's not—"

"It is," I say. "You felt bad because you found out how difficult my life can be. You lost interest in hurting me. I was already invested, though, so you kept playing along, probably hoping I'd break up with you at some point so you wouldn't have to do it yourself. Then you accidentally fell in love. Does that sound right?"

Aaron's staring at me like I reached into his chest and crushed his heart into dust. "Riley," he whispers. "Falling in love with you was never an accident."

"But liking me was." It's fully raining now, but I don't feel the drops hitting my forehead.

"I wasn't a good person. I didn't want you to know . . . how cruel I used to be."

I hear myself laugh dryly. "But sitting on this information isn't cruel?" I demand. "You planned to whisk me off one day to a fixer-upper in the countryside without me ever knowing that the only reason I didn't get my heart broken is because you started pitying me? Do you even actually love me? Or do you just feel so guilty that you've been treating me well to make up for it?"

"It wasn't pity, Riley," Aaron says sharply, his voice strained. "I love you. In every way. Please . . . can we talk about this inside?"

"I'm good," I say, seizing my suitcase handle and dragging it down the driveway, my body one tingling ball of numbness. I should probably feel a lot right now, but it's mostly nothing. My thoughts should be racing, but my head is empty.

"Let me drive you home," Logan pleads, reaching for me, but I evade his grip.

"You're worse," I tell him. "Don't talk to me."

"I know, but please don't walk home in the—"

"You didn't care to save me from getting hurt, so don't pretend you care about my clothes getting wet," I say flatly, muscling past him.

I drag my suitcase home in the pouring rain.

24

My memories are choosing a very inconvenient time to come back.

They hit me like numerous punches to my head back-to-back, a new one surfacing whenever I stride past another driveway. I'm reading a book for the history club, leaned against Aaron's legs and occasionally offering unnecessary two cents while he plays video games. We're slow dancing in the kitchen, covered in flour, our faces flushed from laughter, the smell of brownies wafting through the air. I'm squeezing his waist and shrieking with terror on the back of his dad's motorcycle at midnight while he races down open roads.

I'm touring that campus with him, hand in hand, led by Amy Choi while he points out the quaint little pockets I could study in. I'm yelling at him for being reckless after he fell off his roof and sprained his wrist. I'm letting him do unholy things to me in the bed of his pickup truck atop layers of blankets. I'm flipping pancakes in the Beckham kitchen, listening to his dads bicker about an upcoming project. I'm pinning a flower to the lapel of Aaron's prom suit and thwacking his shoulders every time he playfully tries to grind with me.

I don't want to remember.

I'm kissing him in a bathroom stall at an arcade after winning five games of air hockey against him. I'm enjoying the view while he paints my room sunset-orange in his overalls, his brows pressed in concentration. I'm lying draped around him, sick and dizzy and tired, while he watches a woodworking video. I'm making s'mores over a firepit and crying because Greg is thanking me for taking care of his boy. I'm watching *1917* with Aaron in bed and rattling off historical knowledge.

I'm trying to top Aaron Beckham, but I give up because I'm laughing too hard. I'm crying in his arms because I couldn't have the cookies at the family function since they had butterscotch chips, and it was the final straw after a hard week. I'm at an outlet mall, enjoying the sun under a floppy sun hat while we wander in and out of stores.

I don't want to remember.

I'm drunk and singing an ear-numbing rendition of "All I Want For Christmas Is You" into Aaron's old karaoke set while he tries yanking my Santa hat down over my mouth. I'm kissing him sweetly in the dark corner of a corn maze and enjoying the taste of warm cider. I'm curled up on the bathroom floor, nausea raking me while he rubs my back. I'm giving him the silent treatment after he called Logan a bitch, then letting my frustrations melt when he apologizes and tickles my neck.

"Why now?" I breathe, the rain dripping from my hair, lashes, and chin.

I'm hiding in Aaron's closet because he's grounded and I'm not supposed to be over, and he joins me with a shit-eating grin that tells me he's up to something.

"Stop," I whisper, massaging my forehead.

I'm jumping off the lowest tree branches outside my window and falling into his arms. *Got you*, he breathes in my ear.

"I don't want to remember anymore . . ."

I'm telling Aaron Beckham that I love him for the first time.

I stagger to a stop on the sidewalk, my breaths shortening. I choke on a sob but bite frantically on my finger to keep anything else from surfacing. I don't need to cry, so I won't.

I won't, I won't, *I won't*.

Logan drives beside me, begging me to get in the car, but I ignore him until he gives up and heads home. Mom and Dad leap up from the couch when I push through the front door, my skin purplish and soggy. I give them some haphazard excuse I don't hear and drag my suitcase upstairs to my room, then peel out of my soaked clothes and stand there blankly.

They won't stop.

I'm apologizing for laughing at Aaron's first attempt to whittle a horse. I'm at a beach in late summer, massaging copious amounts of SPF 50 into his paper-white skin. I'm pounding on the wall between our rooms because it's one o'clock in the morning and he's still clattering around with his tools. I'm standing in line at the pharmacy for my prescription and glaring at him down the aisle, where he's winking sexily at me while getting his flu vaccine. I'm dozing off on his thigh while he listens to an online summer course lecture. I'm giving him doe eyes and fluttering my lashes so he'll do what I want. I'm telling him I love him. Again. And again.

It's not fair. These memory fragments are interrupting any progress my brain is attempting to make. Anger and grief battle for the mantle that numbness is currently wearing. I should want to scream and punch the window and cry into my pillow.

I just want to shower.

I crawl into my robe and head into the bathroom, then stand under scalding hot water, hoping it'll wake me from this overwhelming nothingness so I can think. So I can try to understand how I let myself get played so easily. I close my eyes, my breaths short and shaky despite how little I'm feeling.

I'm huddled with Aaron under the warm showerhead, letting him run his soapy hands down my shoulder blades.

I jam my index finger back into my mouth, letting the salty taste of blood center me. The realization of this situation slowly roots into my chest. With every pump of my heart, I feel pain coursing through my limbs, like Logan's words are a physical poison sapping my strength away. I sink onto the floor of the tub, hugging my arms, the water's warmth trickling away.

I shouldn't be surprised that Aaron asked me out because he wanted to use me like a toy in his revenge plot. That he decided to take this secret to his grave—the fact that our relationship was built on a lie. Aaron was always crafty, cunning, selfish. I knew this but agreed to his ploy, hoping I could exchange my time for the safety of Logan's future.

All the while, Logan knew Aaron would try to break me. And said nothing.

"*Protective*," I breathe, watching blood soak into the grooves of my palm. "He knew you were *protective* of me . . ."

Logan and I aren't particularly close. We never have been, aside from a few late-night conversations when we were younger about how Mom and Dad always seemed too busy for us. We're quiet and keep to ourselves, occasionally hanging out when we're bored, constantly passing through each other's radius with a nod. Just because we're not best friends doesn't mean I don't love him. I've always looked up to him for the simple fact that he's my older brother. I've gone to him for advice, for help with homework, for reassurance. He's always been stoic but there for me nonetheless.

I knew we both struggled to win our parents' attention when we were younger, but I didn't know he felt invisible, all because my health issues forced them to look my way. I didn't know he was capable of using someone's struggles to his advantage for the thrill of rebellion and half-assed scoldings from our parents. I didn't know he was the type to put himself before others.

Protective. In what world?

I smear my eyes against my knees, shivering under the assault of icy cold water. I can't find the strength to get up. I hate them. Aaron for not telling me the truth—for planning on *never* telling me. And Logan for everything else.

It's no wonder they despise each other. They each held the other's dirty rotten truth. All the subject changes, guilty eye flitting, dismissive words . . . it makes sense. They were keeping me ignorant to hold up their image. So Aaron could play the *perfect boyfriend* to feel better about wanting to hurt someone as miserable as me. So Logan could continue pretending he cares about me.

I don't answer the tentative knock on my door that night.

I don't answer the tapping on my window, either.

The next few days pass in a numbing blur. I must be getting things done, because nobody's following up with me.

The less I want to know, the more I remember.

The memories sliding into place aren't just with Aaron anymore. I'm awkwardly pitching my case to the history club in the hopes of inviting a local museum curator to the school to host a presentation. I'm throwing axes with my family and trying to navigate out of a Roaring '20s escape room for my eighteenth birthday while they wander around, clueless but happy that I'm happy. I'm kicking my legs under a desk with inappropriate excitement as a bored student gives a presentation on the Battle of Peleliu for our "forgotten moments of history" assignment.

I'm sitting under low lighting at the kitchen table, telling my parents I've decided to live my last couple of months of school, and summer break, for myself. That I'm moving in with Aaron for a while, but I would be back.

Logan keeps trying to intercept me, but there's nothing he can say that I want to hear.

And Aaron. *Aaron.*

He's clearly not the same person he was when he devised his plot to lure me in and then break my heart. The issue is that I'm not sure what to believe about his love. The reason he treats me so well and adjusts his lifestyle for me . . .

Is it love or disguised pity?

If it's the latter, he might not even realize. What if my concerns are valid and he realizes I'm right—that everything he's done has been out of a sense of guilt he's mistaken for devotion?

A conversation would clear this up. The thought of talking to him, though, constricts my throat. I'm not doing well. I don't realize it until I faint while vacuuming the living room.

When I open my eyes, I'm lying in bed with pillows propped under my legs, a bag of gluten-free potato chips and an energy drink on my bedside table. The world pulses around me, and a warm summer breeze from the open window grazes my face. Mom brushes my hair while Logan nervously adjusts my ankles to ensure they're elevated.

"Deep breaths, honey," Mom says tearfully. "Did you take your supplements? Did you forget to eat?"

I can't remember. Fainting tends to be a build of multiple things, so it might be both.

"You have to take care of yourself," Mom says, leaning me upright against my headboard.

I must respond, because she's satisfied enough to walk away. Leaving Logan hovering over me, shuffling his feet, unable to make eye contact. "Can we talk?" he asks.

I stare at him blankly.

"You're been a zombie, Riley. You haven't been eating or sleeping or talking. Please . . . what can I do to make things right?"

I continue staring at him.

"I can't change my decision," Logan whispers, steering his eyes to the bedspread. "All I can do is say I'm sorry over and over until you believe me. In the meantime . . . please eat."

He strides out of the room without waiting for a response. Probably because he knows I don't have one for him.

I pass out again two days later in the backyard. Dad sees it through the kitchen window overlooking the lawn. Normally, I'd be embarrassed for being such a pathetic damsel, but I don't care enough to be annoyed with myself. Any annoyance I do feel stems from recognition of the fact that I truly am a doormat, because I'm less upset with Aaron than I should be. Maybe it'll come in full force later when the numbness leaves, but I know myself. The longer it takes my emotions to return, the clearer I start to think, and the less intense they'll be when it's time to really *feel*.

It seems so anticlimactic. It should come to a boil where I scream and cry and fight his grip as he tries to wrap me in his arms, like in a typical rom-dram movie. I should be seething and sobbing in my room for days. Then I should be approaching a slow realization that I don't need a man to feel fulfilled—that I've grown so much over the course of these weeks that I'm fully confident in myself.

But all I can do is follow my schedule.

I open my eyes and find that Dad has carried me to the couch. He texts the family group chat about the incident, and Logan comes home looking gray and ill.

"Why aren't you being cautious?" he asks desperately while I'm whisking things together in the kitchen, whatever they may be. "What if you faint on the staircase or something and split your head?"

I stare at him wearily until he sighs and leaves.

I try to find the energy to get my supplements when my alarm goes off, on occasions when I hear it. I try getting ahead of the food issue by preparing myself lunch every morning, but sometimes I forget I've made something. Sometimes I don't have the strength to divert attention away from whatever I'm doing to take a break and eat. When I stop moving, it starts to hurt.

So I'll just keep moving.

25

I faint for the third time in a couple of weeks. I can't run errands because I'm recovering from a gluten incident on top of my recent lightheadedness. I don't know what I did wrong—my days are all one jumbled mass. All I know is that I wake one morning racked with chills, nausea, joint pain, and tingly discomfort.

I'm standing from the table after lunch when it happens, and I crash heavily onto the wooden floor. I slide in and out of consciousness for a few minutes while my parents kneel over me and support my head, asking if I'm hurt. It's so ridiculous I could laugh. Can't I be emotionally stunted for a little while without physically falling apart?

When I next come into focus, I'm in bed again, and I'm freezing cold. My fingers are stiff and throbbing. My eyes are unbearably heavy. I'm alone.

I can't stand the AC, so I shove the blankets back and wobble toward the window to let the scorching hot day sear into my room. I toss the curtain aside and grab the window frame to hoist it up.

Logan and Aaron are in the driveway.

I blink in puzzlement. They're talking. Arguing, I think, but their body language is more agitated than aggressive. Aaron is wearing a white T-shirt under a black jean vest and pants. His hair has a naturally tousled look to it, but now it's particularly unruly, his curled black tips flying every which way.

I lift the window quietly so they won't notice me eavesdropping above.

". . . know I've treated you like shit," Logan is saying, his knuckles kneading his temples. "Look, I was a horrible kid. I still am. I know I need to work on it, but I'm asking you for this solid."

"I'd do it if I could," Aaron snaps, leaning against his pickup. "Not for you, but for him. But I can't force him not to be angry."

"The problem is that he's *not* angry!" Logan says desperately. "He's not *anything*, Aaron. He's barely functional. He's not eating, sleeping, taking his medications. It's like he's completely tuned out. He's been fainting again, and I'm worried something will happen when he's alone. My family works through the week, and we can't . . . we can't . . ."

Logan lowers his face, shivering hard enough that I can see it from here.

"We can't take care of him," he chokes out.

"Obviously not," Aaron says coldly. "But I can't just break his window and force myself in."

"It's a matter of safety! What if he passes out with a knife in his hand and falls on it, or hits his head against something? He's barely recovered from the accident." Logan slides a hand through his hair, clutching it with frustration. "I don't understand. Is this revenge? If he's trying to make us worry, it's working."

Aaron barks with unfriendly laughter. "You still don't know a single fucking thing about Riley, do you?" he snarls.

Logan's face contorts with anger, but it quickly vanishes. "I'll let you in," he insists. "Maybe if you talk to him, he'll realize what he's doing—"

"Don't bother," I say.

They jump at the sound of my voice, necks craning to see my second-story window while I lean in the frame, glaring at them. Logan instantly looks guilty, but Aaron's expression brightens.

"Riley," he says softly.

The sound of my name spoken with such sweetness makes my heart skip, but I don't let it distract me. "Quit conspiring," I order. "You can't force me to talk to you."

"We're just worried," Logan says, holding his hands up defensively. "You're not well."

"When am I ever?" I demand.

"Please . . . I can't . . ." Logan falters, gathering the courage for his next words before croaking them. "I can't watch you do this to yourself. This whole time, I've been driving you away from him. But I didn't realize how much healthier you were while living with him. How much . . . *happier* you were with him. If I'd known . . ."

"Then what?" I ask icily. "You would've kept sitting on the truth?"

Logan winces.

Aaron takes a step closer to the tree jutting toward my window. His eyes must be teary, because they're shimmering like little diamonds in the sunlight. "I know I don't deserve your time," he says, "but I'm asking for it anyway. Just five minutes?"

I purse my lips. He's good with his words—do I want to give him the chance to use them?

I decide I still need clarification, so I mutter, "Fine."

I figure he'll head through the front door, but the moment the word leaves my mouth, he's vaulting up the trunk of the tree like a professional climber, and ten seconds later, he's slinking through my window. Immediately, he draws the curtain sideways so Logan can't see us, then checks to make sure my bedroom door is closed. His hairline shimmers with sweat droplets from having been standing in the heat, and the tip of his nose is the color of bubble gum.

"Hey, sunshine," Aaron says with a frail smile. His gaze wanders from my eyes to my ankles, no doubt assessing my pathetic state. I don't need his pity, though, so as he steps closer to hold my face, I slap his hands away.

"What do you want?" I ask.

"To apologize."

I give him a tired glare, then go back to my bed and flop onto the edge, waiting. It's been a couple of weeks since I've seen him, so this moment should feel bigger. *This* is where my emotions should swell to the surface and come pouring out of me in screams and cries.

Naturally, they don't.

"Logan said you fainted today," he says, wisely keeping his distance. "Have you eaten?"

"Does it matter?" I roll my hand irritably through the air. "If you're going to waste my time scolding me, just leave."

"No, that's not . . ." Aaron's shoulders slump with exasperation. "I just wish you wouldn't punish yourself physically when you're hurting emotionally. Can I borrow your kitchen for five minutes to make you something?"

I continue glaring at him, my eyes heavy and burning with fatigue.

Aaron's throat bobs, and he nods, apparently expecting my lack of response. "I don't have excuses, Riley," he whispers. "It's true. I planned on charming you and breaking your heart to get back at Logan. It was disgusting. I didn't see that at the time." His hands clench into pale fists at his navel. "I could only think about how betrayed I felt. How Logan used me for a year, then blamed me for corrupting him. I wasn't thinking about you at all in this revenge plan. You were nothing but a tool I could use to my advantage."

I sit silently, letting my brain absorb the words. I can't tell whether they sting or not. I guess I already know most of what he's saying.

"The other day, I said that falling in love with you wasn't a mistake," he murmurs. "You said *But liking me was*. And it's true. I was never supposed to like you. You were meant to stay this shadowed object in the background of my plans. The problem . . ."

Aaron steps closer, then sinks onto his knees, inches from my legs. ". . . is that you're the sun, sunshine."

I blink down at him in surprise, unswayable but not minding this new position. I can tell he's about to launch into a speech. The thought might normally make me smile if I had the strength or feeling for it.

"I couldn't avoid looking at you," he says quietly, reaching out and clasping my hand, which is limp on my kneecap. "I tried ignoring your brightness without realizing you were already burned into my skin. All it took was a couple of dates for you to melt the anger in my heart."

He begins to stroke the skin between my ice-cold knuckles. He smiles, his eyes distant, as if recalling the memory.

"It's humiliating how quickly it happened. A handful of hours showed me how kind you are. That your humor is as dry as your stare. That you worry more about others than you should—even people you hate. Or rather dislike, since your heart won't hold something as petty as hatred."

He scoops up my other hand to massage away the frost glazing my joints. I allow it because I'm tired of being cold.

"I had a yearslong friendship with someone I discovered was using me. So being around you . . . someone who didn't have the capacity to intentionally hurt me . . . was new. I didn't understand it." He raises my hands to pepper slow, lingering kisses between my knuckles. "The more time I spent with you, the less I thought about Logan. At one point, I realized my feelings expanded beyond liking you. I wanted you. I *craved* you. When we weren't together, I was daydreaming about you. I didn't know what it was to be happy until I became yours."

Warmth blossoms behind my ears and into my cheeks. I must be flustered, though it struggles to break through the ice seal around my heart.

"The revenge plot lasted a couple of dates," he says softly. He's moved on to kiss my shivering fingertips. "That's the thing about you. For as reserved as you are, your existence is explosive to those around you. After a few days, I suddenly wanted to be *better.* Not just for you, but for my dads, and for myself. Being with you made me think long-term, and that's not something I ever used to do."

The heat is expanding downward through my neck. If he keeps talking, the ice will crack.

"I didn't tell you because for so long, you believed I was scum." Aaron leans his forehead against my knee with a frustrated huff. "You weren't wrong. But I was changing, and you started warming up to me. I was scared that if I told you it started as a lie, it would validate all your old concerns and you'd end up heartbroken anyway. I couldn't stand the thought of hurting you. Of losing you."

I feel the brush of his mouth as it curls up into an annoyed smile against my skin.

"I changed, but I've still been acting selfish," he breathes. "I'm sorry for lying by omission. I'm sorry for ever intending to hurt you. For actually hurting you. I promise never to hide anything from you again. But please understand that my love isn't a lie."

He cranes his neck to look up again, his expression resolute. I'm starting to feel bad about how long he's been kneeling on the floor.

"You're everything I want to be," he says. "You deserve someone who treats you with the same consideration you offer everyone else. I promise to continue trying to be that person for you. If you'll let me. Someone who takes care of you and helps you look after your health. Someone who keeps you from huddling up in your room. Someone who doesn't give up on you. Someone who puts you first."

He rises on his knees, bringing my palms together, his own folded around them. He smiles, a mixture of sweet and mischievous, gray eyes crinkling, and I realize I don't stand a chance.

"I love you, Riley Wilson," he whispers. "Thank you for being the center of my everything. My sunshine."

I continue watching him, my body's aches and pains loud enough to disrupt my thoughts. I wonder how long he practiced this. It's thoughtful. Sweet. Charming, like I knew it would be.

All I can manage to mumble is "Not pity?"

Thankfully, he understands. "I just listed several reasons I fell for you," he says, dragging his thumb beneath my dry, tired eye. "Pity isn't one of them."

Okay. My biggest question has been answered. Now what?

"I'm going to make you food," Aaron says, rising to his feet so he can go back to towering. "I won't stick around after that. I won't text or come to your window. The next step is yours. Take as much time as you need to think about what I've said. If you're not willing to see me again . . ."

He winces, like the thought is difficult to bear.

"I'll respect your wishes and hope for a day you can forgive me. Even if I don't deserve it."

Then he leaves. I sit on the edge of the bed, exhaustion rippling through me, the frost steadily webbing through my body without his warmth to keep it at bay. I don't have the strength to know what I should be thinking. All I know is that I don't feel worse.

Aaron returns five minutes later with a sandwich and potato chips, then places the plate beside me. He leans over and kisses my forehead—a parting memento. Then he heads for the window.

"Wait," I say.

He pauses. I stare at the food, blinking slow, my vision blurred at the edges.

"I'm cold," I breathe.

Aaron turns to me, his expression horribly soft.

"I'm cold," I repeat. "And tired. And dizzy. And sore. I'm cold."

I don't know how to ask without sounding pathetic. He understands. I don't think anyone else would. "I won't talk," he assures me, and he returns to my side, sliding onto my mattress and pressing his back against the headboard. He gathers me between his legs and leans me against his chest. His skin radiates heat, like it's convinced it's still outside soaking up the sun.

He holds the plate under my chin with one hand, then brings the sandwich to my mouth. When I bite into it, I can taste the salt of meat and tang of mustard and cheese. Aaron keeps to his word, and I'm too numb to feel awkward about the silence.

Within minutes, the throbbing in my stomach lessens. I'm still shivering, though, and exhausted beyond relief. When I finish, I stay slumped against him, fumbling for the blankets. Aaron hikes them over us, then shifts onto his back with me, making me comfortable on the pillow. He curls around me, pouring his warmth into my body.

It's been a couple of weeks since I've slept in his arms. I forgot how comfortable they are. How safe they make me feel.

I nuzzle into his neck, arms tucked up and limp between us, letting him stroke my back. His lips are nestled into the top of my head, and he's broken into a barely noticeable quiver. I think I understand why. He's wondering if this is the last time he'll get to hold me.

I'm starting to feel. The first emotion that comes back is guilt.

"Sorry," I say, my eyes moistening. I scrunch them shut. "I'm not trying to be difficult . . . or do this on purpose to make everyone feel bad . . ."

Aaron's arms close tighter around me, pressing me flush with his body. "I know," he says. "You don't like to hurt other people, so you take your problems out on yourself. Maybe that's something we can figure out together, if . . ."

He fizzles off, but I know the end of his sentence. *If you can forgive me.*

More guilt needles through me. "Okay," I say. "I'll forgive you."

I expect Aaron to react with a gasp and beaming grin. That he'll kiss me fiercely and thank me for giving him another chance. I'm not sure where my decision comes from—I don't even remember thinking the words.

"No," he says.

That startles me. I draw my head back to give him a puzzled look, and he smiles, his fingertips rising to nudge my hair off my forehead.

"Don't forgive me yet," he continues, his eyes sparkling with fondness. "Not when you're so numb. Give yourself time to think. Let your emotions come back, however long it takes. Be angry. Sad. Frustrated. It's not fair, what Logan and I have put you through." His thumb combs an arch along my brow. "So just *feel*, sunshine."

I purse my lips, a twinge of annoyance in my chest. "What if I change my mind and decide I want nothing to do with you?"

"That's fine. So long as you make your decision when you're thinking straight." Aaron draws my face forward and kisses the bridge of my nose. "Just let me know what you need. I'll meal prep, then bring you food so you don't have to make lunch every day. I'll come over and hold you at night to keep you warm, and promise not to say a word. I'll help you get dressed or wash your hair or get food to your mouth if it's too much. I'll be here. So call me—"

"*—every time. I'll find a way to you. Always*," I say lightly.

Aaron looks thoroughly befuddled. The sight awakens something tingly and warm within me, and I feel my mouth rise at the corners.

"You've said it before. Becoming predictable," I say, poking my index finger scoldingly into his chest.

"Predictable?" Aaron scoffs. "I'm the most spontaneous person you know."

"Yet I clocked what you were going to say immediately." I shrug. "You're losing your touch."

Aaron's smile turns into a sharp and pointy grin, and I think in any other circumstance, I'd be in trouble for saying something so bold.

"Maybe," he says. "Any other insults you want to hurl while I'm at your mercy?"

I consider it. The longer I lay pressed into his chest, his arms folded protectively around me, the more I start to feel. The guilt is waning in place of other things. Comfort. Relief. Amusement. Nothing negative—at least, not yet.

"Would it kill you to add color to your closet?" I ask, clicking my tongue. "I get that you think you look sexy and mysterious in black. But have you ever considered a nice periwinkle? Or chartreuse? Or literally anything else?"

Aaron whistles long and low. "Brutal," he says. "Thank you for teaching me that other colors exist. I'll add *a nice periwinkle* to my list." He waits a couple of moments, then smirks, and asks, "Is that the worst insult you could come up with?"

"I could find something more offensive," I say, huffing.

"Prove it."

My brain works furiously through the haze to conjure something more biting. This might be the only time I can say these things without retaliation—surely there's something else. I confidently say, "Your massages could use some work."

Aaron chokes on his breath. "What?"

"You're too gentle," I say sternly. "Be rougher with me. Like really dig your thumbs in. If you're going to do it, do it right."

Aaron chokes again, but it's on laughter this time. "I'm sorry. I'll be more merciless with you moving forward," he says seriously.

"You're being bratty," I accuse, and his eyes twinkle with mischief.

"That's because I'm a brat. You know this."

I scowl and squirm so my back is to him because I can't stand his smug face. He merely squeezes me tighter and pecks the arch of my neck.

"I knew it," he breathes in my ear. "You're too nice to be mean."

I don't respond because that movement sapped me of my remaining energy.

I can't sleep, despite my exhaustion. I'm cozy lying here, Aaron's breath on the back of my neck a familiar sensation. I roll his words around in my head, trying to determine my thoughts toward them. He says I should allow myself to feel upset before making the decision to forgive him. But after hearing him talk . . .

I'm just not.

It must be the doormat thing. So long as he flashes that pretty smile and uses his charming words, I let him walk all over me, like Logan claimed. But . . . I don't know. Aaron isn't the type of person who would step on me. Not anymore.

Maybe it's okay that I don't have the kind of personality that would let me cling to this and feel overwhelmingly negative. My adverse emotions are always geared toward myself. I'm too fragile, too stubborn, too difficult to accommodate, too everything. Maybe it's fine that my anger and sadness aren't taking shape like they should.

Maybe that's just the way I am.

I think Aaron knows that. But he's giving me the chance to feel them anyway, just in case. The fact that he's encouraging me to be upset, because he knows I tend to jump the gap between *numbness* and *acceptance*, shows just how unwilling he is to take advantage of me. In one hour, he's done more to prove his heart to me than Logan has in weeks.

Because he knows me. He's taken the time to understand how my mind functions. His love for me is genuine, even if I sometimes have trouble understanding what I've done to warrant it. He's shown me his care through more means than words and promises.

I manage to roll toward him again, my nose inches from his on the pillow. Sunlight still gushes through the curtain edges over my window—it's midafternoon. His eyes widen when he realizes mine are glassy. "I hate what you did," I say, scrunching my fingers into his vest. "I hate that you planned to do something horrible to me, and I hate how you hid it from me. I hate that I'm not angry with you. I wish I could be that person. But I'm not."

Aaron smiles, and it's warm. It's him. "I know," he says.

"I've always thought that if I had the energy, I would hold on to things longer," I murmur. The water seeps into my lashes, collecting at the tips. "But I think I just want to see the best in people. I want to believe they're genuine. And maybe that's a good thing. Sometimes."

Aaron's eyes are shining brighter.

"I know people will take advantage of that," I continue. "Even if they don't mean to. Like my family. But I don't think it's my fault. They're the ones choosing to walk on me when they don't have to. They could step around me, like you do. But they don't, because I've allowed them to . . . or they've allowed *themselves* to get used to it."

Aaron brushes his knuckles against my lashes, collecting the gathered tears onto his fingers. He doesn't say anything. He doesn't have to.

"You're giving me the chance to get angry and yell at you because that's what you think you deserve. And maybe you do. I don't know," I admit. "But I don't need to wait to feel because I know the end result. I can't hate you, and not just because it's who I am. It's because you're not the only one who fell in love."

Aaron's smile widens. There's a tremor in his lips.

"My memories . . . they've been coming back. The good ones. The bad ones. Learning what you did will be one of the bad ones. But moments like now . . . the way you're holding me, even knowing I might break up with you . . . it's one of the good ones."

I blink frantically to keep his image from becoming a teary blur. He rolls his knuckles over my lashes again to dispel the water.

"I trust you," I say quietly. "Because you're the only person in my life who chooses not to walk on me, even when I lie down and say it's fine. I am a doormat. Maybe that's okay, if I have someone like you to clean off the footprints once in a while. You make me feel like it's good to be myself. You make me . . . feel. It's been weeks, and now that you're here, it's all I know how to do. That's why . . ."

The tears come faster, equally as hot as my scarlet cheeks and shortened breath. Aaron closes his eyes and leans his forehead against mine, like he's absorbing this moment.

"I love you, Aaron Beckham," I whisper. "I love the way you love me. I love that I can't hide from you. I love how you always know what I need, even when I won't tell you, and how warm you are, and how sweetly you talk to me. I love your smile, even when it irritates me, and I love when you tease and bully me, even when I pretend I don't."

Aaron is trembling fiercely now. His hand spreads along the back of my head, holding me against him.

"I love watching you study wood carvings and fiddle with your gadget toy," I say, nudging my nose against his sunburned one. "I love how your eyes start sparkling when you see me. How you make me feel important. For your sincerity and thoughtfulness and confidence and intensity. For respecting my boundaries, but also knowing when to overstep them for my health and happiness. I love you for making me feel like a person who exists outside of my illnesses, but also for always having my illnesses in mind. I love you for not letting me shove through my pain."

I kiss the corner of his mouth. Every breath he takes shivers.

"You said I deserve someone who takes care of me and puts me first. You want to be that person for me. So I hope you'll let me be that person for you, too. Someone who will be there as you figure things out with your mom, or when you relapse into bad habits, or when you want to talk about something that excites you. Someone who lets you feel like you can be honest, even if I'm having a rough time myself."

I look between his eyes, waiting for him to open them. He doesn't.

"You can cry, Aaron," I tell him.

Aaron's mouth wobbles into a desperate smile, but it only lasts a second before he's pulling away and shoving his palms over his face. "How did this happen?" he chokes out. "I'm the one who's supposed to be comforting you today . . . Somehow it got turned around. How do you always manage to surprise me, even now? In what world do I deserve you? *Fuck*, Riley."

It's my turn to smile. I draw his wrists away from his face, because if I can't hide from him, he shouldn't be able to hide from me. His eyes are rimmed red and his pale face is smeared in tear streaks.

"Ever since the accident, I've been so terrified of losing you," he breathes. "I feel like I've been drowning. I was worried that someone like you falling for someone like me was a fluke—it couldn't possibly happen twice. I said I'd start from square one if I had to, but having to go back to the beginning right after you finally got comfortable saying you loved me . . . it was so *hard*. I've been bottling it up because I didn't want to burden you . . ."

Aaron chokes on a cry and buries his face in his upper arm. I've never seen him like this—not even in the memories that have returned. "Of course I'd fall for you twice," I say softly. "Look at me. An hour ago I wasn't even functional. I could barely move. You give me the energy to exist."

I massage away his tear streaks with my thumb.

"Liking you was an accident," I whisper. "Falling in love with you wasn't."

Aaron's inhale is broken and scratchy. He throws his face into my shirt and bursts into sobs, his arms sliding around my back and clutching me like I'm a lifeline. I hug his head to my chest, letting his tears soak into the fabric, my fingers working through his dark hair. His voice is garbled, but I can faintly hear the words he's choking out. *Thank you. I'm so sorry. I love you. I'm so sorry. Thank you.*

His speech was nice. Genuine. This is even more so.

"I forgive you, so stop apologizing, okay?" I say. "You're starting to sound like me."

I hear raspy laughter that falls away into crying again. I'm not sure which of us falls asleep first.

But we do, curled around each other, arms and legs tangled beneath the comforter.

26

"I moved in with Aaron because I didn't have the courage to talk to you."

My parents stare at me in bewilderment across the dinner table. I twirl my gluten-free spaghetti, hoping it'll keep them from noticing how much my fingers are shaking. Logan's head remains bowed, his expression neutral. He hasn't tried talking to me in two weeks, since the day I made up with Aaron.

"I wanted to see what it was like, living my life without worrying about anyone else's," I say, steadying my voice. My eyes wander to the golden chandelier shedding a calming radiance over the kitchen. "I know it was a shock. I remember your faces the day I packed and moved."

Mom chirps with laughter, poking at her own pasta. I can tell she's nervous. "We weren't expecting it," she admits.

"I know. So I'm talking to you first this time."

Dad's salt-and-pepper brows knit. Logan continues watching the tablecloth, like the pattern is mesmerizing.

"I don't have plans to move out," I say sternly. "But that could change. I . . . I've never been good at setting boundaries. I've always done as I was told because I felt I owed a debt, thanks to the medical complications. There should be a change, though. Especially once college starts."

"You've never owed us for your medical issues, Riley," Dad says carefully.

"But you've been letting me pay it off anyway," I respond.

His eyes widen with surprise, like my words are resonating with him for the first time.

"What boundaries would you like to set, honey?" Mom asks. She's blinking fiercely now, as if combating tears. I guess I've never spoken my thoughts so bluntly before—maybe she's coming to the same realization my dad is.

"Workload." I swallow with difficulty. "I'm happy to help out in the summer when I don't have a job or classes, but I shouldn't be shouldering every errand or cleaning duty. Also, I won't be making two meals every night anymore."

My parents exchange bemused glances. They don't look upset—just startled. I've never confronted them before, so they're probably not sure how to take it. "We're sorry if we made you feel like you needed to carry all the work around here," Mom says softly. "We appreciate everything you've done to keep things running, Riley. But you're right. There needs to be a change."

"We don't mind gluten-free food," Dad tacks on. "Whatever makes things easy for you. And only if you're feeling up to it."

My eyes flit to Logan. I'm not sure he's paying attention, but I don't care.

"When I start college, there should be an even divide in work," I say. "Let's come up with a schedule to make sure everyone has a hand in things. The last-minute requests have to stop, too. Even if it's urgent, don't expect me to drop what I'm doing to get something done. Got it?"

My parents nod vigorously in agreement. Logan plucks at a loose strand in the tablecloth.

"Lastly, Aaron is my boyfriend, whether you like it or not," I say sharply. "He's there for me and makes me happy, so please deal with it."

I rise to my feet, knees trembling as my kitchen chair scratches against the floor.

"I'm going on a trip with him this weekend. Maybe you can talk things over while I'm gone." I clear my throat, feeling awkward about using Aaron in this way but knowing I have his blessing. "Aaron will be monitoring my schedule to make sure I'm not overloaded. I'm not good at noticing it myself. So please make sure whatever you come up with is balanced."

I bring my dish to the sink, then race up the stairs so I can overthink every word I just said.

They don't address the conversation with me for the rest of the week. But my daily to-do list gets noticeably shorter over the next couple of days, and one evening, I find my parents hunched over a spreadsheet on Dad's laptop.

Maybe they'll abide by my rules for a couple of weeks and then subconsciously wane away from them. Maybe I'll even let them without noticing. I'm used to heaviness on my shoulders, but that's why I have Aaron. I've given him permission to ask me every morning about my tasks. I don't know how well this is going to work.

What I do know is that it's a start.

"Riley."

I'm on my way to Aaron's truck with my suitcase when the voice at my back startles me. Aaron is standing near the passenger door, ever the gentleman. His souring expression tells me exactly who's approaching behind me. I turn and find Logan on the driveway.

"I wanted to see you off," he mumbles. "I hope you have fun. You deserve a trip."

I pinch my brows, wondering why he's decided now to talk to me after so many days of radio silence. "Thanks," I say, starting back to the truck, but Logan snags my wrist, tugging me to a stop.

"Why just him?" he asks.

I stare at him in perplexity. "What?"

"You . . . you forgave Aaron." He snaps his hand to his side when he notices Aaron step forward. His scruff has grown longer, but it's patchy and uneven—he hasn't been properly grooming it. "Why did you let him get away with doing what he did, but not me?"

I sigh, kneading the bridge of my nose. "Forgiving someone isn't letting them *get away* with something," I say with a sharp look. "Aaron proves himself every day. He can grow from this. Besides, what he did is different."

"How?" he asks desperately. "We hid the same information from you."

"He hid it because he didn't want to hurt or lose me," I say, holding a palm up to keep Aaron from striding toward us. This won't take long. "You hid it to protect your ego. Not only that, but you chose not to save me from Aaron's plan. You got lucky he didn't go through with it."

"I know, but . . ." Logan pulls at his fingers, clearly noticing that I'm on the brink of walking away. "What more can I do for your forgiveness?"

I consider it. I can't say I *haven't* forgiven him. Rather, I just don't care to hold grudges or cling to people's bad actions. Even so, I haven't felt any desire to talk to him. "I don't know," I admit.

"There has to be something," he pleads.

"Maybe. It shouldn't be my job to find it for you." I turn my back to him with a half-hearted wave. "Make an effort beyond a verbal apology and see where it takes you."

I drag my suitcase down the driveway, leaving him watching in dismay. The moment I'm within range, Aaron reaches out, his palms unfurling around my face. "Are you okay?" he asks softly.

"I'm fine." I tilt my head and kiss the outer edge of his thumb. "Let's not talk about it. I won't let him ruin the day."

Aaron gives me an uneasy look but nods, loading my luggage into the back seat. Within the minute, we're taking off. The farther we get from home, the higher my excitement mounts.

Chicago.

Aaron booked a long weekend for us in the heart of the city as a "part two" of his apology. To which I bitterly asked if he intended to buy my complete forgiveness, and he floundered until I laughed and kissed him. It's a three-hour drive, and my backpack is stocked with gluten-free snacks.

"I'm surprised you've never been there," Aaron says as we merge onto the highway, casting me a curious glance. "It's within driving distance. Did you ever consider asking for it as a present?"

"I wanted to wait until I could go with someone who cares about history." I smile playfully. "Or someone who pretends to care."

"I do care!" he says, though he's clearly pleased that I find him to be a worthy partner for exploration. "Or I care about you. I care that you care. So it's basically the same thing."

"Sure," I say, reaching over to fluff up his curly tips. He's wearing gray cargo shorts and a navy-blue button-down. It's no periwinkle, but I appreciate the effort. "Thank you in advance for letting me yap your ear off."

"Of course. We could've gone sooner, but . . ." Aaron sighs with melancholy. "You had to make me *plan in advance*."

"We can't show up to a major city without a booking or itinerary," I snap.

"So you say."

"We would've been sleeping in your truck."

It's been a couple of weeks since Aaron and I made up. Since then, more of my memories have been slotting back into place, though it's mostly flashes and sensations. I'm less worried about retrieving all of them. Even if they don't come back, what matters is that I'm lucky enough to create new ones.

I try to make time to see Aaron as often as possible. Once, I let my family fend for themselves so I could go out to dinner at our favorite restaurant, and I only felt slightly guilty. I've spent the night at his place a few times, in which our recreational activities span from movie-watching to baking to talking to fiery kisses and wandering hands. Sometimes, he comes over when my family is in bed and vaults through my window because he's dramatic. I told him I don't care if my parents notice the alarm was deactivated, but he likes the tree-climbing thrill.

"And I look sexy doing it," he claims, which is valid.

Aaron told his dads about the state his mother was in when he last saw her, and they've taken on the responsibility of stepping in. Aaron has been in the dark about the details, but it sounds like they're trying to get her help, and hoping to catch whatever habit she's fallen into early. It's been on his mind, but he's also recognized that it's out of his control and not his responsibility. He seems more okay with admitting when he's feeling low about it. I'm proud of him for approaching everything so maturely rather than responding to it by trying to get his adrenaline dose in.

I wonder if I'll ever get to meet her. If that would mean anything to him.

I don't forget what he did. What matters is knowing he won't keep anything from me again, now that he's seen the pain his secrecy can cause me. It'll take time for me to get it off my mind, but I still trust him. I do. Some people might think I'm naive, but he's proven he can change. He's proven that his love for me extends beyond pity.

We get an early check-in at our hotel and drop our luggage off, bringing nothing with us but a backpack. From there, we wander the gridded streets hand in hand, scattering pigeons and needling through groups of tourists and enjoying the incessant breeze whistling between the skyscrapers. We visit the Field Museum first, where my favorite exhibits are ancient Egypt and the Cyrus Tang Hall of China. I'm basically hopping between displays, vibrating in my shoes as I drag Aaron around by the wrist. I explain how the mummification process required removing every organ but the heart and that jade stone discs were buried with high-ranking people in the Neolithic era. Aaron pretends to be fascinated, and it makes me embarrassingly happy.

He takes me to a certified gluten-free restaurant afterward, where we indulge in Chicago-style pizza. I tell him we'll have to try New York City's to compare, and his eyes sparkle with excitement.

We visit the Art Institute of Chicago, which is another museum on my bucket list. Aaron has no complaints in pausing at everything so I can read the placards. I wonder if he's listening when I prattle on, or if he's too busy staring lovingly at me. I decide I'll give him a pop quiz later to test him.

We catch an Uber to the hotel, and by then, we're wiped. But I'm giddy, eager, and fulfilled.

"This is the best trip you could've planned," I say when he exits the bathroom after his shower, dressed in a fluffy towel, his black hair slicked back and his lean body on full display. I've already washed and changed into my leopard-print flannels, because I freeze at night even in the summer. Other than a bedside lamp, the lights are off, and the curtains are partially open to grant us a view of the staggering buildings.

He crawls under the sheets to join me. "I'm glad you're enjoying it," he says, tucking my damp hair behind my ear. "How are you feeling? Rate your discomfort."

"Mm . . . a three," I suggest.

"So like a five," he says, flicking my nose. I scowl and bite at it.

"It's just my legs. My calves are whining about all the walking," I admit. "But other than that, the rest of me is okay."

Aaron gives me a probing look to ensure I'm not downplaying my pain, and I return it with a sweet doe-eyed stare and a flutter of my lashes. Because I remember what works now. Sure enough, the apples of his cheeks redden, and he groans, slamming his face into his pillow. "You do it on purpose," he mutters.

"Do what?" I ask.

He glares sideways at me, face partially buried. I blink innocently at him, and then he's suddenly lunging at me. I squeak in surprise and try squirming away, but it takes five seconds for him to wrestle me beneath him and tickle me. I screech with laughter, shoving his chest as he bends down and nibbles the arch of my neck, the words *little shit* ghosting over my ear.

"I'm sorry, I won't do it again!" I cry out, tears of mirth flooding my eyes.

"Is this rough enough for you?" he asks, jabbing his fingers into my sides, and now I'm laughing harder for a different reason.

"Th-that was for massages . . . Please have mercy . . ."

He stops digging his fingers into my skin but only so he can slide his hands under my flannel shirt and massage my waist. I'm panting at this point, a faint smile etched onto my lips. The city lights slant sideways through the room, pouring through the parted curtains, bathing Aaron in a silvery-white glow. His unblinking eyes are more luminescent than the moon, and it warms my ears.

"What?" I ask self-consciously.

"Nothing. I just love to hear you laugh." He bends lower, brushing his lips against mine. I can't stand how good he looks with his hair pushed back. "Can I spoil you tonight?"

My body temperature soars. "Don't just ask me something like that out of nowhere!" I plead.

"We're in bed. In our own hotel room. On our first vacation together. And I'm naked. How is this out of nowhere?" he asks amusedly.

"The least you can do is set the mood!"

"Sorry." He gives me a slow, achingly deep kiss that makes me fluttery, then pulls back with a lip-smacking noise, and says, "Your answer, then?"

"Brat," I snap.

"Your brat," he counters, stooping over to kiss me a second time. When he draws back, I feel like the world is tilting around me.

"Whatever," I grumble, tossing my arm over my eyes. "Do what you want."

Aaron "spoils" me all night. By the time he's done, I'm ready for another shower, and more exhausted than I've been in weeks. He apologizes, smiling against my ear. I don't forgive him.

But then he whispers that he loves me, and of course I do, because I'm a doormat.

I flop fully on top of him and nestle my head into his chest, preparing to let his steady breathing lull me to sleep. His hand rises to pet my hair, apparently not minding that it's now damp with more than just shower water.

I'm not sure what to expect when we get home. Hopefully, my parents will have a game plan for how to tackle everything. It's been on my mind, but just barely. Because I know, regardless of what happens, Aaron will be my safety net. I can rely on him if my family falls through. Even if *I* fall through. He'll make sure I receive nothing less than what he thinks I deserve.

As for Logan . . . well. He has time to figure it out. I'll put in the effort when he does. For now, though, I'm moving on.

"Where should we go next?" I ask, folding my arms atop Aaron's chest.

"We still have Saturday and Sunday, you know," he says, smirking.

"Yeah, but it's good to think ahead."

He curls his arms around me and nuzzles his chin into my hair. "You're right," he says. "So let's plan the next one. And the next. And the next. I'll make sure you visit every city and museum and gallery you want to see."

As exhaustion carries me into sleep, he presses his smile into the top of my head.

"As long as I get to come with you, sunshine."

CREDITS

VIKING BOOKS AND PENGUIN YOUNG READERS

ART AND DESIGN

Kelley Brady
Lucia Baez

CONTRACTS

Jennifer Skrzypinski

EDITORIAL

Dana Leydig

MANAGING EDITORIAL

Alexandra Aleman
Gaby Corzo
Ginny Dominguez

MARKETING

Alex Garber
Astrid Rojas
Bri Lockhart
Christina Colangelo
Danielle Presley
Emily Romero
Felicity Vallence
Lisa Kelly
Shannon Spann
Talisa Ramos

PRODUCTION

Miranda Shulman

PRODUCTION EDITORIAL

Marinda Valenti

PUBLICITY

Lathea Mondesir

PUBLISHER

Tamar Brazis

SUBSIDIARY RIGHTS

Helen Boomer
Kim Ryan

SALES

Abby Fritz
Becky Green
Emily Bruce
Kimberly Langus
Micheal Gentile

SCHOOL AND LIBRARY MARKETING

Andrea Cruise
Carmela Iaria
Cody Tigue
Gaby Paez
Judith Huerta
Maggie Searcy
Summer Ogata
Trevor Ingerson
Venessa Carson

LISTENING LIBRARY

Emily Parliman
Kelly Atkinson
Rebecca Waugh

NEW LEAF LITERARY

Suzie Townsend

A. M. WOODY is a Metro Detroit–based queer author. They graduated from Central Michigan University with a degree in English and a certificate in creative writing. When not writing and reading happily-ever-afters, they can be found drinking caramel apple cocktails, playing *Hades*, or rewatching childhood shows with their siblings.

You can follow them @AMWoody_.